SABOTAGED

Books by Dani Pettrey

ALASKAN COURAGE

Submerged

Shattered

Stranded

Silenced

Sabotaged

ALASKAN COURAGE,
• BOOK FIVE •

SABOTAGED

DANI PETTREY

BETHANY HOUSE PUBLISHERS
a division of Baker Publishing Group
Minneapolis, Minnesota

IF
Pettrey

Published by Bethany House Publishers
11400 Hampshire Avenue South
Bloomington, Minnesota 55438
www.bethanyhouse.com

Bethany House Publishers is a division of
Baker Publishing Group, Grand Rapids, Michigan

Printed in the United States of America

Library of Congress Cataloging-in-Publication Data
Pettrey, Dani.
    Sabotaged / Dani Pettrey.
        pages ; cm.— (Alaskan courage ; book 5)
    Summary: "Growing up in Yancey, Alaska, Kirra Jacobs and Reef McKenna
were always at odds; now working together to stop an ecoterrorist threatening
the Iditarod and Alaskan lives, Kirra and the entire McKenna family attempt
to prevent tragedy in this final book of the ALASKAN COURAGE series"—
Provided by publisher.
        ISBN 978-0-7642-1196-6 (pbk.)
    1. Ecoterrorism—Fiction. I. Title.
PS3616.E89S23 2015
813'.6—dc23   2014032258

Scripture taken from the HOLY BIBLE, NEW INTERNATIONAL VERSION®. Copy-
right © 1973, 1978, 1984 Biblica. Used by permission of Zondervan. All rights reserved.

Cover design by Paul Higdon with Koechel Peterson & Associates, Inc, Minneapolis,
Minnesota/Gregory Rohm

Author is represented by Books & Such Literary Agency

15 16 17 18 19 20 21   7 6 5 4 3 2 1

To Jimmy
For being the best dad and Pop-Pop
a family could ask for.
We are so blessed by you.

Prologue

Frank woke to a low rumble churning in Diesel's throat.

"Settle." The dogs hated waiting for the restart. He'd moved away from the other mushers up onto the hill, bedded the dogs down on their piles of hay, but the yearning to run was gnawing at them all.

Diesel sprang to his feet, lurching forward, and the rest of the sixteen-dog team followed suit—their hair bristling in spiky waves down the length of their lean backs.

Before Frank's vision could completely adjust to the full-moon-lit night, something sharp pressed against his side.

The dogs broke into a howling chorus, yanking at their line.

A bright light shone in his eyes. Frank pulled his gloved hand from his sleeping bag, the frigid Alaskan air seeping into his cocoon, and lifted it to shield the invasive glare. Was it another musher?

"You fully awake now?" A man knelt over him with a gun in hand. "Because your daughter's life rests in the balance."

"Meg?" Frank bolted to a sitting position, his nerve endings sparking, adrenaline burning through his limbs.

"Tell your mutts to settle, or I'll shoot every last one of them."

It took a harsh command, but they minded his order.

"What about my daughter?" Who were they and what did they want with Meg?

The man held up his phone, streaming video of Meg, bleary-eyed and weary.

A wave of nausea crashed through Frank's gut as desperation clawed hold. "What have you done?"

"Nothing yet, but what happens now depends on you."

"Where is she?" Frank reached for the phone. *Meg.* Anguish teetered on the brink of consuming him whole.

The man whacked his hand away. "She's someplace secure."

"I don't understand." Frank shook his head. "Why take Meg?" Were they holding her for ransom? If so, they'd picked the wrong guy. "I don't have much money, but whatever I have is yours."

"We don't want your money."

We? "Then what do you want?"

"You're going to do a job for us."

1

RAINY PASS, ALASKA
MARCH 10, 2:17 A.M.

Exhilaration pulsated through Reef. Not helpful at two-something in the morning, when he should be sleeping, but he never tired of Iditarod excitement. It was his first year back volunteering since he was a teen at his dad's side, and it'd been an adrenaline-packed thirty-six hours since the restart in Willow.

He rolled over, facing the cabin-turned-communications-bunkhouse front window. A dull sliver of moonlight crept around the curtain's edge—enough to make out a shape moving across the room toward the door.

Odd.

He propped his weight on his elbow, studying the form he'd been studying far too much lately. *Kirra.* What was she up to now?

He couldn't believe that, of all the search and rescue volunteers working the Iditarod, he and Kirra Jacobs had been paired as a team. He also couldn't help but wonder if one or more of his siblings had influenced that decision. Not that he actually minded—and quite frankly, that's what scared him.

They'd been assigned to sweeper duty. Keeping an eye out for any lagging mushers. The snowstorm whipping through Skwentna and on into Finger Lake was slowing the mushers' time by hours—except for the leaders, who were already through and on to Rohn before the worst of the storm hit, creating an even greater than usual gap between first and last place. When he and Kirra had reached their shift to sleep, there'd still been a couple dozen mushers out.

Slipping to his feet, he crept across the cold wooden floor to intercept Kirra. His hand wrapped around the doorknob a fraction of a second before hers.

Her breath hitched.

He leaned against the door, the frigid outside temps seeping through the frame.

"Reef!" she hissed under her breath, glancing over her shoulder. "Get out of my way." She shoved against him, but he easily held his ground. A good half a foot shorter and, he'd wager, seventy pounds lighter, did she seriously think she could just nudge him out of the way?

A smirk danced across his lips. He liked her style. "If you haven't noticed, it's close to ten below out there, not to mention the middle of the night. Where on earth are you headed in such a rush?

"Wait a minute . . ." His smirk turned into a grin. "You're not headed out for a middle-of-the-night rendezvous, are you?" Not the perfect and prim Kirra Jacobs? A thrill shot through him. Was there more than expected beneath the straitlaced exterior of the lady who'd oddly enough been haunting his dreams?

She adjusted her gloves with oomph. "Don't be ridiculous."

He lifted his hands with a chuckle. "You're right. What *was* I thinking?"

"I don't have time for this." She elbowed him in the ribs, hard, opened the door, and jetted past him. "My uncle's missing."

"What?" He yanked his jacket and gear from the peg and headed out after her.

The sub-zero temps stole his breath, searing his lungs with a cold burn. "Kirra, wait!"

She headed for the barn around back where the snowmobiles were stored.

"You're seriously going to race out into the night after him?"

She yanked the snowmobile keys off the hook overhead. "I've waited long enough." She shook her head. "I can't believe I fell asleep before he checked in."

"The mushers come at all hours, especially with this storm. You can't stay awake 24-7."

"I slept too long. I just called the checkpoint. Frank still hasn't checked in. Something's wrong."

He rested his gloved hand over hers as she slid the key into the ignition. "Maybe he's just running behind. This storm is causing havoc."

"He's been at the front since the race's start. Even if he took a rest at Finger Lake, he'd have been here by now."

Reef lifted his hands, letting large flakes cling to his flattened palms. He gazed up at the tendrils of white descending down on them. "Not if he's waiting out the storm."

"He'd never wait out the *entire* storm. No one but a rookie would. You'd fall so far behind, you'd never catch up."

"Fine. Then we'll wake the team and do this search right."

"Ben will never order a night search. He'll make us wait until morning and the storm lightens, and then they'll have the Iditarod air force take a look first."

"And what's wrong with that? It makes good sense."

"Really? *You're* lecturing me on good sense?"

Touché. "I'm just saying it's dangerous."

She cocked her head to the side. "I thought you thrived on danger."

Not anymore . . . He didn't mind the occasional adrenaline rush that extreme sports provided, but this wasn't that. Heading into the Alaska Range alone at night could get Kirra killed.

"You're not talking me out of this." She started the snowmobile. "Now, please get out of my way."

He exhaled, his mind racing through the options. "Fine." He climbed on the back.

She stiffened as he settled behind her. "*What* do you think you're doing?"

"I'm your SAR partner. I'm going with you."

"Look, that's nice and all, but—"

"You know me well enough to know I'm not budging on this one." He wrapped his arms around her waist.

"I really don't think this is a good idea."

"Sitting here arguing when we could be out looking for Frank? I agree."

She wiggled, trying to break free of his snug hold. "That's not what I meant."

"Look, I've got all night, and I'm not going anywhere." He relished the feel of her in front of him, and that gave him pause—as did the shock waves bolting through him.

12

"You're being ridiculous!" She squirmed some more.

He grinned. "Actually, I'm rather enjoying this."

"Ugh." She released a highly offended exhale. "You really are ridiculous."

His grin widened. He loved getting under her skin. In fact, he was thinking of all the ways . . . *Whoa!* This was Kirra Jacobs, and he was no longer that guy. "Look. You either come back in the shelter with me or I'm going with you. End of story."

"Fine." She ground out, then thumbed the throttle.

Kirra tried to ignore Reef's arms wrapped around her, his body molded to hers on the snowmobile. She considered insisting on some distance, but she wasn't foolish enough to refuse the only available source of warmth. Every inch of her body was covered except her eyes, and still the cold permeated her bones.

Loath as she was to admit it, Reef was right—this was crazy. But leaving her uncle and his dogs out to fend for themselves in this weather would be akin to murder. Frank always ran in the top ten. *Always.* Something was definitely wrong. They needed to reach him before he froze to death.

Thankfully she knew his favorite *parking spots*, as the mushers were prone to call the places they stopped to rest the dogs and themselves. She'd start with the spot closest to Rainy Pass, arriving from Finger Lake's direction, and work her way out from there. Maybe one of Frank's dogs had been hurt and he'd had to hunker down before reaching the checkpoint. If that were the worst of it, she'd be thankful, but she couldn't shake the sense of dread lodged in the pit of her stomach, the quivering that wouldn't ease.

Leave it to Reef to play the chivalrous knight. *Seriously? Reef?* Just her luck she'd gotten paired up with him again.

She exhaled, trying to release the pent-up tension from her body, the warmth of her breath quickly swallowed by the cold. The more time she spent with Reef, the more he surprised her. And she *hated* surprises, especially when it came to men.

Accelerating, she pushed the engine to its max, as snow-flakes the size of half dollars pelted her face. She blinked, the simple motion made difficult by the ice crusting her eyelashes. Was she putting herself and Reef in danger being out in such harsh elements—yes—but she didn't have a choice. This was Uncle Frank.

She took the last upswing to her uncle's favorite resting spot at full speed, the front of the machine lifting over the rise. Reef's laughter echoed over the roar of the wind and the purr of the engine. She slid to a stop and left the engine idling.

Reef hopped off beside her. "I'm impressed. Didn't know you had that kind of speed in you." His face was covered from the nose down, but she could see his smile in the crinkle of his eyes.

She adjusted her headlamp and pulled the flashlight from her jacket, pressing it on. She fanned the light out across the thick cascading snow, so thick it was difficult to make out where the ridge began and where it dropped off.

"Thank God." Her uncle's voice echoed along the fifteen-foot crevice that bordered the ridge. "I hoped you'd think to come looking for me here."

"Frank." Relief swarmed inside as she moved toward his voice.

Reef's strong arm grabbed around her waist, yanking her back. "Whoa!"

Her feet dangled in the air over the dark emptiness below, her flashlight dropping into nothingness.

Was Frank on the other side of the crevice?

Reef swung her back and set her down, his hold remaining firm.

She pushed at his forearm.

"I'm not letting go unless you promise to be more careful."

She nodded, her heartbeat whooshing in her ears.

He let go, and she instantly missed the warmth of his embrace.

"Kirra," Frank yelled.

"Yeah." She moved with great care toward the edge, Reef keeping in close stride with her. Thick trees on that side prevented the moonlight's penetration—she couldn't see anything.

"I need you to listen. We don't have much time."

"Are you hurt? Are the dogs?" Why was he on the opposite side of the crevice from the race trail?

"We're fine, but your cousin's not."

"Meg?" What did she have to do with any of this?

"Some men have taken her."

"What?" A nervous laugh escaped her lips. He couldn't be serious. "What are you talking about?"

She yanked the secondary flashlight from her pants pocket and shone it across the space. She could barely make out Frank's form silhouetted by the snow. His dogs stood in a line in front of his sled, harnessed and ready to go.

"Listen carefully." The edge in his voice deepened. "Some men kidnapped her. They're holding her hostage until I do something for them."

She sensed Reef shift, as if he intended to say something,

but she was thankful when he said nothing, allowing her to take the lead. "What do they want you to do?" What could they possibly want from her uncle?

"I can't tell you. I have to do what they say or they'll kill her. But you might be able to help."

"Anything. How?"

"Find Meg before I reach the finish line in Nome. If you find her, I won't have to finish the job."

"Job? What job?"

"Stop asking questions and listen. You find Meg and then find me. If I know she's safe, I won't finish the job. Otherwise, I fear a lot of others may be hurt too."

"I don't understand."

"You don't have to. Just do what I say and find your cousin before I reach Nome."

"I'll call the cops as soon as we get back to Rainy Pass."

"No! No cops. They said if they saw a cop anywhere around, they'd kill her. Promise me, Kirra. No cops. I can't lose Meg."

"Okay. No cops."

Diesel growled and Frank's eyes widened. Kirra looked over her shoulder and saw a light approaching through the gloom. The rumble of a snowmobile drew near.

"I took too long. They're here."

"Who's here?" She looked again to the light and then back at Frank, but he was gone.

"Frank! Frank!" She fanned her light along the opposite ridge, finding nothing but snow.

The snowmobile stopped but remained idling as a man stepped from it.

She lifted a hand, shielding her eyes from the floodlights

mounted on the front. "Ben?" Had he followed them? "Thank goodness." He could help them track Frank down, get him to sit still so they could make sense of what he had said.

Reef grabbed her hand, tugging her close. "I don't think that's Ben."

"What?"

The man, hooded and in full snow gear, stepped toward them, his head angled down. His right arm lifted, his thinly gloved hand gripped around a gun now aimed straight at them.

Kirra swallowed, her mind too muddled to wrap around what was happening.

"What did he tell you?" the man grunted.

Reef stepped back, pulling her with him toward the tree line.

"Nah-uh." The man extended his arm, his gloved finger hovering over the trigger, his face covered with a ski mask. "Stay right where you are." He stepped forward, snow crunching beneath his boots. "What did Frank Weber tell you?"

"Who are you?" Reef asked, trying to buy time while he figured out a way to get Kirra and himself closer to the trees. This was only going down one way. He could read it in the man's eyes.

"None of your business," the man replied.

Reef moved his hand to Kirra's wrist, strengthening his grip on her. If they could just make it to the trees, they'd have some cover. Only a few feet . . . He held up his free hand, inching back. "Look, we don't want any trouble."

The man's arm stiffened. "I said stop moving!"

Reef held in place, his lungs burning. Adrenaline heating his veins. His legs itching to move.

"*What* did Frank tell you?" the man gritted out.

"He told us he was fine, that he didn't need any assistance," Kirra said.

Reef looked to her. *Smart*.

"What else?"

"That's it." She shrugged. "He didn't check in at Rainy Pass, so we came looking. He said he was just running behind."

"That's it?"

"That's it. The storm has held up a number of mushers."

"All right. Well, then I suppose it's a shame I'm going to have to kill you over nothing, but I can't risk it."

Reef didn't waste a moment. He yanked Kirra into a run, pushing her in front of him. "Go!"

The gun fired, the explosion reverberating with a hollow *ping*. They wove through the trees as the gun fired repeatedly. Fierce heat lanced Reef's side.

Kirra screamed as the ground gave way beneath them.

Reef's jaw slammed onto the rock-strewn ice as he barreled down a steep incline, pain throbbing afresh with each bump and bounce. Everything whirled white around him as gunshots echoed. His free fall spun in a rapidly increasing rate until he slammed into something solid with bone-shattering pain.

"Reef?" Kirra crawled to his side. "Are you okay?"

He nodded, ignoring the pain surging through him. "Are you?"

"Yes. Come on." She tugged his hand. "I know where we are."

"What?"

Her gaze darted up the hill. "He's coming."

Reef made out the form stumbling down after them.

"Come on. I know where we can hide."

He scrambled to his feet. The pain was throbbing, but he pushed forward.

The man's footsteps crunched after them, unrelenting as the howling wind.

"Hide?" Had Kirra said *hide*? "Shouldn't we keep going?" Keep moving. Nausea roiled through him.

"We can't outrun him. Not with you injured."

"I can keep going."

"I don't doubt that, but this is best. Trust me." She clamped hold of his hand.

Jagged slits of breath burned his lungs, moisture seeping down his right side.

"It's just ahead . . ." She surveyed the terrain as if suddenly uncertain, then pointed. "There."

All he saw was snow. "I don't see . . . anything."

"That's the point. He won't either." She bent and pulled him down. He crumpled against the snow. It felt cool against his face.

"We have to go low from here," she said, tugging him.

Swallowing the pain, he crawled forward, following Kirra into deeper darkness.

Branches and undergrowth slashed at their jackets, scraping the fabric with slithering sounds.

"Keep low," she said.

The moonlight around them dimmed, debris thickened beneath them, the earth growing . . . *warmer*?

"Just follow the sound of my voice," she instructed. "Only a little farther . . ."

Queasiness sloshed in his gut.

"Here," she finally said. "Sit down."

Exhausted, he slumped against something hard.

2

Kirra insisted Reef sit still while she set to making a fire. He was thankful that, though he was injured, she wasn't. Pain throbbed in his side. Something had taken a chunk out of it, or so it felt.

Before long the comforting scent of pine smoke filled the cave Kirra had dragged him into, wood crackling in the fire pit she'd fashioned.

Warmth permeated his skin, firelight dancing along the dark, arched ceiling. They needed the fire to survive the night in these temps, but wouldn't the man see the light? "Won't the fire give away our position?"

"We're too far in for this to be visible. Don't worry. He won't find us back here."

Nor, he worried, would anyone else. When the rest of SAR was launched in the morning upon finding them missing, they'd never be found back in a remote cave. How did she even find this place?

"Now that I've got the fire started, let me take a look at that wound." Unfortunately they'd had to leave what cold weather gear he'd grabbed with the snowmobile, which he

SABOTAGED

was betting was disabled at best, long gone at worst. Frank had said *they* were coming. How many more were on the way?

Kirra scooted closer, reaching for him. "Let me take a look."

"It's not that bad. The pain is less."

"Just let me look."

"Okay." If it made her feel better. He grabbed ahold of the right side of his jacket with his left hand and slowly inched it up. Kirra helped lift the additional layers he had on, her fingers cold to the touch but filling him with warmth all the same. Her skin was soft and delicate, just like her eyes had become. When they were in school, those eyes used to always be so vibrant, full of fire, but the light was not there when she came home from grad school. What had happened to vanquish it?

He trembled as her fingers slid up his chest.

"Sorry." She pulled her hands back and rubbed them together. "They haven't fully warmed up yet."

"You're fine." *Better than fine.*

Worry filled her eyes, and he followed her concerned gaze down along his side, the light flickering off his pale skin covered with blood.

Kirra carefully examined the wound and then sighed with relief. "The bullet just grazed you, thank God."

He'd been shot? He'd heard the gun's report, felt a hit, but it hadn't felt that bad. Had the cold and adrenaline combined to stall the pain? He closed his eyes. *Thank you, Lord.*

"We don't have supplies to clean or bandage the wound, but . . . hold on." She turned away.

"What are you doing?"

"Tearing my shirt." The fabric ripped.

He kept his thoughts focused on the visual of the plaid fabric tearing and not on what the material covered. "You can use one of my shirts," he said, wanting her to stay warm.

"No need. I've got plenty of layers." Another rip.

Maybe if they were back in the warm cabin with a heating stove, or even if they had decent sleeping bags . . . but with temps hardly breaking zero, even in the cave, she wouldn't be warm enough. *They* wouldn't be warm enough.

"Seriously," he said. "Let me use one of mine."

"Already done." She turned back, holding two jaggedly ripped flannel sleeves.

She knotted two ends together and then reached carefully around Reef's back, pulling the two open ends around his waist, moving gingerly as the fabric covered the wound.

He watched her work, her lithe fingers smoothing the green-and-purple fabric against his bloodied skin.

She shifted the open ends to his good side and knotted them, creating a sash to bind his injury. "There," she said, lowering his shirt. "You should be okay until we get you back to Rainy Pass."

He grabbed her hand before she could move away. "Thank you."

She tilted her head, her gaze appraising him, searching. "You're welcome." She'd been looking at him like that a lot lately, and he wondered what she saw.

Kirra stood, caught off guard by Reef's sincerity. He just kept surprising her. "I found a good amount of debris. The fire should hold until morning, or close to it." But it wasn't enough to keep them warm. Not in these temperatures. Not in such a large cave.

"And then?" he asked, his husky voice deeper than usual.

She cleared her throat, trying to shake off the pleasure the sound of his voice resonated in her. "We head back for Rainy Pass."

"How'd you know this cave was here?"

"Uncle Frank's been running the Iditarod for years. He took me and Meg out on practice runs several times, and we usually stopped here. Plus my family loved camping in this area." Or at least they had until everything fell apart. Her father still didn't look at her the same; her mom's eyes always filled with pity. It was agonizing just being around them—the disgrace always bubbling to the surface.

Her parents' relocation to Juneau and then to Arizona, of all places, rather than sticking with the plan of her running Nanook Haven at her dad's side was for the best, even if it had destroyed one of her long-held dreams. The loss of a dream stung less than having to look her parents in the eye every day or avoid doing so. Uncle Frank and her cousin Meg . . . they were different. They looked at her the same. They were her only family to do so.

"You betting the snowmobile's gone?" Reef asked, giving her a reprieve from the painful thoughts.

"Yeah." She dropped more kindling in the fire. "At the very least, he disabled it before he left."

"Who was he?"

"I have no idea."

"And what your uncle said . . . ?"

She hunched down, stoking the fire. "I have no idea." It was crazy. Someone kidnapped her cousin? At first she'd thought the cold and the rigors of the race might have gotten to Frank. Disorientation, even hallucinations could happen with mental and physical exhaustion, but the man with the gun proved her uncle's story true.

"Do you think . . . ?"

"He was hallucinating?" She shook her head. "I already ran through that scenario, and no, not Frank."

"Why not?"

"For one, he's the strongest man I know, both physically and mentally." He'd shown great fortitude when Aunt Sarah died and he'd been left to raise Meg on his own. "For two . . ."

"The man holding us at gunpoint, demanding to know what your uncle told us."

"Right." She nodded.

"So someone has your cousin."

She tried not to let the horror of that sink in, tried not to think of the fear that must be coursing through Meg. She'd often prayed no one she loved would ever have to suffer what she herself had suffered—to be at someone's mercy. It was the most degrading and helpless feeling in the world. She prayed the man or men who had Meg actually possessed some mercy, because she'd found none.

"I'll call Landon and Jake as soon as we're back at Rainy Pass."

"No."

"No?"

"No cops. You heard Frank."

"Yes, but I—"

"No buts. I gave Frank my word. We can't risk the man seeing any cops, even if they're your family."

"Okay, then how do you propose we find your cousin?"

"We work search and rescue. She's our missing victim." She cringed at the word—loathed it.

"All right, but—"

"No buts, Reef. I understand if you don't want to be a part of my search, but no cops."

"You can't seriously think I'm just going to walk away from this?"

She shrugged.

"What kind of guy do you think I am?" Hurt flickered in his eyes. "Wait. Don't answer that."

"Look, I appreciate you wanting to help." She did. It was just . . .

"I'm coming. End of discussion."

"You have a gunshot wound."

"It's just a graze."

"Yes, but—"

He straightened, his movement ginger. "Let me stop you right there. We know each other pretty well."

"How do you figure that?" They'd hung in totally different circles their entire lives. For a while last summer they'd been thrown together in the search for Kayden, but since then—except for periodic search and rescue missions—they'd seen each other only occasionally. She'd often wondered why—

"Because we both see past the surface."

She'd always thought she had . . . until William.

"You know I'm as stubborn as you are, and the fact is, you're stuck with me."

She opened her mouth to argue.

"If you won't let me get the cops involved, then I'm absolutely not going to let you go it alone. It's not safe. Whoever has Meg clearly has someone watching you."

"Me?" She'd thought he was watching Frank.

"He came from behind us. Not Frank. He chased after *us*. And I bet he's going to be watching to see what we do next."

"Which makes an even better argument for you not to join me." She stood, moving closer to him, yet keeping a wall of distance between them—her arms wrapped tight around her knees as she sat. "I know you and Meg had a thing a couple years back."

Reef's brows lifted. "She mentioned us."

Us? That stung . . . surprisingly. "She said it wasn't anything serious."

"It wasn't."

"So why do you care so much about finding her?"

"Wow. You really do think so little of me."

"I'm just saying . . ."

"That I'm the type of guy that's going to walk away when a lady is in trouble. Or in this case, ladies. What Meg and I had wasn't serious, but I still consider her a friend, and when a friend's in trouble, I help."

"Fine. You can help." Otherwise she couldn't trust him *not* to go to the police. "But I'm calling the shots."

He grinned. "Don't you always?"

Gage McKenna woke, uneasiness stirring him, the sensation something was wrong biting at him. He rolled over and propped his head on his hand. It was dark, the bunkhouse still. He'd heard a snowmobile revving a while back, but surely it had been a dream. All SAR and communication hands were accounted for. Perhaps mushers were still lagging behind, but with the storm, that was to be expected. So what was nagging at him?

He turned over and tried to quiet his mind, but a frustrating half hour later, he climbed from the warmth of his sleeping bag and hopped down from the bunk. Darcy was sleeping in the back room with the rest of the ladies. He padded across the frigid floor—the stove required more wood. He glanced out the window. The snow was still surging and the wind whipping it in dancing frenzies across the whitened landscape. He glanced back, and his gaze fastened on Reef's empty bunk.

3

"Don't you always?" Reef's last words to her flitting, no stomped, through her mind.

Ugh! Was there a more infuriating man alive?

She dropped the final pile of scrounged wood into the fire, praying it would last until sunup but knowing better. They were going to run out of heat before they could take the chance their attacker was not still outside searching for them and get moving.

"Man." Reef whistled. "I really get under your skin, don't I?"

"Ha." She bit the inside of her cheek as the flames flashed higher, devouring the newly added branches.

"Good comeback."

She took a deep breath, expelling it in a rush. "Contrary to what you think, *you* have *no* effect on me whatsoever."

"Your heartbeat skipping along the curve of your neck seems to suggest otherwise."

She grabbed her neck, praying her face didn't redden. "If my pulse is elevated, it's because I'm worried about Meg." It was a boldfaced lie. She *was* worried about Meg, but it wasn't the cause of her infuriated pulse. It was *him*. They'd known each other since they were five and yet he still managed to rattle her. She despised him for it.

His smirk slackened. "I'm worried about her too."

"Really? You worry about all your flings?" It was harsh, but she was flustered.

His bright blue eyes narrowed. "If I didn't know better, I'd say that's jealousy snapping."

"Me? Jealous over you?"

He smiled softly, his eyes alight with playfulness. "I tend to have that effect."

"Wow. You really think highly of yourself, don't you?"

"*This* has nothing to do with how I think of myself."

"No?"

"No."

"Then what does it have to do with?" She should have known better than to ask.

"What *you* think of me."

"Why do you care what I think of you?"

He fidgeted with his jacket zipper. "I keep asking myself the very same thing."

Meaning . . . ? He *did* care what she thought? Well, that was interesting.

"Gage, you know the protocol," the head of Iditarod Search and Rescue, Ben James, said. "I can't authorize a sweep with this storm still raging."

"But Reef and Kirra are missing, along with a snowmobile."

"They should have known better than to take off during the night."

"Clearly they thought someone was in danger."

"Or Reef talked Kirra into a joyride."

"I wouldn't have put something like that past the old Reef, but he's changed. And Kirra is the last person I'd expect to take a joyride with SAR equipment."

"Her uncle still hasn't checked in," Ethan said.

Ethan Young had been paired with Gage and Xander Cook on race communications, and he, along with everyone else in the tiny cabin, was now wide-awake.

"Have you confirmed with the checkers? Perhaps he came in while we were sleeping," Ben suggested.

The checkers were on duty 24-7 and were stationed out in the tents for ready availability.

"I'll go see." Ethan slipped on his coat and boots.

Gage nodded. "Thanks, man."

"No problem."

"What's all the commotion?" Xander asked as he stumbled into the room, his hair mimicking Heat Miser's.

"Two SAR team members are missing, along with a snow-mobile," Gage said, quickly catching him up to speed.

Reef let Kirra's insults roll right off. He'd heard them his whole life. For the most part they were deserved, but from Kirra, they ached deep in his soul. He wasn't the same man he'd been—wasn't that same playboy, wasn't the reckless man intent on drowning his feelings in a world of distraction. What he felt was very real, and to his complete surprise and slight bemusement, what he felt was growing love for Kirra. God certainly had a sense of humor. Reef only prayed it wasn't the ruin of him.

What irony. He'd finally allowed himself to really feel, only to be consumed with genuine feelings for Kirra Jacobs—a woman who would never love him back.

He shifted in the dwindling firelight, the darkness closing in on them.

Kirra sat a dozen feet away, her knees hugged once again to her chest, her hood draped over her head.

"The fire's not going to last." The cold was already swallowing its warmth.

"We'll have daylight in a few hours."

"A few hours is more than enough time for frostbite or hypothermia to take hold."

"So what do you suggest?"

"Body heat."

"Nice try."

"You really think I'd try to make a play on you—and under these circumstances?"

She gave him an are-you-kidding-me look.

"Fair enough." The old him would have in a heartbeat, but he was working hard at being a gentleman. "But that's not what this is. We need to conserve our body heat." He held out his arm. "Come here."

She hesitated.

Was he that repulsive to her? "No funny business. I promise."

After another moment's hesitation, she stood and moved to his side.

"Come on. I don't bite." He tugged her to his good side, pulling her close.

She stiffened.

"Relax."

"I've heard that one before."

He arched a brow.

"Never mind."

Ethan entered the cabin along with a frigid blast of wind. He kicked the door shut behind him, rubbing his arms.

"What's the word?" Gage asked.

"Frank Jacobs hasn't checked in."

"We need to contact Finger Lake and see when he checked out."

"On it," Xander said. "I'm sure they're going to appreciate the middle-of-the-night call, especially since all mushers have no doubt at least arrived at that checkpoint."

Gage laid out the grid map of the area.

"What do you think you're doing?" Ben sat on the corner of the desk. "You know I'm not sending you out in this. It's suicide. Wait until the storm passes and we have daylight, and I'll send one of the air force to take a scan."

The Iditarod air force, as it was called, consisted of a dozen single-engine planes manned by expert bushmen who volunteered their time to help fly in supplies and pick up dropped dogs or seriously injured mushers. They also helped with searches and sweeping.

"We've still got two hours until sunrise. They could freeze to death in that time."

Kirra lay gingerly beside Reef, trying not to enjoy the feel of his embrace, but it was a lost cause. She hadn't been held like this since before William, hadn't allowed herself to be close to any man, not like this, since William had . . .

She squeezed her eyes shut, hoping doing so would keep the nightmares, the gnawing fear that returned whenever she thought of William, at bay. This was Reef, not William, and he was only trying to help. He felt good. He smelled good—like evergreens and a crisp winter day. The dwindling fire crackled at her feet, Reef's body heat warming her. She was tired, but relaxing to the point of sleep seemed impossible—not while in a man's arms.

"You okay?" he asked.

"Fine. Why?"

"You're awfully tense. Like I said, I won't bite."

She tried laughing it off. "I know. I just . . ."

He brushed back her hair from her face, careful to keep her hat in place. "You just what?"

"Will feel better when we're safely back at the checkpoint." And around other people. Not that she believed Reef would do anything—but then again, William had been the last person she'd expected to . . .

"There you go. Tensing up again. Do I really make you that uncomfortable?"

She heard the hurt in his words. "No. It's just awkward."

"Because it's me?"

She arched back to look at him. "What do you mean?"

"I know how you felt about me when we were growing up. I guess that hasn't changed much."

No. His sister was right. He clearly was different. He was changing, growing, maturing. And, truth be told, there'd always been a part of her that had been drawn to Reef McKenna. Something about a moth to a flame. It was dangerous, but magnetic. In the past she'd been smart enough to keep her distance, to not pursue that attraction, but now . . . ?

Her attraction for him was only growing, and this time, frighteningly enough, strong feelings were growing right along with it.

"Gage, calm down," Darcy said.

"How can I calm down when my brother is out there?"

"You don't have a choice until the sun's up."

"I can go on foot."

"And how is that going to help them? If anything, it'll just give SAR one more person to search for, taking away some of the concentration on finding them. We only have a couple more hours."

"Why didn't he take a sat phone? Why leave in such a hurry? Why not wake anyone else up?"

"Probably because they knew Ben wouldn't approve the search, and I'm betting Kirra was deadset on finding her uncle."

"And Reef?"

"Probably saw her going and refused to let her go alone."

"I'm sure that went over well."

Ethan and Xander stepped back into the room.

Gage turned. "Any word?" The two men had been on the line with anyone and everyone who might have spotted Frank, or Reef and Kirra.

Ethan shook his head. "No sign of any of them. I'm sorry, Gage."

Reef reveled in the feel of Kirra in his arms, even if she remained stiff. It didn't take too long for her head to bob as she finally drifted off. Within a few minutes she was completely out. Slowly the tension eased from her body, and she swayed into him, her limbs limp. A soft purr escaped her lips as she snuggled deeper into his hold. He remained perfectly still, terrified that if he moved, he'd break the moment. She felt incredible, and even more frightening . . . *right*. He'd held a lot of women in his arms, but none had ever felt like Kirra did right now—a perfect fit.

She murmured, her silky hair caressing his stubbled neck as she nuzzled into him, resting her head on his shoulder.

Her breathing was rhythmic, her eyes fluttering in a dream. The smile on her lips said it was a good one. She shifted on a sigh, another murmur escaping her lips.

"Reef," she said sleepily, her eyes still shut and fluttering.

He was terrified to speak and ruin the moment, so he released a soft sound of affirmation. She tilted her head upward, toward his lips, and knowing better, he lowered his to hers. Her mouth opened, inviting him in. Slowly, passionately, she kissed him—a million sensations ricocheting through him.

She pulled back on a satisfied sigh, her head resting in the crook of his neck, her breathing once again rhythmic and deep in slumber.

He sat there, shock and endorphins warring for purchase of his body and mind. *Man, am I in trouble.*

He braced for the wrath to come.

"What happened?"

Clearing his throat, he held the satellite phone close to his face, the storm still raging around him. "I lost them."

"How?"

"They ran, but I hit the guy."

"So you're saying you managed to let an injured man get away?"

"The wilderness is huge, and they clearly know their way around this area."

"And Frank?"

"They swore he didn't tell them anything."

"Of course they did."

"I think they were telling the truth."

"Okay, even if they were . . . your threatening them at gunpoint is going to raise their suspicions. Even if he didn't tell them anything, because of your actions, now they *know* something's going on."

"You told me to make sure Frank didn't talk to anyone, especially the girl."

"And I told you to make sure to take care of her if he did."

"I tried. I wounded the man."

"The man's inconsequential. It's Kirra Jacobs we have to worry about. If she figures out what's going on. If she interferes . . ."

"I'll make sure that doesn't happen."

"See that you do, or this entire venture could be compromised."

"I'll take care of it." He grunted. "How's Meg?"

"Cooperating just fine."

4

ROUGHLY 20 MILES OUTSIDE OF RAINY PASS
MARCH 10, 8:03 A.M.

Kirra stirred, half awake. She felt warm and protected. She'd had a delicious dream—it danced on the tip of her lips. She blinked, opening her eyes and surveying her surroundings. It took a moment for her memory to jog. She was in a cave. And a man with a gun had shot at them. Then she'd lain in Reef's arms and . . .

She swallowed. Reef's lips had been pressed to hers.

She bolted upright, jarring Reef in the process, and scrambled to her feet. Turning her flashlight on, she shone it in his face.

"Whoa! Easy there," he said, his wide eyes so blue, with such dark lashes. "You all right?"

She straightened her jacket, zipping it the fraction of the inch it had slipped down. "Fine. We should be going."

"Is it daylight?"

She looked in the direction of the cave's opening, seeing a

sliver of light breaking the darkness of the cave. "Yes. Let's get going. I fear we've got quite the hike before us." No way the man had left their snowmobile intact. Not unless he was waiting nearby, using the machine as a trap to pounce once they returned.

"Okay." Reef shifted, slowly lumbering to his feet. "Give me a minute."

She bit her bottom lip at his tenuous movements. "How's the wound?"

"A little sore, but no big deal."

She wasn't so sure.

He straightened and readjusted his outerwear.

"Are you going to be all right to walk?"

"I'll be fine."

It was roughly a twenty-mile hike back to the Rainy Pass checkpoint. On flat terrain and on a good day, they could make it in under five hours. With the storm conditions and the most rugged terrain of the Iditarod race fixed between them and Rainy Pass, not to mention Reef's injury, it could easily take until nightfall for them to reach shelter. And, they wouldn't survive another night out in the elements. Not without proper gear. They had to make it back to the checkpoint before nightfall.

Leading the way back outside, relief filled Kirra as the vast openness of wilderness stretched before them. The storm had halted for the time being, and sunlight poked through the dark clouds brewing overhead. It lit the snow with a beautiful orange hue. The crisp, frigid air bit at their exposed skin, and they both yanked their hoods over their heads, tightening them around their faces, attempting to block out the stinging wind.

Reef's breath danced in the morning air, creeping out from his hood in a swirl of smokelike appearance. "I'm guessing we're still at close to ten below."

"Should we risk seeing if our snowmobile is still working?"

"I think we should at least scope it out."

"What if the man's waiting for us?"

"If the snowmobile's still there and not visibly disabled, we can assess from a distance before we approach. I think it's worth a look. It would save us hours."

She nodded, unsure but willing to give it a shot. "I don't think hiking back up the way we fell down is the wisest choice." They'd tumbled down some of the roughest terrain in the area, the jagged formations a serious antonym to their name—Happy Steps. There was nothing *happy* about them. "I think we need to track back and come up around from the east, like we originally came. If the man is watching, I doubt he'll expect us to come from that direction."

"Good plan."

He shifted in the snow. Squatting for hours was taking its toll.

Forget it.

He stood, shaking the snow off his boots. "This is a waste of time. I'm telling you, they couldn't have survived stranded out here all night with no equipment."

Bruce maintained position. "He said we had to be certain."

"How long does he expect us to stay out here? This isn't where our focus should be."

"If they survived, they could compromise our entire operation."

"And Frank? You're supposed to be watching him. How do we even know he's following orders? Staying on track?"

"Our man inside has got that covered. He knows exactly what's going on and where everyone is."

Kirra led the way back around to where they'd left the snowmobile. To Reef's surprise, it was right where they'd left it.

He pulled Kirra down behind a giant spruce. "I think you were right. He's watching." Crouching, Reef scanned the trees surrounding them.

"What do we do?"

He debated the risk and closed his eyes in prayer.

Please, Father, help me know what to do. Should I go check the snowmobile or should we head back on foot? Please guide me so I can lead Kirra safely back.

"Reef?" She nudged his arm. "You all right?"

"Just praying for guidance."

Her eyes widened. "Oh."

He scanned the tree line again, a knot tightening in his gut. "And?"

"I think we need to head back on foot." It'd take them hours longer, but if he moved for the snowmobile and the man was watching, he'd be shot before he could reach it, and then Kirra would be on her own. He couldn't let that happen. He'd see her back to safety.

Kirra shifted to look him directly in the eyes. "Are you sure you're going to be all right for the hike?"

"I'll be fine."

"All right, let's hit the trail." She started to move.

He halted her. "No. Sticking to the trail is too dangerous. He could be watching it. We're going to have to stay off the race trail."

"But the snow could be up to our waists off trail."

"If we want to make it back safely, it's the wisest course."

"Don't you think Ben and the rest of the crew have figured out we're missing by now? Don't you think they'll come looking for us?"

"Probably, but who knows which direction they'll even search? And most if not all of the mushers are already headed on to Rohn. They've got to move forward with the race."

She nodded, obviously letting that sink in.

He grasped her gloved hand. "Don't worry. We'll make it back, and then we'll regroup and find Frank."

"And Meg."

He swallowed, praying she was right. "And Meg."

Hours had passed, and he was done. "I'm outta here."

"But he said—"

"I know what he said, Bruce, but I'm not spending days out here waiting for two dead people to show."

"You can't be positive they're dead."

"No, but waiting here isn't doing any good. I'm a man of action, not patience. You should know that by now."

"So what do you suggest?"

"Instead of sitting here freezing our bums off, I suggest we start sweeping the area between here and the checkpoint. If they miraculously survived, it won't be for long."

Time evaporated in the white desolation surrounding them, the flakes falling with fury once again.

Numbness rendered Reef's feet nearly useless. He was still moving, but not sure how. He'd lost all feeling from his knees down.

Kirra was a trooper, trudging on ahead, icicles dangling from the furry ridge of her hat and hair that poked free. Her movements were thick, her stride tin-man-like. Frostbite was nipping at them both.

"We should walk together," he said.

She turned, what he could see of her forehead pinching. "We are."

"No." He shook his head and tugged her into his embrace. "Closer. We're losing too much body heat."

"I don't think—"

"Trust me." She fit perfectly against him. "It's necessary."

After a moment's hesitation, she huddled fully against his left side, molding her curves along the slope of his torso. It took a few practice steps, but soon they moved forward in unison—their labored steps somehow easier when taken together.

They sunk in the snow, the white powder cresting Reef's thighs and Kirra's waist. Trudging, they continued on.

Snow lashed Gage's face as he whirred through the white mass ahead. Ben had given him the okay to search for Reef and Kirra, but after finding their snowmobile abandoned, his fear grew. Something was very wrong.

Darcy's arms wrapped tight around him. He wished she'd stayed at the checkpoint, but trying to force Darcy to stay behind when someone was in trouble was like trying to make a bull a house pet. While he loved her determination to help others, he wished she gave a fraction of the same concern to her own safety.

He crested the next step, the snowmobile tilting. When he leaned hard right, Darcy followed suit. Fortunately she'd spent enough time on the back of his sports bike to understand how to move with the turns.

He tightened his grip on the handles. *Where are you, Reef?*

Reef guided Kirra toward the trail. Numbness now consumed his legs, his limbs feeling like tree stumps—heavy and clumsy. Kirra teetered with each step beside him. They needed to get out of the snowdrift, and the only way out was to move to the trail. It was risky, but they couldn't continue on like this. They stepped from the snow onto the trail, and Kirra's leg caught on a sled rut, flailing her forward. His tight hold kept her from hitting the ground, but it took a moment to get her mostly upright. A whimper escaped her lips as she planted her feet on the ground and shifted clumsily to take the weight off her right foot.

"You okay?"

"Just twisted my ankle. I'm fine."

The pain etched on her pale face said otherwise. A face that was too pale and slightly puffy. Hypothermia was setting in. They needed to reach the shelter and soon.

The purr of a motor sounded in the distance, and his heart dropped.

"One of the SAR team?" Kirra said with hope.

He prayed so, but chances were . . .

He yanked her back toward the trees, moving in a diagonal toward the icy-covered rocks cresting the edge of the woods. It was a dangerous maze to maneuver but would hide their footprints. Unfortunately the ones on the trail were still visible despite the heavily falling snow.

Kirra bit back a grunt, clearly favoring her ankle, but kept up with his pace.

Reef nestled them behind the copse of trees.

"You think it's him?" Kirra whispered as the snowmobile pulled into view.

"I pray not."

A second snowmobile came into view, both with single riders.

Reef's chest tightened. It had to be their attacker, and he'd brought a friend.

5

Reef signaled Kirra to remain still. The snowmobiles pulled idle.

"Why'd you stop, Bruce?" Irritation edged the second snowmobile driver's voice. Their attacker—he recognized the voice.

"I thought I saw movement." The other man's gaze swept over the tree line.

Reef pressed his back firmly against the tree, praying, *Please, Lord, don't let them see us. Mask us with this storm. Hide us and protect us.*

"It was probably a moose," their attacker said.

"I don't know . . ."

"What I don't know is why we're even still out here. I told you there's no way they survived the night."

"I'm being thorough. Something you don't seem to grasp." Their attacker stiffened. "Excuse me?"

"If you had been thorough, they would have been dead."

"They are dead!"

"Show me their bodies."

"I hit the man."

"And the girl?"

"Please, like she could survive out here, on her own, with no equipment. She probably holed up someplace and died."

"He said to make sure they aren't going to be a problem, and that's what I'm doing."

"Fine, but I'm moving on. It's not my responsibility to traipse all over this frozen wasteland looking for two dead people."

"It was your *responsibility* to make sure Frank didn't tell them anything. If he did and they managed to survive, our entire plan could be compromised."

"*Our* plan?"

"Yes. *Ours*. It belongs to all of us."

"Fine. Then, let's get back to it instead of chasing after ghosts."

Bruce scanned the tree line once again, then climbed off his snowmobile, moving toward where Reef and Kirra had broken through the snow.

Their attacker rose up in his seat. "What now?"

"Something came through here."

"Like I said, probably a moose. Look, I've had enough of this. I'm heading back in. You do what you want." He took off, leaving a spray of snow flying in his wake.

Bruce cussed and returned to his snowmobile. He started the engine and sped off in the direction of the Rainy Pass checkpoint.

Reef slumped against the tree, relief and apprehension streaming through him. "Thank you, Lord." He'd masked and sheltered them. He prayed God would continue to do so as they worked their way back to the checkpoint.

What plan was the man referencing? And where were they

headed? The checkpoint? Surely they wouldn't show their faces there. Reef hadn't seen much of them, with their hoods and ski masks on. But the first man's voice—the one who'd shot him—that he'd definitely recognize.

Kirra peered around the tree. "We should get moving. I think we're safe to stick to the trail now."

"I think you're right." No way they'd catch up with the men on snowmobiles.

Wind whistled through the trees, growing in strength as Kirra's body heat slipped away. It was bone-chillingly cold. There was no warmth left in her, but she kept moving. Movement was essential to keep the blood flowing. Frostbite was definitely setting in. She wasn't feeling much pain from her sprain, but she didn't know if that was because it wasn't as bad as she'd feared or because her ankle was freezing.

She'd spent the day trying to forget the feel of Reef's lips on hers, but the intense memory still replayed through her mind. She'd thought it'd been a dream until she licked her lips and tasted him.

He hadn't brought it up. Maybe he'd thought it a dream too, maybe he didn't remember, or maybe he just didn't care. Whatever the reason for his silence on the matter, she was thankful. It had been a mistake. A wonderful mistake, but a mistake all the same.

When she'd learned a couple years back that Meg was dating Reef, jealousy had reared its ugly head. It was ridiculous. He had never been hers, nor would he ever be. But the jealousy had tugged all the same. The two had first met when Meg visited Yancey the summer between Reef and Kirra's junior and senior year of high school. How they'd managed to meet up years later in Anchorage, she didn't know, but it wasn't worth asking. He owed her no answers.

She exhaled. Back then she'd wondered what it felt like to touch Reef's body, his lips. Now she knew, and it was every bit as wonderful as she'd imagined. *More so.* But it was still ridiculous. Reef McKenna fell for girls like her cousin Meg, not her.

Meg. Kirra's heart winced. What was her cousin enduring right now while they moved like snails back to Rainy Pass? If only she could will her legs to move faster. But all it seemed she could focus on was that heady kiss. Why did everything turn sideways when she was around Reef?

She forced herself to shake off the delicious yet unnerving thoughts and turned her attention to the sky overhead. What minimal light there was in the endless gray blanketing the sky was vanishing. It'd be night soon, and based on the last landmark they passed—the trail split at Wallow's Creek— they still had a few miles to go.

She lumbered on. Her right foot caught on something, and she pitched forward as pain ricocheted up her leg.

"Kirra!" Reef's strong arms kept her from colliding with the ground once again.

She tried to fight the weariness engulfing her, but it was too much. She was holding him back. He could have been to the shelter by now, and he was the one with a gunshot graze. It was ridiculous. "You go on. I'm holding you back."

"You're crazy if you think I'd leave you out here."

"You can send help back for me after you reach the shelter." After he was safe.

"I'm not leaving you out here." He bent over her, slipping his arms beneath her, and hefted her up.

Was *he* crazy? "What are you doing?"

"Carrying you."

"You've been shot, and *you're* carrying *me*?"

"It was a flesh wound, Kirra. You said it yourself—the bullet just grazed me. I'm fine. Besides, the cold numbs the pain. I haven't felt anything in hours."

Great. So they'd both die of frostbite and hypothermia.

"You can't carry me."

He smiled, the ice cracking around his lips. "I already am."

"Reef . . ."

"We don't have far to go. I'll be fine."

"We've still got a couple miles."

He tightened his hold. "Is that all?"

The man was crazy.

Kirra prayed the men weren't watching this last portion of the trail, but she feared otherwise.

"I'm going to take us off trail for this last part," Reef said. "Not far, but—"

"The men might be watching from near the checkpoint." She finished his thought, or rather he'd finished hers.

Reef nodded.

The wind whipped hard, slashing against Kirra's back as they moved from the trail. Fighting her instincts, she pressed tight against Reef's body, letting him warm her, and positioning her back to take the brunt of the wind.

Please, Father, let us make it. I've never been this cold.

"Gage." Darcy's hand rested over his on the gearshift. "We need to head in."

"We've got a little while longer."

"It's almost dark, and you're heading away from the shelter."

"Just one more sweep."

"Ben's already let us sweep way longer than he originally agreed to." Night and another storm were closing in. The other communication and SAR volunteers had already moved on to Rohn to get ahead of it, leaving them on sweeper duty, but they were seriously pushing the limits. Continuing the search with the burgeoning conditions was beyond dangerous, but this was his brother's and Kirra's lives at stake.

Gage increased the throttle.

"Maybe we're going about this wrong," Darcy yelled over the roar of the engine.

He glanced over his shoulder. "What do you mean?"

"We've been sweeping the trail."

"Right?"

"Maybe they aren't sticking to the trail."

"Why wouldn't they be on the trail?"

"Why would they leave their snowmobile?"

"Because the spark plugs were missing."

"Which brings us to ask, who would take their spark plugs while they were away from the snowmobile?"

"We can ask them that when we find them." He'd been wondering the very same thing, but he had to remain focused. Finding his brother and Kirra was what mattered. Whatever occurred with the snowmobile and why his brother and Kirra weren't with it was troubling, but hashing and rehashing the possibilities with no way of knowing the answers would be of zero help in locating them.

"I still think we should be looking for them off trail," Darcy said.

"No air force pilot is going to fly in this storm. Not until it eases some."

"Then *we* search. Direct our headlights or the floodlight off trail."

Not a bad idea. "Definitely worth a shot."

An hour later he approached the edge of Rainy Pass. He'd kept Darcy out too long. It was time to drop her off and head back out, regardless of the danger. He couldn't in good conscience stay warm in the shelter when his brother and Kirra were out there.

Gage approached the checkpoint from the west, slowing along the last tree line leading in. Darcy swung the floodlight she'd brought across the snowy expanse.

"Wait!" she hollered.

He pulled to a stop.

"What?" He scanned the ridge.

"Reef?" she hollered.

"Darcy?"

Relief swarmed Gage at the sound of his younger brother's voice.

Reef's hunched form stepped into the light. He was carrying Kirra. What had happened?

Back at the Rainy Pass station, Reef settled into the chair by the wood stove, but only after he'd made sure Kirra was being seen to. He feared the lingering effects of frostbite.

Gage hunkered down beside him, handing him a steaming mug of broth. "Here. Drink this."

Reef clasped his cold fingers around the warm ceramic. "Thanks."

"So you care to explain what's going on? Why were you out there? And, why weren't you on the trail?"

"He was still looking for us. Off trail seemed safest."

Gage frowned. "Who was looking for you?"

Reef explained all that had happened—their encounter with Kirra's uncle Frank, his cryptic message, the man with the gun, the sabotaged snowmobile—Gage had told them the spark plugs were missing—and the second man helping track them today.

"What do the men want with Meg and Frank?"

"I don't know. That's what Kirra and I have to find out."

A slight smile tugged at Gage's worried face.

Reef arched a brow. "What?"

Gage shook his head. "Nothing."

Reef considered prodding but decided it was probably safer to let it go. He knew that look, knew it had to do with Gage's observation of him and Kirra—and he wasn't ready to go there. He had no idea what was going on with them. Well, he knew he had feelings for her, but when it came to her, he doubted she felt the same, or felt anything other than irritation for him. But that kiss . . . The memory of it had been the only thing keeping him warm in the ferocious elements.

Kirra sat back, letting Darcy pull off her socks. She feared what she would find. Her toes were red with blue tips and swollen, indicative of at least second-degree frostbite. The digits felt hard and frozen.

Darcy swallowed. "Let's get these in some warm water." She turned to the propane stove with water warming on it, and carried the kettle over to a large basin she had placed on the floor beside Kirra. "You're lucky," she said, slowly lowering Kirra's feet into the warm water. "It looks like it's only second degree. You should heal rather quickly."

Kirra winced as her frosted skin made contact with the warm water—electric-like currents pulsating her feet as the heat engulfed them.

"I'd say you were minutes away from the next degree of frostbite."

And possibly permanent damage. Kirra swallowed. If Reef hadn't insisted on carrying her, on not leaving her behind, at best she would have lost some toes—at worst she could have lost her life. Now she'd be okay and it was all thanks to Reef. "How is he?" She looked toward the door where Reef was receiving treatment on the other side.

"Gage said he'll be fine. They are treating him with antibiotics just in case and gave him a tetanus shot." She poured more water in the basin, fully submerging Kirra's feet, which were finally adjusting to the warmth of the water, the cold slowly fading away. "You did a great job taking care of him, Kirra."

"He did the same for me." Why was it so hard to simply acknowledge the emotions she'd felt while tending to Reef— the compassion that filled her at the sight of his wound and her overwhelming desire to help him? It was the first time in two years she'd felt compassion for a man, felt anything other than wariness.

"What happened out there?" Darcy asked, turning to the stove to bring Kirra a warm cup of broth.

Kirra swallowed, wondering what Reef was telling Gage. Or rather, how much he was telling Gage. She carefully weighed how much she could trust Darcy not to tell Landon or Jake, and went the safe route. "My uncle Frank never made it to this checkpoint."

Darcy handed her an owl mug—two wide eyes staring her down. The aroma of rich, buttery chicken broth swirled beneath her nose.

"We know that much," Darcy said.

Kirra took a sip, buying time before she responded. The warm liquid coated her throat, spreading heat across her chest. So good.

"Kirra?" Darcy prodded when she'd finished her sip.

She swallowed, the motion less painful now. "I'd like to talk to Reef."

Darcy eyed her appraisingly. "Okay."

"Could you get him for me?"

"Right now?"

"Yes, please."

"Okay." Darcy disappeared through the doorway. Kirra heard murmuring and movement, and then Reef lumbered through the door, a blanket draped over his shoulders, a mug in his hand. No doubt filled with the same rich chicken broth.

He smiled, warming her more than the broth. "Hey there."

She shifted her hair behind her ear, remembering the feel of his soft lips on hers and glanced down as heat rushed to her cheeks. "Hey."

"What's up?" He sat down beside her. "Darcy said you wanted to talk?"

She looked past him at the open doorway, at Darcy standing beside Gage in the front room—Gage's arm wrapped about Darcy's slender waist, both of their eyes fixed on her and Reef. "What did you tell him?"

"The truth."

Her heart plummeted. "How could you?"

"I couldn't lie to my brother."

"And how long do you think it'll take him to call Landon?"

"He promised he wouldn't. Not unless we told him otherwise."

She frowned. "What? Why would he do that?"

"Because I asked him to."

He'd do that for her? "But I thought . . . ?"

"I know how much finding Meg means to you, and if you're not willing to let Landon and Jake in on it, I'm not going to force you."

"But you think I should?" Frank had said no cops. Landon Grainger, Reef's brother-in-law, was sheriff of Yancey and Jake Cavanaugh his deputy. Both amazing cops, but Frank had said . . .

"I think they could be of great help, even if they are only involved as a resource."

She narrowed her eyes. "What do you mean . . . as a resource?"

"Gage had a great idea. He said we could call them, and whichever one of them is available can—with one of my sisters in tow, no doubt—take over our responsibilities in the race. That way they could be close, could offer advice and assistance, but in a way that's not likely to draw a lot of attention."

She narrowed her eyes. "What do you mean 'take over our responsibilities'?"

"Well, I assumed you wanted to get going on our search right away. That likely means we will be stepping away from our volunteer duties."

Kirra closed her eyes and nodded. "I see what you mean."

Reef put his hand on hers. "I'm thinking our first step is to track Meg by her last-known whereabouts, which means the race start, if she was there."

"She wasn't, which I thought was odd. She's always there to wish Frank good luck, but now that she's transferred to U of A, Fairbanks, from the community college, her schedule is tighter and she's farther away, so I just assumed she wasn't able to make it down."

"And we can't confirm that without talking to Frank."

"Which means tracking him down . . ."

"Or talking to Meg's friends or roommate on campus."

Campus? Her stomach flipped. "I imagine her roommate, Ashley, would know if Meg had headed to the race start or not. They're pretty tight. I'll give her a call."

"You'd probably get more information if you talk to her in person," Darcy said from the doorway.

Gage stood behind her, his hand resting on her shoulder. How long had they been listening?

She bypassed that question for the more pertinent one. "Why in person?" Not that she'd do it, but she wondered why Darcy felt it would be better.

Darcy stepped into the room and Gage followed. "I've found that you get a lot more information in person. Besides, depending on what Ashley tells you, you may need to interview other people on campus."

Kirra's stomach churned, acid rising in her throat. Could she do it? Go back to campus? Back to . . . "I appreciate your insight, and you may be right, but I can't go to Fairbanks."

"Why not?" Reef asked.

She scanned the room, all their curious glances fixed on her. "I need to find Frank."

"No, Frank asked you to find Meg. Jake or Landon can help search for Frank when they arrive."

"But . . ."

Reef clasped her knee. "Are you okay?"

"I'm fine. Why?"

"Because you just got really pale."

"It's just . . . I feel it would be better if I remained with the race."

"Someone's got to determine Meg's last-known whereabouts," Darcy said. "If you'd prefer, Gage and I can go."

"No," Kirra said, a little too forcefully.

Darcy cocked her head, curiosity dancing across her furrowed brow.

If they went, they might learn, might hear, might discover . . .

Darcy was too good a reporter.

No, if anyone was going to go, it had to be her. At least that way, no one else would find out about her history in Fairbanks. "I just meant, if you really feel it's best, I should be the one to go. I know Ashley. She's much more likely to talk to me."

Darcy nodded.

"Okay . . ." She took a deep breath, trying desperately not to think about what she'd just agreed to. "I guess I better see if one of the air force guys can give me a lift to Anchorage. I can catch a commuter flight from there to Fairbanks."

"Great." Reef stood. "So we'll go to Fairbanks while—"

"Whoa," Kirra interrupted. "What do you mean *we*?"

Reef smiled. "I'm going with you, of course."

"Of course? Why *of course*?"

"Because there were two men tracking us with guns. It's not safe for you to be on your own."

58

"I appreciate your concern, but I'll be just fine on my own." If Reef came . . . if they ran into someone from her time on campus . . . Horror filled her gut. If they ran into William . . .

"You sure you're all right?" he asked, concern cresting his brow.

"Fine." She took a deep breath, trying to calm the panic racing through her like a herd of thoroughbreds run wild.

"You're awfully pale."

"Reef, she just spent the last day out in the elements—as you said, chased by two men with guns. It's no wonder she's pale," Darcy said.

He nodded, though clearly suspecting there was something else.

Kirra smiled at Darcy, thankful for her support—though she wondered if Darcy really believed what she'd said or if she was just trying to help Kirra cover for the true turmoil cascading through her. Was Darcy that observant? Good thing she wasn't the one going to Fairbanks.

Kirra took a deep breath. "Look, Reef—"

"Again, you can argue until you're blue in the face, or . . . pale as Casper, as the case may be. Regardless of what argument you concoct, I'm going with you."

"And if I refuse?"

"I'll follow you."

Great. "You're not leaving me any choice."

"No, ma'am."

"Then let's get this over with." She lifted her feet from the water, which was now cold, dried them, and stood, willing her legs not to wobble as she moved toward the front room.

How could she possibly return to Fairbanks? She sighed. With Meg's life at stake, how could she not?

"Wait a minute." She paused in the doorframe, using the doorpost for added support. "How will the men watching us react to our departure? What if they realize we're going to track Meg? We're supposed to be working SAR for the duration of the race."

"Based on our little adventure in the woods, it would make sense that we pull out and defer to two fully healthy people," Reef said.

"We're healthy." Nothing but a little frostbite, and her sprained ankle was nothing more than a slight inconvenience. She wouldn't feel anything within a day or so.

"Yes, but no one but the four of us know that," Gage said. "Believe me, if you pull out due to injuries, it'll probably make the men following you feel a whole lot better."

"We'll just make a show of you two heading back to Yancey for treatment or something of the like," Darcy added. "They'll think they got you two out of the way."

Kirra frowned. "You really think they'll buy that?"

Reef smiled. "We can hope."

Why didn't that make her feel better?

6

NIKOLAI, ALASKA
MARCH 11, 11:30 A.M.

While waiting for Jake and Kayden to arrive, Reef, Kirra, Gage, and Darcy had moved to the Rohn checkpoint and then on with the rest of the SAR team and Iditarod communications crew to the village at Nikolai. They were caught back up with the race, thanks to the air force pilot who'd flown them out early.

Once the storm ended, Jake and Kayden had flown from Yancey and were due to arrive any minute. Kayden would then transport Reef and Kirra back to Anchorage airport, where they could catch a flight to Fairbanks. If all went as planned, they would be in Fairbanks by nightfall.

The first of the mushers had left Nikolai in the early morning hours, a good portion having only taken a four-hour rest, while the slower mushers, running as far as twenty-five miles behind, according to the latest update, were still passing through.

Nikolai was large compared to Rainy Pass—the first Native

American village the mushers passed through on the Iditarod course. Houses and cabins lined the low, sloped hills, and the checkpoint building offered mushers a place to crash and enjoy a hot meal.

Kirra paced the metal building, her coat on, a chill permeating the trailer-like walls. *I'm heading to Fairbanks.*

Suffocating fear threatened to swallow her.

She needed to focus on Meg, on the terror her cousin surely was going through. Kirra couldn't imagine. She needed to step past her own fears and do this for Meg.

"Hey," Jake said, entering the building, followed by Kayden. She'd be joining the Iditarod air force for the remainder of the race. It was the perfect cover for her to try and track Frank down. He'd missed the checkpoint at Rohn, which if he didn't pass through Nikolai would make three missed checkpoints. He was clearly out of the race but hadn't notified anyone he'd scratched. So far none of the other mushers they'd talked with had seen her uncle. It was as if he'd simply vanished.

Reef had suggested they ask the volunteers at the checkpoints where Frank had made food drops ahead of the race to check if any of his supplies had been touched. It was possible he'd snuck supplies when the volunteers were distracted. His dogs needed food, and so did he. He couldn't go the length of the race—nearly nine days, at bare minimum—without food and hydration. They were still waiting to hear back.

Assuming someone could be planted amongst the race personnel, they'd been very careful to watch their conversations, to speak of their true intentions and plans only when alone. Who knew how long the people responsible had this planned? They could have accomplices posing as communications helpers, checkers, or any number of volunteer positions.

It was hard to stop something they knew nothing about. If Kayden and Jake could locate Frank, maybe they'd be able to get more answers, discover what job the men had him doing, and figure out how people were going to get hurt if they didn't stop it.

Reef led the group into an unoccupied room and shut the door. It was small, the size of a storage closet, but it'd been turned into a bunkroom—every inch of space needed when the mushers came through.

Reef clasped Jake's hand. "Thanks for coming, man."

"Of course."

He stepped past Jake and hugged Kayden. "Hey, Kayd."

"How you holding up? I heard you took a shot."

"Just a graze. I'm fine."

Her gaze shifted to Kirra. "Hey, Kirra, how are you?"

She shrugged. "I've been better, but I'm okay." The frostbite seemed to be affecting only her feet—and even that was less painful than she'd expected. And her sprain was not a factor.

"As soon as you're ready to leave, I'm ready to head out."

"Won't your leaving to fly us to Anchorage cause suspicion? You just arrived to help with the race."

"Nah," Jake said. "She's simply flying two wounded searchers back to race headquarters. Nothing suspicious in that." He smiled. "In the meantime, I'll try and track your uncle. At the moment, he's the only musher missing from the race, so he gets concentrated SAR efforts. Hopefully, I'll be able to locate him and get some more answers."

"I doubt he'll talk. He looked terrified on that ridge, and we are starting to understand why."

Jake leaned against the windowsill beside Kayden. "I'll do my best to make sure I'm not followed."

Darcy took a seat on the bottom bunk. "While Jake is tracking Frank, I'll be researching his background."

Frank's background? "What for?"

"It seems the men who took Meg wanted Frank *specifically*. We need to know why. Unless you already know that, some digging will be required."

"I have no idea what they'd want with Frank."

"Well, you're in good hands." Gage squeezed Darcy's shoulders. "Darcy can find anything, and I mean *anything*."

Anything? She was definitely thankful Darcy wasn't going to Fairbanks. But she couldn't fathom what she could possibly find on Uncle Frank.

"What can you tell me about your uncle?" Darcy asked, flipping her notebook to a clean page.

Kirra sat in the chair opposite her, feeling awkward even having this conversation. "What do you want to know?"

"Everything." Darcy clicked her pen. "The more I know about him at the start, the quicker this'll go."

Kirra shifted. It seemed weird talking about her uncle, her family, to others. It wasn't like Frank had done anything wrong. He was such a private man. Sharing the details of his life with people he barely knew seemed wrong somehow. "I'm sorry, but I don't understand how knowing about Frank is going to help us find Meg." Meg was the one being held at gunpoint, not Frank.

Darcy leaned forward, her gaze sincere and direct. "The men who took Meg chose your cousin and your uncle for a particular reason."

Jake pushed off from the windowsill. "You said Frank told you they wanted him to do a job. What job? And, more importantly, why do they need *him* to do it?"

That made sense. "Okay, what do you want to know?"

"Let's start with where Frank lives," Darcy said.

"Anchorage."

"How long has he lived there?"

"As long as I can remember. Twenty years, at least."

She scribbled that down. "So your mom's family is from Anchorage?"

Kirra's brow pinched. "My mom's family?"

Darcy looked up. "Frank's last name is Weber, not Jacobs. I assumed he was your mother's brother."

"Oh. I see the confusion. My uncle Frank was adopted. Sometime after he became an adult, he legally changed his last name to his biological surname."

Darcy quickly glanced at Jake, then back at Kirra. "So Frank knows his biological parents?"

"I guess so." She ran past conversations through her mind. "But I don't recall him ever mentioning them."

"Interesting." Darcy tapped the pen against her lip. "That could come in helpful."

"Why?" What could Frank's biological parents have to do with any of this?

"Because that gives us two names to search under."

"Then, good thing you asked, because I would have never thought to mention it." It was just part of who Uncle Frank had always been.

"So, tracking back . . ." Darcy tapped her notebook, the purple pen bouncing up and down. "Your dad's family is from Anchorage?"

"No. Kodiak. I believe my dad said Uncle Frank moved to Anchorage sometime after high school."

"For college, perhaps?"

"Yes. He graduated from U of A, Anchorage."

"With a degree in . . . ?"

"Mechanical engineering."

"Okay, so he's lived in Anchorage, probably since college, and has gone by Frank Weber since around that same time. He's married, I assume?"

"Was. Aunt Sarah died ten years back. Automobile accident."

"I'm sorry."

She missed Aunt Sarah, but not nearly as much as Meg did. Worry for her cousin swirled inside. She understood Darcy's reasoning for the questioning, but it was taking up time—time she should be using to look for Meg. "Look, I want to be helpful, but Meg's out there and—"

"You want to go." Darcy smiled. "I understand. Just a couple more questions and we could be halfway to finding her."

How could that be? They hadn't even started truly searching. "How do you figure that?"

"Like I said, it's clear the men who took your cousin want something specific from your uncle. Determining what that is may lead us to the kidnappers."

"All right, a couple more questions, but then I'd really like to go." If she had to go to Fairbanks, she just wanted to get it over with. Finding Meg was what mattered, not a history lesson on Frank. Besides, they wouldn't find anything she didn't know about. Frank was as straightforward as they came. Private, but what you saw was what you got.

"Where does Frank work?"

"I don't know exactly. I think he does different consulting jobs."

"Like a contractor or free agent?"

"I think so. I can ask my dad. He may know." Though

the two had never been close. Her dad, for whatever reason, always looked down on Frank. Unfortunately she knew the feeling.

"Contacting your dad would be great, but remember to play it casual if you don't want him picking up on the fact that something's wrong," Jake said.

"Good point. My dad would call the cops regardless of my pleas otherwise." Which was ironic, considering that when she'd needed him to call the police for her—silently prayed he would—he'd let her down horribly.

A few more questions, and as promised, Darcy set her notebook aside. "That's a good enough start. I'll let you get on your way. But if you think of anything else that might be helpful or if your dad tells you anything that seems important, let me know."

"Will do." Kirra gathered her stuff. "And you'll do the same?" She hefted her duffel over her shoulder. "You'll keep me in the loop?"

"Absolutely," Jake said, walking them to the shelter door.

"Ready?" Kayden asked, hand on the knob.

Kirra nodded, and Kayden opened the door—the bitter wind swirling in.

Jake leaned over and gave Kayden a slow, tender kiss. "Be careful in this mess."

"Always." She winked.

He smiled. "We both know better."

Gage squeezed Darcy's shoulder as she typed away on the laptop. The thrill of the hunt was practically vibrating from her.

He leaned over her shoulder, his lips hovering by her delicate ear. "I know that look in your eyes. You're on to something."

She shivered as his breath danced along her neck, then smiled, leaning into him.

Jake cleared his throat.

Gage glanced over at him reclining in the chair catty-corner to them and straightened. "Didn't see you there."

An amused smirk twitched on Jake's lips. "I know—hence the cough. And for what it's worth, I agree, Darcy." He kicked his socked feet up onto the stool. "You're clearly on to something and I'm betting it has to do with Kirra's earlier comment."

Darcy smiled. "You got it."

"Yeah. Red flag went up straightaway."

Over what? Gage glanced between Darcy and Jake, curious which red flag he was apparently missing. When those two caught a scent . . . found a breadcrumb . . . they were like bloodhounds. "I hate to interrupt this cryptic interchange, but would either of you care to share your revelation with this mere mortal?"

Amusement danced across Darcy's lips.

"What's so funny?"

"Nothing." Her smile widened as he spun her chair around so she faced him. "That was just the most humble description I've ever heard you use about yourself."

"What? *Mortal?*" He leaned over, bracing a hand on either side of her chair, effectively boxing her in. "The fact that I'm just mortal should make all this"—he dipped his chin, and her gaze followed his physique—"all the more impressive." He gave a playful wink.

She attempted to smother her laughter, but it bubbled out. "You're ridiculous."

"Ridiculously handsome I know." He swooped in for a kiss.

"Please." Jake groaned. "Of course I would get stuck with you two lovebirds."

Gage lifted a brow. "I've been stuck with you and Kayden a time or two, and trust me, that's way worse."

"How do you figure that?"

"Dude, she's my *sister*."

Jake lifted a hand in surrender. "Point taken."

"All right, boys," Darcy said. "Let's get back on topic."

Jake nodded. "Right."

"So . . . where were we?" Gage snagged a biscotti from the glass cookie jar on the weathered plank counter and flopped sideways over the battered gray sofa.

"Discussing the curious fact that Frank Jacobs chooses to go by Frank Weber."

"So he chose to go by his biological last name," Gage said, crunching off a bite of almond biscotti. "Why's that curious?"

"Because it means there was either discord in his adoptive family or . . ." Darcy glanced at Jake.

"He needed a name change," Jake obliged.

"Yep." Darcy smiled. "Which in itself usually points to one of two things."

"Trouble with the law," Gage said.

"Yes, or . . ."

"He doesn't want to be found," Jake added.

"Isn't that the same thing?" Gage asked.

Darcy shook her head. "Not necessarily."

Jake leaned forward on an exhale. "All depends on who he was hiding from."

He settled into his tent, reclining on his cot. "How's Meg?" he asked over his sat phone.

"Still cooperating."

He chuckled. "You still haven't said what you are going to do with her when her daddy reaches the finish line. Surely you're not going to let her go. She knows too much." She knew *him*.

"You let me worry about that. What about the niece and her boyfriend?"

"Unfortunately they're still alive." He braced for some serious displeasure. "But they've left the race."

"What do you mean *left*?"

"They pulled out to nurse their injuries. Headed back home according to race headquarters."

"According to headquarters?" His voice tightened. "Please tell me you didn't just take their word for it."

"Of course not." He draped his leg over the cot's side. "I saw them leave myself."

"And go where?"

"They got in a plane. I assume for home."

"You *assume*? Are you kidding me? There is no room for assumption in our plan. Head to wherever home is and get visual confirmation."

He sat up. "I can, but I don't see . . ."

"I'm not asking you to see—I'm asking you to *do*."

Man, his cousin had gotten bossy and cranky since this all started. This was his cause too. Best he didn't forget that.

7

"Hi, Dad." Kirra clutched her cell to her ear, trying to hear over the heightened noise of the terminal. They'd spent the last few hours waiting for their flight and the anxious moths dancing a jig in her belly hadn't eased yet. Time to get the call to her dad over with.

"Kirra?"

"Yeah, Dad. It's me."

"You calling from the race?"

"Yep."

"Everything okay?"

"Yeah, fine. Just calling to check in."

"Oh. Well, everything's good here. Your mom and I are getting ready for our Caribbean cruise. Your mom's arthritis has been acting up, so the warm weather will do her good."

"Dad, you guys live in Arizona. Isn't it always warm there?"

"Normally. But we've only had highs in the sixties lately. Besides, she's ready for a change of scenery."

71

An escape. Her mom could only deal with reality for so long, and then she had to run away for a vacation or a weekend trip to the spa. Anything to forget whatever was upsetting her—whether it was health-related or life changes in general.

"How's the race going?"

Leave it to her dad not to ask how his brother was doing specifically. "Well." She swallowed, knowing she could only stall so long. "Hey . . ." She slipped her hair behind her ear, shifting to see Reef sitting across the corridor from her. For whatever reason—she didn't want to ponder too deeply why—his presence gave her courage. "I was just thinking . . . I don't know a lot of specifics about Uncle Frank, and since I'll be seeing him throughout the race, I thought it would be nice to have some talking points."

"O . . . *kay*. What do you want to know?"

"What's he doing these days for a job?"

"Last I heard he was working with the oil rigs."

"When was that?"

"Last I heard."

"Which was a few months ago, a few years ago?"

"I don't know, Kirra. Why does it matter?"

"Just curious. Any idea which oil company?"

"I don't exactly keep tabs on my brother. What's with all the questions?"

"I told you, I know I'm going to see Frank, and it got me thinking—"

His huffy laugh cut her off. "Well, you do tend to overthink things."

Just like he believed she'd overthought the rape, that perhaps that wasn't what *really* happened? She'd been drinking, and either way, what good would come of dragging both their names through the mud? Private matters should remain private.

"Thanks, Dad." *For nothing.*

"Do you want to talk to your mom? I'm sure I can pull her away from the greenhouse, if you really want to talk with her."

"No. Don't bother. I've got to go."

"All right. Take care of yourself."

She was the only one who would.

She strode back over to Reef, her gut hollow.

"Hey," he said as she slipped into the vinyl chair beside him. "You okay?"

"Yeah." Her jaw tightened. "Fine."

"Did your dad have anything helpful?"

Hurtful, yes. Helpful, possibly, she supposed. "Maybe. He said last he heard Frank was working on an oil rig."

"Did he say which company?"

"He didn't know."

"How long ago was this?"

"He didn't remember that either."

"Okay." Reef raked his hands through his hair. "I'll call Jake and update them. It's at least a place to start."

"You're going to have to wait until we reach Fairbanks." She gestured to the plane loading.

"Gotcha." He grabbed their duffels.

She reached for hers. "I can take that."

"No problem." He slung it over his shoulder. "After you."

She still wasn't sure what to do with a chivalrous Reef.

He put their bags in the overhead compartment and settled into the aisle seat beside her. The commuter plane was small, with only two seats on either side of the aisle.

She studied him as he settled in. His family was so different than hers. *He* was so different from the memory in her mind of a reckless and arrogant teen.

She shifted, facing him. "Your family is great."

"Yeah." He smiled. "They really are."

Was he excluding himself from that?

"You all seem really close, always ready to come to each other's aid." And hers, Frank's, and Meg's—they weren't even related. Why would the McKennas go to all the trouble they were just to help her family out? Well, part of her family. The only part that mattered.

"Yeah. It's a tremendous blessing. One I don't deserve."

"Your family doesn't seem to feel that way."

"No." He smiled. "They don't."

"That's got to make you feel good."

He turned, arching a brow. "You say that with regret. Is your family . . . ? I mean, I thought you had a nice family."

"Oh, they're *nice* all right."

His brows arched.

She shook her head. "Never mind. Tell me more about your family."

"Like what?"

"Anything. I love listening to Kayden talk about all your adventures and family antics. Gage seems hysterical."

"Yeah. There's never a dull moment."

They spent the next hour talking about the McKennas, and she reveled in the fantasy of being part of such a loving family. Not that her parents weren't loving. . . . They just didn't know how to react to the difficult parts of life. And in her opinion, that's what real family was—being there for one another during the hard parts of life, supporting and standing up for one another.

Reef smiled.

Kirra shifted. "What?"

"Nothing. I just haven't heard you this talkative in years."

"Meaning?" Was that a good or bad thing?

"It's a compliment. It's nice having a real conversation with you."

"Real?" What did that mean?

"You know . . . one where you aren't lecturing me." He winked.

"Is that who you really think I am?" That she only lectured or bossed? Though, based on their history, she could see where he was coming from. His thoughtful stare and slight smile curving on his lips sent a jig aflutter in her belly.

"I used to."

She swallowed, drawn to his deep blue eyes and the sincerity resting in them. "And now?"

His smile slowly widened on one side—a sexy lopsided grin. "I feel like I'm beginning to see the real you for the first time."

She was dying to ask if he liked what he saw, but she wasn't brave enough.

She stared out the plexiglass window as they made their descent into Fairbanks, her heart thudding in her throat.

8

Kirra followed Reef through Fairbanks International Airport. What was she doing? She couldn't be back here. Her alma mater held some of her best memories, but also her very worst. But Darcy was right—the university was their best resource for determining Meg's whereabouts.

She prayed Meg's roommate, Ashley, knew when Meg had left campus. Knowing when she left and where she was headed would give them the first piece of the puzzle, and Kirra was anxious to start filling in the empty slate before them.

"Hey." Reef nudged her arm. "It's going to be okay."

She straightened. "How can you possibly know that?"

"Because I have faith."

The statement seemed odd coming from Reef. Oh, she knew people could change—she'd witnessed change in Reef already—but Reef McKenna was talking to her about faith. . . . God certainly had an ironic sense of humor. "Sorry to tell you this, but even people of faith are let down sometimes."

"Trust me." He hefted his duffel higher on his shoulder. "I know."

She bit her bottom lip. His parents had both been strong

believers, and both died young. Reef had endured his share of sorrow and suffering.

"But that doesn't mean we shouldn't have faith," he said, holding the glass door open for her. "Jesus doesn't promise us a life without trouble. In fact, for His followers He says the exact opposite."

The verse from John 16 sank into her veins. *"In this world you will have trouble. But take heart! I have overcome the world."*

Reef was right. She'd had trouble, but she continued to believe in God. What she struggled with were the *why*s. Why hadn't God stopped William from raping her? Why hadn't He brought the healing she so desperately desired?

Looking back, she had to admit she hadn't prayed about her decision to join William at the party before she acted, before she took that first drink or the second. She certainly hadn't heeded the voice inside saying he wasn't right for her, that time spent with William was not beneficial. Boy, how she wished she'd listened. Would it have stopped William from doing what he did? Maybe not, but it would have changed the circumstances it happened under, and that would have made a huge difference in how Tracey viewed her, how others viewed her. Being let down by those she loved and trusted most had nearly brought her to her knees.

"Hey." Reef's fingers brushed hers—lingering long enough that heat transferred. "You still with me?"

"Yeah." She swallowed, knowing she should pull back but, for the first time in two years, not wanting to lose physical contact. His hand was soothing, his skin soft.

"Kirra?" He dipped his head to look her in the eye. His fingers softly tangled with hers.

"Sorry." She shook her head. "Got distracted."

"Not in a good way."

She frowned. "What?" He was the one who'd reached for her hand.

"Your face scrunched all up. Whatever you were thinking about, it wasn't pleasant."

Could Reef really read her that well? Was she that transparent? Panic slid up her throat. She needed to change the subject, quickly. She eased her hand back, slipping it in her coat pocket as they stepped outside to the rental car lot. "So . . . how long did you and Meg date?"

He cocked his head, clearly caught off guard by the question. "A couple months. She was in her first year at the community college and I was running snow-kiting lessons out on Twenty Mile River. Meg came for a class and . . ."

"You two started seeing each other."

"We grabbed a bite afterward."

"And?"

"And hung out some for a while."

Why did that sting so? "How come it didn't last?" Probably because Reef rarely stuck anything out—though to be fair, neither did Meg.

Kirra loved her cousin, but Meg certainly wasn't flawless. Maybe that's why she'd been the one to stick closest by Kirra after the rape—because she understood what it was like to be judged.

"I guess I just felt it was time to move on. Looking back . . ." He raked a hand through his hair. "Meg was young and I was immature. It was a bad combo."

"Do you two still stay in touch?" Why was jealousy rising in her throat, spreading heat across her chest? So Reef had dated her cousin. So Meg knew the soft feel of Reef's lips. So what?

It wasn't like anything would ever happen between Reef and *her*. He was too dangerous, lived too fully.

"I'll get the occasional text or FB message," Reef answered, his brow arched, a smile tugging at his lips. Did he find her jealousy amusing? "Our exchanges are random and certainly not serious."

Relief filled her, and that frightened her. Why should she care about Reef's relationship with Meg—or with any woman, for that matter? She needed to stop spending so much time with him. Her vision was getting clouded.

So they'd shared an intimate conversation on the plane and a dreamy kiss in the cave—which he still hadn't brought up, thank goodness. The cold, hard fact was he was completely opposite of what she needed, so there was zero point in letting herself get attached.

A more frightening concern was *why* she was growing so attached in the first place? This was *Reef McKenna*. He dated women like Meg—free-spirited, fun, and risk takers. She, on the other hand, had taken one big risk in her life, and it had cost her a piece of her soul.

She'd prayed and prayed and prayed for God to fill the void. She believed God could make her whole again, but for some reason He hadn't yet. There was still a hollowness eating away inside her—one she attempted to hide, one she tried to fill by taking care of her dogs, but one that wouldn't go away.

She'd been holding on to hope for two years and still the emptiness remained. Maybe she'd better get used to the idea that she might never be whole again.

She stared out the rental car window as they headed for

a restaurant Reef had recommended. She hated taking time to stop for dinner, but she was starving. Besides, returning to campus at night would only heighten her anxiety. It was near the same time of year that—

She cut off the thought before a panic attack set in. She couldn't let Reef see her like that.

They'd decided they would get a couple hotel rooms for the night and would approach Meg's roommate first thing in the morning. There was no sense heading over when classes weren't in session. They needed to be able to question whomever Ashley might direct them to, and that was far more likely to happen during the day.

The restaurant he chose was surprisingly quaint—seating a total of thirty patrons. White tablecloths covered small round tables, and lit white lanterns on the center of the tables added an intimate ambiance. As she sat on a dark wooden chair carved with nautical themes along the back, she felt sheltered and protected—two things she'd been yearning to feel for two years. How did Reef keep doing it?

His gaze remained on her throughout dinner—their conversation kept to a minimum. The silence was nice, the food delicious. God was giving her a moment of peace before the storm she was about to walk into.

9

FAIRBANKS, ALASKA
MARCH 11, 10:15 P.M.

Reef drove their rental car around the back of the hotel, where they'd requested adjoining rooms. Neither of them had sensed anyone following them from Nikolai. Kirra prayed the men who had tracked them on snowmobiles, or whoever might be keeping tabs on them, had bought their story of heading back to Yancey to heal, but it was better to be safe than sorry. Better to stay in secluded places and keep a low profile.

Kirra took in the hotel room as Reef ushered her inside. It ranged about midway between scary and nice. It was older, but clean. Run by an elderly man and his wife. The wife's touches could be seen in the lace doilies topping the nightstand and matching pine dresser.

Reef remained in her room while she got settled, taking a seat at the small table by the curtained window. "You hardly touched your dinner," he said.

"I wasn't that hungry."

He leaned forward. "I know you're worried about Meg, but we'll find her."

"How can you sound so certain?"

"She's got a lot of good people looking for her, and we have time. The race doesn't end for another week, and that's just the leaders."

"A week isn't long." She riffled through her duffel for the third time since they'd checked in, not even knowing what she was looking for—simply trying to distract herself from the encroaching panic.

Reef stood and moved to her side. He clasped his hands around hers. "I have faith God will get us through this—all of us."

She choked back tears, praying his faith would be enough for them both, because hers seemed to be sorely lacking at the moment. The events of the past two days had weakened her, and being back in Fairbanks, all the spiritual questions that had plagued her following the rape were whispering in her ear. *Where was God? Why did He allow it to happen? When would He make her whole again? Would she ever be whole again?*

She'd sought out a Christian counselor when the pain had nearly consumed her, and the woman had been of help. The questions had quieted, and Kirra had begun to rebuild her relationship with the Lord, but now, being here, so close to it all . . . It was as if she'd been slammed back two years, and the emotions were raw and pricking at the surface.

"Come here." Reef pulled her into his embrace. He'd been doing a lot of that lately. Was he making a play, or did he just realize she was aching for comfort, for security? To her surprise, she believed the latter.

"Thanks," she said, pulling away after a moment. "I appreciate you being here, but we should both get some sleep."

"Right." Reef slid his hands in his jean pockets. "Important day tomorrow."

She cringed. He had no idea.

He arrived in Yancey shortly before dawn. No doubt a good twelve hours behind Reef and Kirra. But they'd had quick access to a plane. He'd had to call and get one sent in. It was surprising he was only twelve hours behind, given the circumstances.

Yancey was a small town, which made his job easier. He'd quickly locate the pair and discern if they really were letting the incident go. Glancing through the Internet White Pages, he searched for Kirra Jacobs' vet business and sled dog shelter—Nanook Haven.

He put out his cigarette, crunching it into the snow with the tip of his boot as the rental car agency opened for the day. Thankfully he'd only had to wait an hour.

Now for a drive out to Nanook Haven.

University of Alaska, Fairbanks
March 12, 8:10 a.m.

Kirra hadn't seemed quite right to Reef since Darcy first suggested they interview Meg's roommate in person. Did the two not get along? Was there something about her time at University of Alaska, Fairbanks, that left a sour taste in her mouth?

She moved quickly across campus, not looking up, not making eye contact with anyone. Her frame was stiff, her jaw tight. What had happened here?

He wanted to ask if she was okay, but he knew she would again insist she was fine. She'd skirted the subject of her discomfort during their flight, turning the conversation instead to his brief relationship with her cousin Meg.

His time with Meg had resulted in a handful of dates—barely enough to be labeled a relationship, but Kirra had used that term multiple times. The fact that he'd dated Meg bothered her. He could read it in the tightness of her jaw and brow. Perhaps she wasn't thrilled that her cousin had dallied with the wild McKenna brother. Or, more likely, she knew he wasn't good enough for Meg—which definitely meant he wasn't good enough for her.

That was true, but he'd been praying, hoping, maybe she'd begin to see him differently, and there were moments when he thought she did—the passionate, yet tender, kiss being one of them; their frank conversation on the plane another.

She still hadn't mentioned the kiss, and he wondered if she even remembered it. She'd been half asleep. Either way, the memory of it *was* burned fast and foremost in his mind.

He'd never experienced the sensations he had in that kiss. It left him aching for more. For more of her—not physically but emotionally. He wanted to get to know her better, to figure out what made her tick, to be able to ease the furrowed lines from her brow, to be of comfort and support to her.

She made him want to be a better man. That's why he was here. He would help her find Meg. He'd prove he could see something through, that he could be a reliable friend, that he cared about them both—Meg as a friend, and Kirra as infinitely more, even if she never reciprocated the feelings. He'd screwed up so much in life, had not been there for those he loved, had not followed through. He wasn't screwing up this time, wasn't walking away.

They entered the dorm building, Kirra moving quickly up the concrete stairs to the third floor.

"Have you met her before? Meg's roommate?"

"Yeah. When they came to visit Yancey over Thanksgiving break."

"That should help." It wouldn't be two total strangers showing up at her door.

"Meg is in room 304." Kirra followed the door numbers. "Here."

"Let's hope Ashley's in." Otherwise they'd have to try and track her down on campus.

Kirra knocked on the door.

A moment later, to Reef's great relief, it opened.

A petite woman with long, obviously dyed hair greeted them. "Yeah?" She looked up and smiled as her gaze locked on Kirra. "Kirra? What are you doing here?"

"We're looking for Meg."

"She's not here."

"We know."

Ashley frowned. "What's going on?"

"You may want to take a seat," Reef suggested as she let them in.

The room was typical of a college dorm. Two twin beds were lofted, one with a desk and workstation underneath, the other with a dresser and mounds of clothes—*Meg's*. So opposite Kirra's organized nature.

"Okay, you're kind of freaking me out," Ashley said, moving across the blue carpet to her chair. "What's going on, Kirra?"

Kirra rubbed her arms. "I don't know how best to say this, so I'll just come out with it." She paused until Ashley sat, then exhaled. "Meg's missing."

Ashley's eyes narrowed. "What do you mean *missing*?"

"It's what we've been told," Kirra said, leaning against the wooden bed frame.

"Told?" Ashley's brow creased. "By who?"

"Her dad."

"Oh." Ashley exhaled, the tightness in her face easing.

Kirra's brows arched. "What?"

Ashley swallowed, slipping a strand of her crimson-dyed hair behind her ear. "I'm sure this is all just a bit of confusion."

"What do you mean?"

"Well, you know Meg always goes to see her dad off in the Iditarod . . ."

"Right," Kirra said.

"Well, when Meg was getting ready to leave and I said, 'Say hey to your dad for me,' she gave me this strange look."

Kirra's delicately arched brows furrowed. "Strange, *how*?"

"Like that wasn't where she was really going."

"You think she lied to you about going to the Iditarod?"

"I don't know." Ashley shifted, pulling her knees to her chest, the swivel chair shifting with her. "Meg's been kind of different lately."

"Different?" Kirra asked. "How?"

"She's been hanging around with this new crowd. Kind of getting edgy."

Getting edgy? What was Meg into?

"What kind of crowd?" Kirra asked.

"And edgy how?" Reef added. In his experience, Meg

already straddled the line between acceptable and wild behavior. Had she moved completely over?

Ashley rested her chin on her knees. "This environmental group on campus. ROW. Rescue Our World. They're all jazzed up about saving the world—well, the environment. They're always edgy. I think it's a persona they purposely work to give off, but if you ask me, I'd say they're just twitchy because they ingest too much caffeine. They are always going on and on about one cause after another. Always complaining about this thing or that. I mean, I'm sorry, but a little hairspray isn't going to bring the world to the brink of destruction. A girl's got to have good hair. Am I right?"

Kirra smiled and nodded, but Reef could tell she was itching to get down to business.

"This group," Kirra said. "Do you know any of the members?"

"Meg tried bringing a few of them to our parties, but they were always too busy sitting up on their high horses, preaching to everyone else, to ever enjoy themselves. Kind of a downer, you know? After a while she stopped bringing them."

"You think she stopped hanging out with them?" Kirra asked.

"Nope." Ashley stood, retrieved her messenger bag off the fraying blue carpet, and stepped to her desk. "I think she just decided to keep her friend groups separate."

"Why?"

"I don't think she liked getting flack from us about hanging out too much with those eco-nuts, and I'm just as certain they gave her equal flack for hanging out with us."

"Why?" Kirra frowned.

"Because we weren't into '*the cause.*'" She shoved a couple books in her bag. "It made things awkward with Meg. It was like this point of tension neither of us talked about, but it was always there."

"Could we get some names from you?" Reef asked.

"Of the eco-nuts?" Ashley shrugged. "Sure." She grabbed a notebook and fluffy pen and started scribbling. "I only know a couple of names, but you could always talk to Professor Baxter."

"Professor Baxter?"

"He's head of the Environmental Science department, and the eco-crowd reveres him like a god. I'm sure he could give you some names, probably even tell you about Meg's interest in the cause."

"Was she a student of his?"

"She's taking three of his classes this semester."

"Three? Wow. She must really like him."

"Likes what he has to say." She shoved the last of her books into her bag and swung the flap over, hiking the strap across her shoulder. "He's the one that fires the rest of them up."

"Any idea where we can find him now?"

"Sure. His lecture starts in fifteen minutes."

"Okay, is there anyone else you think we should talk to? Any other professors, a boyfriend, ex-boyfriend . . . ?"

"Her most recent boyfriend was Garret Bale—spends most of his time in the weight room. He's a senior, but Meg dumped him last week. As for professors, she only has Baxter and William Daniels."

Kirra stiffened, her skin paling.

He grazed her arm. "You okay?"

She flinched. "Yeah, fine."

Ashley covered her mouth. "Oh, Kirra. I'm sorry, I—"

Kirra held up a hand, cutting her off. "Don't worry about it. I didn't realize he was teaching or that Meg had a class with him."

Who was William Daniels, and why did his name have such an effect on Kirra?

"You sure you're okay?"

"I'm fine." She nodded.

He looked back to Ashley. Why did he have the feeling he was the only clueless one in the room? "Where can we find Professor Daniels?"

"We don't need to talk to him," Kirra said.

"Why not?"

"He has nothing to do with environmental science."

"And he hardly knew Meg," Ashley added. "I mean he knew who she was because of . . ." She looked at Kirra with a pained expression. "I mean . . . she was one of several hundred in his intro class, and she went out of her way to avoid him. You'd be wasting your time talking to him."

Reef's gaze shifted between a mortified-looking Ashley and a queasy-looking Kirra. What was going on?

"I'm sorry I have to rush off." Ashley clutched the handle of her messenger bag. "But I've got a test in ten minutes that counts for a third of my grade. I can meet up with you two after . . ."

"That's okay," Kirra said. "I think we got everything we need, but give me a call if you think of anything else."

Ashley nodded and mouthed "Sorry" to Kirra as she slipped through the doorway.

Reef waited until they were alone at the end of the hall before asking, "What was that all about?"

Kirra slipped her hat back on before stepping outside.

Snow had started to fall. The burgundy knit cap was a striking contrast to her golden hair and the white flakes swirling around them. "What was what all about?"

"Professor Daniels?"

Kirra slinked her hands into her pea coat pockets. "Like Ashley said, he'd be no help to us. He's a waste of time."

She trudged on in front of him, her shoulders rigid, and her head down. Was she shaking?

He increased his stride and draped an arm around her slender shoulders.

She stiffened. "What are you doing?"

"Trying to warm you up. You're shivering."

"Oh. Right. Shivering. Thanks."

"No problem." He'd hold her in his arms anytime. "So where are we going?"

"To see Professor Baxter."

"What do you mean they aren't there?" his cousin roared over the phone as he pulled down the drive.

"I checked her place. She's not there."

"And McKenna?"

He looked at the McKenna family home in his rearview mirror. "I posed as a delivery guy saying I needed a package signed personally by the recipient—Reef McKenna—and the gal who answered said her brother was at the Iditarod."

"Okay, so if they aren't in Yancey and they aren't at the race, *where* are they?"

He swallowed, acid bubbling up his throat. "I don't know."

"Then, find out!"

The line went dead.

He popped the lid off the Tums and tossed a couple in his mouth. He should have known that Kirra Jacobs would be a nuisance. She had trouble written all over her.

Kirra stepped into the auditorium, her heart in her throat as a million different emotions crashed through her. Her mind drifted back to her first class in this very room, her first day as a grad student, ready to take on the world. It was the day she met William—the sparks had been instantaneous, but in the end they'd burned her.

The room swirled around her, and she sank into an open seat, trying to catch a breath before she passed out.

Reef gazed over at her as the lights dimmed and the professor stopped talking. A video appeared on the large screen at the front of the auditorium.

He leaned toward her and whispered over the deep voice of the narrator, "You okay?"

She nodded and kept her gaze pinned on the wildlife frolicking across the screen. *This is going to end very badly.*

10

BETWEEN TAKOTNA AND OPHIR, ALASKA
MARCH 12, 8:30 A.M.

Kayden flew while Jake scanned the frozen ground several hundred feet below. He tried to ignore the tiny black pouch nestled in his front jean pocket, the outline of the ring pressing against his thigh. He'd been about to propose when the call came in from Reef. Now he'd have to wait for the opportune moment, but keeping silent was burning his lungs.

Kayden dipped the nose of the Cessna, making another sweep of the rugged trail as the sun rose full in the sky—a rare sight, and one they didn't expect to have for long, since the infernal gray cloud cover was moving in again. They'd flown over a couple of the lead mushers, who were pressing toward Ophir after only taking a few hours to rest in Takotna—unlike the majority of the mushers, who had chosen to take the twenty-four-hour rest required at some point of the race in the well-equipped village.

The twenty-three-mile route between Takotna and Ophir was a series of switchbacks climbing up the ridge, making travel difficult for the mushers and dogs alike. So far there was no sign of Frank, his neon-green coat always an Iditarod standout.

Kayden swung around the last of the switchbacks, and Jake hollered, "There."

"What?"

"I think we've got a musher in trouble." He peered down at a sled flipped sideways along the northwest side of the ridge.

"I'm going to have to track west past the trail to find a landing spot."

He peered at the dogs tangled on their line, no sign of the musher. He could be pinned beneath his sled. "Do it."

Kayden landed the plane—skis attached to the wheels—and they disembarked. They took time to pull on their necessary winter gear. It'd be a couple-mile hike back to where he'd spotted the downed musher, and the temps were still below zero.

The air was frigid, but crisp—just how Jake liked it. He appreciated the sun peeking through the cloud cover, but it wouldn't last long—another storm was headed their way.

When they reached the overturned sled, the dogs howled at their approach.

"Hello? Who's there?" a man asked.

"Iditarod SAR," Jake answered, following the sound of the man's voice.

"Thank goodness. I'm down here."

Jake peered over the ridge to find Warren Hunt—two-time Iditarod champ—clinging to a narrow outcrop, his body flush with the ice-covered rock wall. Jake took in the hundred-foot drop below—Warren was one lucky man. "Hang on. We'll get you up."

He looked back at Kayden, who was already assessing their options. She scrounged through Warren's gear bag. It had been tossed twenty feet from the sled but remained intact. She pulled out a rope and held it aloft.

Jake held out his hand. "Toss it here."

"I can climb down to him."

Of course she'd want to go the adventurous route. "No need. I'll anchor the rope and send it down to him. He can climb up."

She exhaled. "Fine. I'll right the sled."

"Wait and we'll help you."

"I'm quite capable."

"I have no doubt where that's concerned, but the dogs might try and bolt when the sled's upright. Better him"— Jake gestured with a tilt of his chin to Warren—"handling the dogs while you and I right it."

Kayden nodded, agreeing but clearly not pleased. Always so strong willed and yearning for adventure—it was a big part of why he loved her. Why he wanted her to be his wife.

Jake secured the rope around his waist and lowered the rest of it down to Warren. Digging his boots into the snow, he braced himself to hold Warren's weight. Slowly but steadily, Warren climbed up hand over hand, his feet wrapped around the rope. He crested the edge of the ridge, and Kayden, lying flat on her stomach for stability, hefted him up onto solid ground. Warren moved straight for his team and exhaled in relief to find none of them injured.

"What happened?" Jake asked after they'd righted his sled and he'd seen to his dogs. "Get too close to the ridge?" It was easy enough to do, even for an expert musher like Warren Hunt.

"Only because a snowmobile nearly ran us right off the mountain."

"What?"

"I caught a glimpse of Frank Weber off course, down there . . ." He gestured to the valley beneath the ridge. "I tried to wave him down. See if he needed help. He's been off grid since Rainy Pass. Before I could flag his attention, this snowmobile came out of nowhere. I had to bank right to avoid being hit head on and ended up where you found me."

The first visual on Frank in nearly three days. What was he doing? What could the kidnappers possibly want him to do out in this rugged, desolate part of the state they loved? And why try to take out Warren? Just because he'd spotted Frank? Probably because he could report Frank's location to SAR volunteers, and the men behind the kidnapping wanted to keep Frank isolated and on track.

"Can you describe the snowmobile or its rider?" Kayden asked.

"Obnoxious." Warren situated himself on the sled. "Probably some bored kid who lives out here and thought it'd be funny to shake things up a bit." He shook his head with a disgusted sigh and swung an arm toward his team. "His idea of fun could have got us all injured or killed."

"I'm just glad you're okay," Kayden said.

Jake nodded in agreement. He was thankful Warren and his team were safe, but he didn't share his assessment of a foolish youth looking for a thrill as the cause of his accident. It was the man watching Frank, making sure no one intercepted or interacted with Frank Weber. He felt confident of it. "Is there *anything* you remember about the man or his ride?" he asked.

"It happened so fast. I think the snowmobile was white, which is why I didn't see it until it was right upon us. I heard the engine but couldn't lay eyes on it. Then, all of a sudden, it was whirring across our path."

"And Frank?"

"No idea. I hope he's not still off course. Once you stray from the path . . ." Warren gazed at the storm burgeoning along the darkening horizon. "Especially in these conditions. It's easy to get lost—permanently." He hunched his shoulders against the wind, tightening his hood around his face. "Speaking of weather—you two had better hurry on to Ophir or back to Takotna, or you'll be grounded."

"Thanks. Just one more thing."

"Yeah?"

"Can you tell me exactly where Frank was? Which way he was headed?"

"He was on the north side of Furrow's Ridge continuing north."

Which made no sense, when the race course dropped south. But it gave them a place to start searching, and that was something. "Thanks." Jake extended his hand.

"Thank you," Warren said, giving his dogs the order to mush, and moments later he and his team disappeared into the white void.

Jake slid his gloved hands into his coat pockets. "What do you think?" He studied the sky—dark and massing with thick cloud cover. "Do we need to head back in?" They'd finally gotten a bead on Frank. If they missed this opportunity, who knew when, or *if*, they'd have another.

"Probably." She leaned against him, warming him instantly.

"But . . . this is our best shot at finding Frank. I say we give it a quick sweep before heading back."

His thoughts exactly.

"You're going to do what?" Gage said over the radio.

"We've got a bead on Frank Weber. We're going to make a quick sweep over the area," Jake repeated.

That's what he thought Jake had said. "You know the weather is worsening. Zero visibility soon."

"I know. We're going to give it fifteen. If we don't see a sign of him by then, we'll head in."

"Okay, but you know if you go down with zero visibility no one can come to help until this passes."

Jake paused, then exhaled. "We're aware of the risks."

Gage shook his head, knowing he and Darcy—infuriatingly dogged woman that she was—would do the exact same, but he didn't have to like their decision. That was his sister out there.

"Those are some dedicated volunteers," Ethan said as he entered the room and settled back in the open chair beside him.

The two had been volunteering for the Iditarod for years—Ethan on communication and Gage typically on SAR. But this year they were both on communications, along with Xander Cook—another volunteer Gage had seen around the race before.

Gage reclined in his chair, stretching his legs out. "You don't know the half of it."

"Are they talking about Frank Weber?"

"Yeah. He's been MIA since Rainy Pass."

"I heard he pulled out of the race," Xander said, coming up behind them with three cans of soda. He tossed them each one, then popped his own open.

"Missing checkpoints means he's out whether he wants to be or not." Ethan took a swig of root beer.

"So why are they still searching?" Xander propped himself on the corner of the folding table serving as a desk.

Gage set his soda down. "To make sure he's okay. It's odd for a competitor to bail on a race but stay out in the field."

Ethan swiped his mouth. "You think Frank's lost?"

"Perhaps." Though his avoidance of the checkpoints certainly seemed intentional.

"Or injured?" Xander offered.

"Another possibility." But it appeared he was not, from what Jake had said about Warren Hunt's sighting.

"Well, he's lucky your sister and her boyfriend are so dedicated." Ethan glanced at the data streaming in on the laptop screen.

Gage leaned forward. "Anything interesting?"

"Storm's moving in, but you already know that. No mushers missing, other than Frank Weber."

"That's good." Gage got to his feet. "I think I'll take my break and grab a bite."

Ethan glanced back at the kitchen. "Enjoy that gorgeous girlfriend of yours."

"Always." Gage smiled. She was the light of his life.

Entering the kitchen, he found Darcy hunched over her laptop at the far table.

"How's it going?" he asked, swooping in beside her.

"Gage!" She swatted him. "You scared me."

"Sorry. Didn't mean to." Okay, maybe a little. He loved getting the best of her—it happened so rarely.

"Guess I was engrossed." She smiled, finally looking away from her work for more than a millisecond.

Gage lifted an orange from his sack and started peeling it—citrus infusing the air. "I'm guessing you found something?"

Darcy glanced around the room and slid closer to Gage so her shoulder was flush against his. Now he was engrossed.

She lifted her notes, glancing around again to be sure no one was paying particular attention to them and then whispered, "I'm waiting to hear back on a couple favors I called in, but it looks like Frank Jacobs has a record."

He tried to ignore the tantalizing feel of her breath along his neck, her vanilla scent mixing with the citrus. "Really?"

"Yep. Frank Weber is clean, but Frank *Jacobs* was involved in a breaking and entering on Kodiak that appears to have gone very wrong." She couldn't hide her smile. Uncovering the truth was what she lived for.

An hour of disturbing images later, the video mercifully ended.

Reef leaned over and whispered, "I see what Ashley means about kindling a fire."

Kirra nodded.

She'd been doing a lot of that lately. Nodding silently—which was so unlike the Kirra he knew. Normally, he couldn't shut her up. Here she was different. Sullen. Guarded. She was afraid of something or someone on campus. He'd sensed it the moment she'd reluctantly agreed to visit the university, and her increasing discomfort with each passing minute was palpable. Something was wrong, something that reached far deeper than Meg's disappearance.

The lights switched on, and the professor answered a few questions before dismissing the class.

Reef and Kirra headed against the flow of traffic, moving down the steps to the front of the auditorium as the rest of the students piled out the exit doors at the rear of the building.

"Professor Baxter," Reef said.

The man turned from slipping his laptop into his brief-case. "Yes?"

"Can we talk to you for a moment?"

"My office hours are from two to four, Tuesday and Thursday."

"This will only take a few moments of your time, and it's vitally important."

"I appreciate your attempt at brevity, but when it comes to the state of the environment, believe me, there are no quick questions or answers for that matter."

"This isn't about the environment."

"Oh?" He frowned.

"We'd like to ask you about one of your students. Meg Weber."

He slid his laptop in the case. "I'm afraid I'm not at liberty to discuss my students."

"She's my cousin," Kirra said, "and she's missing."

"Missing?"

"Yes."

"A lot of college students *appear* to be missing now and again, but they always turn up."

How could the man be so nonchalant about such a topic?

"It's their first time away from home, their first taste of

real freedom, and when they embrace it, they are often assumed missing by overbearing, frantic parents whose need to control borders on the obsessive."

Reef was guessing the man didn't have a college-age daughter or he'd probably view the situation very differently.

"No. She's definitely missing," Kirra said, her voice tight.

His brows hiked up. "If that's the case, why aren't the police here?"

"It's a long story," Reef said.

"I see." He rocked back on his heels. "Well, I'm sure the police are doing what they can. Now, if you'll excuse me." He stepped past them, heading for the door.

"Please, wait," Kirra said. "She *is* missing and in danger. It's complicated, but if you could just tell us the last time you saw her, it could be of great help."

He paused on a long exhale. "Who did you say your cousin is?"

"Meg Weber."

"Meg Weber . . . Ah, young redhead."

"Yes."

"I think she was in my Friday lecture, but I can't be certain. You've seen the size of my classes."

"She was supposed to leave Friday afternoon for Anchorage to see her father off in the Iditarod, but we believe she went elsewhere."

"Such as?"

"We don't know. We spoke with her roommate, and she mentioned that Meg was really getting into fighting for the environment," Reef said, hoping he worded his sentence in a way that would grab the professor's attention. As of yet, he seemed disinterested at best.

"And so you assume . . . what?"

"Her roommate didn't know the names of Meg's new friends, but she thought you might. She thought maybe they might have seen Meg last or known where she was headed."

"Seems farfetched."

"Right now it's our only lead."

"Well, that's pitiful."

"Can you help us?"

"I'm not going to give out student names, but I will tell you that the ROW group is meeting in the student union right now. The students that are currently on campus, at least."

"And where would the rest of the group's members be?"

"At a Save the Whales rally in Seward."

"Thank you, Professor Baxter. If you think of anything else that might be helpful—anything at all—would you give us a call?"

Kirra fished out a business card for Nanook Haven and scribbled her cell number on the back.

"Kirra Jacobs?" He tapped the card. "That name . . ."

Kirra shrunk back, nearly hiding behind Reef.

"She graduated from here," Reef said. "Maybe she took one of your classes." He looked to Kirra.

"No. I didn't." She tugged Reef's arm. "Come on. We've taken up enough of Professor Baxter's time."

"When did you graduate?"

"She graduated from the vet school two years ago," Reef said as Kirra practically dragged him toward the door.

"Huh. Well, I'm sure it'll come to me . . . Kirra Jacobs." His hand stilled. "Kirra. *You're* the one who . . ." Contempt oozed from his voice.

Kirra's shoulders dropped as her hand wrapped tight on the door handle.

"I suggest you wrap up your business and leave campus immediately."

Leave? Reef looked to Kirra, who looked mortified.

"If she's *your* cousin, I'm sure the circumstances surrounding her supposed disappearance have been greatly exaggerated," Baxter said.

Reef turned, moving back for Baxter. "Excuse me? How dare you insinuate . . ."

"Come on, Reef." Kirra tugged him through the door and shut it behind them.

"Be careful with that one," Baxter hollered after them, his angry voice echoing down the long cinderblock hall. "When it comes to insinuation, she's a pro."

Kirra's heart raced in her chest, her stomach swirling in a rapid pull that threatened to knock her to her knees.

"Why did you yank me out of there?" Reef asked. "He can't talk to you like that."

She was shocked that's all Professor Baxter had said. She'd forgotten how close William and he had been—the mentor and mentee, now apparently colleagues in the same department. William had clearly covered his tracks by staging *his* version of the events with his mentor. She could just imagine the conversation, the lies William had told Baxter.

An icy chill shot through her and she pitched forward.

"Whoa!" Reef's strong arm wrapped around her waist. "You okay?"

She grabbed the wall for support, her head spinning. "I'm fine. Just need"—*to get away from here*—"some fresh air."

"You're shivering." He pulled her into his embrace, and she fought the urge to simply collapse into his hold, but he wasn't her savior.

This was Reef McKenna, after all.

Despite the changes she'd witnessed in him, and the change in her feelings toward him, she couldn't throw caution to the wind. Couldn't trust him to keep her safe or to be the man she'd been praying for. This was Reef—irresponsible, playboy, and risk taker. Far too much like William.

"Hey, relax." Reef rubbed her arm, trying to warm her. "I've got you."

"Can we go please?"

"To meet with the ROW group?"

Ugh. She couldn't leave. Not until she'd followed every possible lead. Her cousin's life hung in the balance.

"Yeah," she said, trying to compose herself and feeling like an utter fool for letting Reef see her fall apart. Maybe she really was the drama queen William claimed her to be. The thought reduced her to tears, but she quickly covered them with a false sneeze.

Reef appraised her. "Are you . . . ?"

"Sneeze made my eyes water." She inhaled and swiped at her eyes, shouldering her strength for the next step—visiting the ROW group. "Let's go. Baxter said they're meeting now. We don't want to miss our opportunity."

Reef followed after her, his worried expression saying he wasn't buying any of it. *Great.*

Please, Father, give me the strength for this. I may make a show of being tough, but I feel like a lost little kid. But I'm not alone. Your Word says you'll never leave me or forsake me. Help me cling to your promises and know you are the one I can always trust. Shelter me under the shadow of your wing until I'm out of this horrid place.

Reef followed closely behind Kirra. She was walking strong and purposefully, but her entire physique was tense. What was going on? What was she battling by returning here, and why wouldn't she confide in him so he could protect her?

Baxter's words, along with his arrogance and condescension toward Kirra, had Reef's ire fully riled—his Irish heritage had spurred him to confront the insult head on. But the utter desperation in Kirra's eyes and voice when she'd pleaded for them to go had nearly broken his heart. He needed to get her off campus as quickly as possible. But for Meg's sake that couldn't be quite yet.

He took a deep breath and slowly released it, preparing for a battle he'd fallen in the middle of. A battle he knew nothing about, other than that it had reduced Kirra Jacobs to tears, and that gnawed at his soul.

Kirra led Reef into the student union, praying with all her might that she wouldn't run into William. The thought alone strangled her. She'd been able to avoid him thus far, and for that she was immensely grateful.

It took a while to locate the correct meeting room, but they knew they'd found it when they heard the words "annihilating Mother Nature's glorious work."

Everyone in the small room—all eight members—turned at their entrance.

"Hi," Kirra said, scanning the room. "Sorry to interrupt, but I'm looking for friends of Meg Weber's."

A lanky young man stood. "And you are?"

"I'm Meg's cousin, and she's missing."

"What do you mean *missing*?" a second man asked.

Kirra explained what she could to the group. "Can any of you help us? Do any of you remember when you last saw Meg?"

A brunette about Kirra's size raised her hand. "I saw Meg Friday afternoon—right before she left for Seward."

"Seward?"

"Yeah, there's a week-long Save the Whales rally going on up there. A contingent from ROW went, and Meg joined up last minute."

"Why?"

The lanky man looked at her with disgust. "Because she cares that innocent sea creatures are being slaughtered by commercial fishermen who are heartlessly chasing after their daily quota."

"I didn't mean *why* she wanted to *be* there. I meant, why did she sign up last minute?"

"Oh." At least he had the decency to try and look sheepish. "I think she was torn between going to the rally and supporting her dad at the Iditarod."

"But she decided on the rally?"

"Yeah." He nodded. "She was really pumped about it."

"Did she travel with anybody or go alone?" Reef asked.

The lanky guy looked at the brunette. "Emma?"

Emma crossed her legs. "I think she hitched a ride with Sam and the guys."

"Sam?" Kirra asked.

"Sam Matthews. He's our group leader. I'm pretty sure she decided to ride with him."

"Could we get Sam's cell number from you?"

"Yeah, but he didn't bring his phone."

Kirra frowned. "Why not?" Who didn't carry their cell with them?

"Sam didn't want to be distracted while at a protest or rally. Part of his creed."

Kirra fought the urge to question said creed, but it was vital they stay on topic.

Emma stood and moved for the snack table. "If you want to talk to Sam, you'll have to head up there."

Seward was an eight-hour drive—in good weather. If they were following the wrong trail, it would cost them valuable time, but they had no other leads.

11

"Well, that gives us a place to start," Kirra said, stepping from the room, thankfully looking more relaxed than when they'd entered.

"Yeah. Now we just need to interview Professor Daniels and we can go."

Kirra stopped dead in her tracks. "Professor Daniels?"

"Yeah." What was wrong? Why had all the color drained from Kirra's beautiful face? And why did she look as if she was getting ready to pass out again? "Ashley said he was Meg's other professor and indicated the two didn't get along. I think it would be incomplete investigation-wise to leave campus without speaking with him."

"Ashley said it'd be a waste of our time. We should head to Seward." She glanced at her watch. "If we leave now we can make it by midevening."

"The rally is sure to be dispersed by the time we get there. Arriving in the morning is a better plan."

"Morning? You don't plan on staying *here* tonight?"

"On campus. No. But with a rally in town, Seward lodging is bound to be booked up. I say we head up that way and stop somewhere around Whittier, then drive the last hour and a half in the morning."

"Fine. Let's get going." She headed for the main door leading out of the student union.

Reef kept stride with her. "Okay, so we talk with Professor Daniels and then . . ."

Kirra stopped and turned to face him. "I'm telling you he's a dead end."

"How can you be certain?" *Why so much resistance?*

"Because he has nothing to do with Meg's new crowd."

"How can you be certain?"

Her gaze darted around the open space. "Because he's not into the eco scene."

His eyes narrowed. "Do you know him?" Had he been one of *her* professors?

Was that why she didn't want to visit him?

"Yes." She exhaled. "Which is why I can tell you without hesitation that he has no information to offer in the way of Meg's disappearance."

"That seems like a huge assumption."

"Why are you so insistent on talking to him?"

"I just think to be thorough we should interview everyone."

"Really? You want to interview *everyone* on campus?"

"Of course not." Why was she being so obstinate? "However, Meg's professors and her recently dumped ex-boyfriend seems like a reasonable place to start."

She adjusted her scarf, the burgundy floral print bringing out the bright blue of her eyes, and then exhaled. "You're right."

"I am?"

She turned, heading back across the foyer from the direction they'd come. "We should talk to her ex-boyfriend."

"And Professor Daniels?" he asked, catching up to her.

"I think Ashley said his name was Garret."

"No. William. William Daniels."

She shivered at the mention of his name but kept walking. "I meant the ex-boyfriend."

"Oh. How should we go about finding him?"

"Let's hit the gym."

Reef frowned. "Why the gym?"

"Ashley said he spends most of his time lifting weights. Which doesn't surprise me at all, because Meg always goes for the jocks." She looked him up and down. "The ones like you, at least."

Reef arched a brow. "Ones like me?"

"You know. Athletic, but not your traditional jock. Meg likes her men a little south of respectable."

"Excuse me?" He laughed in shock. Had she really just said that?

"What?" She shrugged. "Oh, come on, you really think you fit in the traditional jock category?"

"No."

"Then why are you getting all huffy?"

"It's the *south of respectable* that has me huffy."

"I'm sorry. I didn't mean it as an insult."

How else did she mean it? And, more importantly, what did that say about how Kirra liked her men?

Kirra led the way into the campus gym. She prayed talking with the ex-boyfriend would eat up enough time that William would be off campus before Reef insisted they locate him.

A sculpted guy with surfer blond hair skipped to her side. "Haven't I seen you around here before?"

Really? Was that the best he had? "I'm looking for Garret Bale."

"Bummer for me."

"Do you know him?"

"Yeah. He's over on the bench press." He kept pace with her, smiling. "Are you sure I can't interest you in a detour? You know . . ."

"I'm good, thanks." She beelined for Garret, feeling Reef close on her heels. "Garret Bale?"

The brown-haired, brown-eyed guy bench pressing one-fifty answered. "Yeah?" He glanced over, appraised her, and smiled.

Really, Meg, what do you see in these men? Reef excluded. She shook her head. Never thought she'd think that. She extended her hand to Garret. "Hi."

He lifted the weights, setting them back on the bar, and pulled to a seated position. "Hi, yourself."

"I need to speak to you about Meg."

"Oh, please tell me she didn't send some friend of hers to try and get me back." He laughed, and the dudes nearest him followed suit.

Kirra's jaw tightened. Time to cut to the chase. "She's missing."

"Sure she is." He laughed.

"I'm not joking."

His smug expression faded. "Well, if it's true, I had nothing to do with it."

"With what?"

"Anything. I haven't even seen Meg since we split."

"You're telling me you're both on campus and you've managed not to see each other since you broke up?"

"Okay, I saw her a couple days later with one of Sam's crew."

"Sam Matthews?"

"Yeah."

"When you say one of his crew . . . ?"

"One of those environmental junkies. Ever since Meg started taking Professor Baxter's classes she's gotten strange."

"Strange, how?"

"Hanging with those losers, carrying on about saving animals and the water and all that junk."

So Meg *was* serious about the environment. Meg was never serious about much outside of shopping and guys. *Hmm.* Maybe this whole environmental thing hinged on a guy. That seemed more like the Meg she knew.

"I've heard Sam's name mentioned twice now," she continued. "And you said Meg was hanging with one of his crew. Do you know the guy's name?"

"No. I'm pretty sure he doesn't go to school here."

"Then why's he in Sam's crew?"

"I think he was a friend of Sam's or he used to go here." Garret shrugged. "I don't know. I just saw him hanging around campus now and then."

"With Meg?"

"Maybe once or twice."

"But after she broke up with you?"

"I never said she broke up with me. Is that what she told you?"

"No. She didn't say anything."

"*Whatever.* I know what happened. She can say whatever she likes. It doesn't make it true."

They were veering off course. "Can you tell me anything

about this guy she was with? What he looked like? Ever hear his name?"

"He had some hippy name like Sky or Rain. Can't believe Meg would actually waste time with a dude like that."

"A dude like what?"

"A hippie wannabe."

She asked a few more questions but had clearly tapped out Garret's depth of knowledge on the subject.

"Thanks, Garret. If you think of anything else, would you give me a call?" She scribbled down her cell number on the back of her card—wondering if Professor Baxter had shown the one she gave him to William. Did he know she was on campus? If so, could she convince Reef they should leave before he found her? She could only imagine how he'd react.

Garret looked at the number and then up at her with a smile. "Cool."

"I doubt that's the last time you'll be hearing from him." Reef chuckled as they exited the gym.

"Glad his leering amused you."

"I'm surprised you gave him your number, that's all."

"He may think of something helpful." Whatever it took to find Meg—*minus* speaking with William. She wished she were stronger, but she didn't have it in her. Her embarrassing lack of composure after Baxter recognized her made that humiliatingly evident.

She sincerely believed William had nothing to do with Meg's disappearance. Not that he was innocent; he was absolutely a predator, just a predator of a different kind.

If Meg's safety hinged on talking to William, Reef would have to do it, but it terrified her to imagine what William might say to Reef, or what Reef might choose to believe about her. As hard as it was for her to admit, for the first time in a long time someone's opinion mattered, and to her great surprise, it was Reef's.

"You're heading where?" Jake said loudly. The commotion of the checkpoint whirred at a high pitch in the background.

"Seward," Reef said.

"Why Seward?"

"Because Meg supposedly went to a rally there instead of heading for the Iditarod."

"So you think she was taken from there?"

"Seems the logical course. Any sign of Frank?"

"He picked up his dogs' rations at Takotna sometime during the night, and Warren Hunt spotted him about halfway up the switchbacks to Ophir, running off course through the valley."

"He's on a mission, and it no longer involves the race."

"But he's keeping near the path. We're going to keep an eye on the other drop sites. Maybe we can catch him at one of those."

"Maybe."

"How's Kirra?"

Reef turned his back to her. She sat at one of the cafeteria tables, looking piqued. "Something has her spooked."

"A kidnapped cousin will do that."

"No. I mean here on campus. I think it has to do something with a Professor Daniels. You should have seen the visible relief on her face when I went to talk with him and learned he was already off campus for the day."

"Odd."

"That's what I thought."

"You want me to ask Darcy to do a little digging?"

He looked back at Kirra. "No. I don't think it has anything to do with Meg's disappearance. I think this has something to do with Kirra's past, and if that's the case, her past is her business."

"Speaking of pasts . . . we got two distinct histories on Frank."

"*Two?*"

"Yeah. First we looked into the oil rig thing you mentioned on our last call."

"And?"

"Looks like Frank moves around as a consultant a lot, so it's hard to track his employment history, but we're working on it."

"Kirra and I are trying to figure out what working with oil rigs would have to do with the race. There aren't any along the Iditarod trail except near Anchorage and, of course, off the coast of Nome."

"Wait a minute," Jake's voice lowered. "When you spoke with Frank, didn't he say something about Nome?"

"Yeah. He said if we didn't find Meg before he reached Nome, they'd both be dead and a lot of others would be hurt."

"You think these men could be holding Meg hostage in order to get Frank to do something to the rig off Nome's coast? Maybe that's why he's racing so far in front of the group. He needs to reach the rig and do his job before the rest of the racers cross the finish line."

"But why an oil rig?"

115

Reef ran a hand through his hair. "Oh man."

"Why don't I like the sound of that . . . ?"

"It's just all day long we've been hearing about how tight Meg's getting in with the environmental crowd."

"You think maybe she got in too deep? Overheard something? Told someone what her dad did for a living?"

"Could be." Now he was even more anxious to get to Seward and start questioning people at the rally. "Meg's ex said she'd recently started hanging around a guy from the group who he's pretty sure isn't a student."

"This guy have a name?"

"The ex wasn't sure, but said it was something like Sky or Rain."

"So not his real name?"

"Seriously doubt it. I can ask around when we get to Seward. See if he's there or if anyone knows him."

"Reef, I don't know Meg at all, so please don't take this as an insult, but I've got to ask."

"Yeah?" He feared he knew exactly where Jake was going.

"You don't think Meg could be in on this, do—"

The line went dead.

"Hello? Jake?"

Kirra stepped up behind him. "Problem?"

"The line went dead."

"I've been watching the news." She gestured to the giant flat screen mounted on the wall of the Quad. "They say a massive storm is moving into the interior."

"You worried about your uncle?" He was alone, away from the shelters and the help of the race volunteers.

"A lone man and his dogs in a blizzard." Kirra rubbed her arms.

"Frank's tough." He had to be to run the Iditarod, not to mention his four wins. "He'll be fine."

Kirra tried to smile. "I pray you're right."

"You ready to go?" he asked, and she gratefully nodded.

As uneasy as Kirra was on campus, there was no need to question her about the possibility Meg could be involved while still there. He hated to ask—period—but it needed to be done. Just in case. And, he needed to finish his conversation with Jake. Needed to find out what Frank's second history involved.

12

How on earth was he going to broach the subject of whether Meg might be in on the kidnappers' plan? And should he even bother? Did he really believe Meg could be a part of something like that? He wanted to think not, but during their short time together he'd quickly learned Meg was even wilder than he had been. Ready to push the limits, ready to experience the *extreme*, as she liked to put it.

But would she really put her father through this? Letting him think she'd been kidnapped if she'd gone willingly?

That seemed too far, but during their weekend trip to British Columbia, her dad had texted repeatedly trying to find out where she'd disappeared to, and it was only at Reef's persistent prompting that she'd even bothered to respond to one of her dad's texts. Even then she'd simply texted back that she was an adult and for him to chill. To be honest, he'd been even worse about keeping in contact with his own family, but something about her dad's desperation had tugged at his heart.

Could the environmental cause really have gotten to Meg?

Did she believe her dad's work—whatever it was—with the oil rigs was so awful that she was willing to go along with a ruse to get him to do . . . what? Compromise a rig?

"A penny for your thoughts," Kirra said.

Reef smiled. "That's a cute expression." One he hadn't heard since he was a child.

"My grandma Alice used to say it all the time."

"I remember her. She used to always wear those fancy brooches to church." She'd been the only Sunday school teacher who actually seemed to enjoy his company.

Kirra stopped in her tracks. "Yeah, she did. How'd you remember?"

"I don't know, I—"

"You've got some nerve coming back here." A woman, tall and curvy, stormed toward them, her long brown hair flying in the wind across her shoulders.

Kirra's heart sank. *Tracey.* How had she known? Had William learned of her presence and told Tracey?

Her stomach lurched. *Is William here too?* Her heart thudded in her chest—each *thwack* resonating in her ears—her pulse growing rapid, her breathing shallow. She glanced around. A few people milled at the edge of the parking lot, most distracted. But Reef . . .

Please, Lord. Not now. Not in front of him.

Hot shame and mortification sifted through her. She lifted a hand, willing Tracey to stop, but she kept coming. "I'm just looking for my cousin Meg, Tracey. She's missing," Kirra managed, praying the truth of her purpose here would keep Tracey at bay.

Tracey stopped just shy of her—it'd only been a couple

years, but she'd changed. Her dark hair had auburn streaks and she'd put on a good ten pounds.

Tracey cocked her head with a snarky smile. "If she's related to you, she's probably off playing the trollop." Her hot pink nails tapped along her silver heart belt buckle. "I'm sure it runs in the family." She turned to Reef, her gaze raking over him. "Who are *you*?"

Reef looked at Kirra, confused. "I'm Kirra's friend."

Tracey planted her hands on her ample hips. "Then, you'd better be careful. She tends to stab friends in the back."

Anger churned in Kirra's throat. *Injustice. Lies.* "That's not what happened." It had been completely the other way around. "It was William! He—"

"Ah, I see you're still sticking with that pathetic lie?"

"Your boyfriend is the liar." And the one responsible.

Tracey held up her hand—the lowering sun glinting off the pear-shaped stone on her ring finger. "My *husband*."

She'd actually married the man?

"Now." Tracey squared her shoulders, her faux-fur coat grazing her artificial tanned cheeks imbued with anger's flush. "I suggest you get out of here."

She would like nothing better than to leave, but Tracey's stab at intimidation was only raising Kirra's ire. Her betrayal, William's lies, the injustice of it all . . . Strength filled her. A confidence she hadn't felt in two years. "Or what?"

Tracey took a step closer. "I'll make you." She shoved Kirra.

The small group at the edge of the parking lot had grown in size—everyone now watching them.

"Whoa!" Reef stepped between the two. "I don't know who you are, lady, but I suggest you back away."

Tracey peered around Reef at Kirra, her smile tinged with

malice. "So . . ." She looked back at Reef. "She hasn't told you? Well"—Tracey pushed up her jacket sleeves—"let me enlighten you."

Horror vibrated up Kirra's throat, rendering her speechless.

"Tracey!" a man roared.

William. His voice jolted Kirra greater than a hundred volts ricocheting through her could.

"Will?" Tracey turned. "I told you I'd handle this."

"And I told you to let it be."

Kirra refused to look at William, refused to make eye contact, afraid if she did it would all come rushing back and consume her with terror.

Reef wrapped a protective arm around her. "Time to go." He guided her toward their rental car.

"We aren't done here," Tracey called, her boot heels clacking along the pavement behind them.

Reef opened Kirra's car door and settled her inside. "*Yes.*" He shut the door and turned to face Tracey. "We are."

She looked past Reef at Kirra. "Running away again. I suppose that's what liars and skanks do—run away in shame."

Kirra rolled down her window as Reef climbed in the car and started it, finding her voice again. "I'm not the one who should be filled with shame." But she was. "And William knows it." She braved a glance in his direction. He remained on the periphery, letting Tracey fight his battle, coward that he was.

"You liar." Tracey spewed out a string of expletives as Reef started to reverse out of the spot.

"That's it!" He shifted the car into Park and stepped out to stand behind the open door. "What's wrong with you, lady? How can you talk to her like that?"

"She deserves it."

"No way. Not Kirra."

Tracey linked her arms across her chest. "Then clearly you don't know who you're dealing with."

Reef tried to keep his eyes on the road, but he couldn't keep his worried gaze off Kirra.

She was hunched over, nearly balled up against the passenger door, her face pale, her body shivering.

He cranked up the heat. They needed to find someplace to rest for a while—grab something to eat and get a good night's sleep. But not yet, not until he got her farther away from that horrid woman.

A lot of different scenarios raced through his mind, but none of them matched up to what the woman said and who he knew Kirra to be. Even if they weren't close, he knew her. He'd spent every year of grade school in the same class with her, shared the same homeroom in high school. He knew her character. And all the ugly things the woman spewed were incongruent with the person he knew Kirra to be.

He glanced over at her again. "You wanna talk about it?"

She shook her head.

"Okay."

They drove in silence for the next two hours, making it to the southern border of Denali before Reef reached the lodge he and his family had stayed at so often while he was growing up.

The two-story, arched-frame wooden lodge was just as he remembered it—down to the bronze statue of a moose standing guard by the front entrance—it'd been his sister

Piper's favorite part of their trips there. A gorgeous twenty-thousand-plus-foot mountain stood prime for exploring right in the lodge's backyard, but no, his sister loved to sit out front by the moose statue and read.

Kirra frowned as he cut the ignition. "Why are we stopping here?"

"Because you need a good meal and a decent night's sleep."

"But Meg . . ."

"We wouldn't reach Seward before midnight. Everyone will be dispersed for the night. We might as well rest where we know we can find a room and head out early. If we leave by five, we'll be there by noon."

Kirra swallowed but didn't argue as she stared up at the lodge. "Nice place."

"My family used to come here every year." Until his folks had passed away.

The valet opened Kirra's door as Reef stepped out of his. He moved around the car, conferred with the valet, and stepped to Kirra's side, linking his arm with hers. He opened the main door and ushered her inside, thankful to have her on what he considered safe territory—at least familiar territory for him.

The tension racking her body hadn't eased, but after what had transpired, he couldn't blame her. It was going to take a while for her to settle down.

"Let's check in and then head for the hotel restaurant."

She nodded.

Reef secured rooms in Moose Hall—the wing of the lodge his family always stayed in because of Piper's adoration of the silly-looking animals. He understood their majesty, but cuteness? But that was Piper—able to see beauty amidst ugliness or even plain ordinariness. She'd seen the best in him when he didn't deserve it. He still didn't deserve it, but he was working toward being a man his sister, his whole family, could be proud of.

Kirra dropped her bag on the bed, not even bothering to take in her surroundings. She couldn't imagine what Reef must be thinking. She silently followed him back down to the lobby, where the restaurant was located.

Dark wood tables filled the center of the dimly lit dining area, with cushioned booths lining the walls. In the center of the red-and-white-checked tablecloth stood an old bloomed-bottom bottle with a cream-colored taper candle wedged in the top. Wax trailed down in rivulets over the green glass surface. She hadn't seen one like it since she was a kid in her parents' favorite Italian restaurant. Just seeing it—the flame dancing along the wick—brought back the scent of garlic bread to her mind.

She waited until after their meat loaf specials arrived to get the conversation rolling—she had to do it sooner or later. Better to get it over with. He'd think of her what he would. It was how she chose to react that made the difference. But first a report of Reef's conversation with Jake. "What did Jake have to say?" she asked while digging into her meat loaf with a fork. It was so tender and juicy, it simply fell apart.

Reef poured ketchup onto his plate. "We can talk about that later. It's been a long day, hasn't it?"

A long day. That was a considerate way to put it. He may not have asked what Tracey was talking about during her rant, but he'd been thinking about it. How could he not? Besides, she could always tell when he was contemplating something—his forehead creased. Had since the first day of kindergarten when the teacher had asked him his favorite color. She'd asked all of them the same question, but only Reef's answer had left a permanent impression on Kirra. He'd said it was blue that day. When the teacher asked if it would still be blue tomorrow, he'd replied tomorrow was a new day. Even then he'd lived for the moment. It had drawn her attention; *he'd* drawn her attention, in a *good* way—right up until he'd called her a stinky girl at recess. Then he'd become memorable for an entirely different reason—he'd become her nemesis that day and remained so all the way through high school.

Now he sat across from her, and heaven help her, she yearned to share the weight crushing down on her, but why? Simply because he was available? No, because, for whatever crazy reason, she longed for *his* understanding. His comfort.

"Penny for your thoughts?" He smiled softly.

She smiled back. Grandma Alice's words were a soothing balm to her suffering soul. "You first."

He set his fork aside.

Never a good sign.

He exhaled. "Jake said it's been difficult tracking down Frank's most recent employer, but Darcy's on it."

Was that all? "I'm sure she'll figure it out. She seems quite determined."

"I actually think she rivals Piper in that area."

"Now, that's saying something." She poked at her meat loaf, apprehension stealing her appetite.

"You know Piper." He cleared his throat and glanced around

the mostly empty room. Only an hour until closing, few customers lingered.

She shifted uncomfortably. Why was he hedging? Had Darcy found something on Frank, or was he just working up the nerve to ask her about Tracey? "Anything else?"

"A couple things, actually. Jake said something about Frank having two distinct histories, but we got on to another subject and before we could get back to it, the line went dead. Any idea what that means?"

She sat back. "No clue."

He shrugged a shoulder. "I guess we'll have to wait until they are able to get back in touch before we can find out."

"I guess . . . And the other thing?" He'd said there were a couple.

He twirled his unused straw in hand, his gaze focused on his fingers. "Jake's just trying to be thorough and work every angle . . ."

"And?" Where was this going?

His hand stilled, and he finally looked at her. "Is there any chance with Meg's new devotion to the environment and Frank's ties to the oil rigs . . . that she's part of whatever's happening?"

Her eyes narrowed. "Part of as in . . . ?"

"Could she be in on it?"

Had he seriously just asked her that? "No way. How can you think that?" He'd dated her cousin, for goodness' sake.

"Jake is . . . *we're* just trying to view every angle, every option."

"Well, Meg being involved isn't one of them."

"Are you positive?"

She shook her head. "I thought you knew Meg."

"I do."

"Yet you still think her capable of staging her own kidnapping?"

He leaned forward, lowering his voice. "I'm not saying that . . . exactly."

She scooted toward him, hunching over the table. "Then what are you saying *exactly*?"

He exhaled. "That maybe she got in over her head. Maybe her new friends saw an opportunity and . . ."

"And what? Meg just went along with it? Set up her father? I know Meg's not the most responsible person . . ."

"She can take off without notice."

"What do you mean?" She knew exactly what he meant. Meg had once done it at the worst possible time.

"When we were seeing each other, she liked to just take off. A weekend skiing in British Columbia, another—"

"What a minute!" She cut him off, heat flaring in her cheeks. "Are you saying you were with her *that* weekend in B.C.?"

"That weekend? I don't know what *that* weekend is."

"It would have been in March."

"Yeah, we '*dated*' "—he used air quotes—"from January until the end of March a couple years back."

"Two years back?"

"Yeah, like I said, Meg was in her freshman year at the community college in Anchorage."

Her stomach dropped. Meg had ditched her *that* weekend for a getaway with Reef?

"What does a weekend in British Columbia have to do with any of this?" Reef asked.

She collected her thoughts, forcing herself to remain as focused as she could manage. "I'm just saying Meg's heading for Seward is similar to that weekend—a guy talked her into taking off for the weekend, even though she was already committed to something . . ."

"Trust me." He sat back, lifting his hands. "I wasn't the one who suggested the getaway back then."

"You're saying Meg did?" She gripped the edge of the table. Meg had initiated the getaway? Her cousin had made it sound as if she'd been swept away, that she hadn't really wanted to go but the guy she'd been dating had insisted. Kirra had tried not to blame Meg for ditching her, but now . . .

"Yeah. If you don't believe me, ask her." His face softened. "When you can. I mean . . . when we get all this sorted out."

She swallowed. If that was true, it meant . . . She shook off the thought. *Focus on the matter at hand. Deep breaths.* "Taking off for a weekend is a lot different than staging a kidnapping. She would never do something like that to her dad." She may push the line, may disappear for a weekend of fun, but she'd never lead him on to believe she was in danger if she wasn't. Reef and Meg hadn't dated long, but surely he knew at least that much about her cousin.

Reef reached across the table and clasped her hand. His touch felt warm, secure. She was tempted to pull back, but she didn't.

"I agree," he said. "I don't believe she would do that, but I had to ask."

"Did you?"

"If I didn't, Jake would have."

"I would have preferred it coming from him." Because he didn't know Meg.

"I'm sorry. I didn't mean to upset you."

He hadn't upset her. He'd made her mad, but at least it'd

distracted her from the hurt Tracey had inflicted. And . . .
Frank's two distinct histories? What was that all about?

He landed in Fairbanks, already sick of all this travel. All
because he had to chase after some stupid girl. At least their
man inside had tipped them off and he'd be able to arrange
transportation again. He only hoped he wasn't too late this
time. It'd taken a little research, but he'd tracked down Meg
Weber's roommate and was approaching her now. He was
one step closer to Reef and Kirra, and he was gaining ground.

13

TAKOTNA, ALASKA
MARCH 12, 10:36 P.M.

"Any luck?" Ethan asked Gage as Jake struggled to get reception.

Gage shook his head.

A massive blizzard raged outside, creating complete whiteout conditions. Every musher except Frank was either safely secured ahead at Ophir or bunked down with them at Takotna, waiting for it to pass before they could move on. It was suicide to move now.

Weather reports—the last they'd gotten in before all communication went down—said the storm would last well into the early morning hours but should subside by daybreak.

Frustration prompted Gage to his feet. He hated being stuck when there was work to be done, or in Darcy's nonstop mind, a case to be solved.

She flopped down on a cushy brown sofa as he paced.

"I hate this," she said. "I feel completely useless."

"Chill," Xander said. "The storm will pass soon enough. What are *you* working on anyway?"

"Reporting on the race." It was her job, and a great cover for her investigative work.

"Okay, but the race is stalled. No one is actually racing. There's no reporting to do, so chill."

Darcy's mouth twitched but finally moved into a smile. "You're right."

"Of course I am." Xander winked. "I'm heading to the kitchen—anyone want some grub?"

Ethan joined him, but everyone else declined.

Gage took a seat beside Darcy and squeezed her knee. "I know you were dying to say something."

"I know I can't."

The thought that someone in the checkpoint building with them could be part of Meg's kidnapping made Gage's skin crawl. If there was a threat, you dealt with it, didn't tiptoe around it. But Jake said if they jumped the gun—if the men responsible for Meg's abduction knew they were on to them, knew they were trying to track them—Meg's life could be in jeopardy, so Gage played along.

He could see she was bursting to share something she'd found. He peered through the open door at the empty hallway. Now at least they could talk. He gave Darcy the go-ahead signal by lifting his chin.

"I discovered who Frank's current employer is before we lost connection with the outside world. NorthStar Oil."

"What do we know about them?" Jake asked, resting a boot on his opposite knee.

"They own a series of off-shore oil rigs, right?" Kayden said.

"Right." Darcy nodded. "And they're laying the new interior pipeline."

Jake straightened. "They are?"

"Yeah."

"I remember all the news coverage of the protests when they first broke ground." Kayden took a seat on the arm of Jake's chair.

"Any chance Frank has worked on the pipeline?" Jake asked.

Darcy leaned into Gage, and he wrapped his arm around her shoulder. "I'll check as soon as the Internet is back up. But I think his role in the breaking and entering is a far more intriguing angle."

Reef stood awkwardly near the door to Kirra's room as she shuffled back and forth between her duffel bag and the nightstand—laying out her iPod, plugging in her phone charger. She hadn't made any indication she wanted him to leave, and he had no desire to go. Today had been crazy, and all the events and emotions of it pumped through his system in a rush.

"I think I'll order some dessert from room service," Kirra said, picking up the menu. "You want something?"

"Sure. Milk and cookies."

She arched a brow.

He smiled and pushed off the wall he'd been holding up. "I know it sounds childish, but it's a lodge specialty. Warm, gooey cookies and ice-cold milk." It was the perfect combo of opposites, kind of like him and Kirra.

She lifted the phone with a smile and ordered milk and cookies for two.

"You can sit." She gestured to the sofa area.

"Okay." He looked to the cold hearth. "Would you like me to turn the fireplace on?"

She rubbed her arms. "Sure."

He moved to the stone hearth and switched on the electric fireplace before taking a seat on the sofa.

Kirra sank into the armchair. She kicked off her boots, and he was surprised to find her wearing neon heart fuzzy socks. "You're right," she said, stretching out.

"That's got to be a first." *For those words to be coming out of Kirra Jacobs' mouth.* His gaze fastened on her mouth, on the delicate curve of her full bottom lip. *Whoa!* He straightened. This was Kirra. She deserved the best, and he certainly wasn't it.

She smirked, drawing his attention back to her supple pink lips. "Don't get used to it."

"Wouldn't dream of it. So . . ." He leaned forward with a wink. "What am I right about?"

She glanced around the room. "This lodge is wonderful, and stopping was a really good idea."

An hour later she set her empty mug on the room service tray and turned to face him. "Those were the best milk and cookies I've ever had."

He laughed.

"What?"

"You've got a milk mustache."

"So do you." She swiped at her lip. "Only I wasn't going to tell you about it."

"Brat," he said playfully and instantly regretted it. Even if he'd said it completely in jest, she'd been called enough names today. "Sorry. I shouldn't have . . ."

She frowned. "What?" Then it hit her. "I know you were just playing, Reef." She strode back to her seat. "Don't worry about it."

Reef took a deep breath and spoke what was pressing on his heart. "Look, I don't know what happened between you and that woman, or with that William guy, but I do know what she said, what she called you—she was wrong."

She linked her arms tight against her chest, nearly hugging herself. "What makes you so sure?"

He leaned forward, bracing his hand on the edge of her chair. "Because I know you, and none of those words describe you."

She nodded but remained silent.

He scooted closer. "Sometimes talking about it helps."

She bit her lip. "And sometimes it makes it much worse."

Kirra rolled over in bed, her heart aching so hard she struggled to draw a decent breath.

Tell him.

I can't.

Tell him, child.

But, Father, I—

God cut off the thought, filling her with the overwhelming need to share her burden and to share it with the most unlikely of people—Reef McKenna.

She pulled to her feet and yanked a sweatshirt over her pajama top. Sliding her feet into her slippers, she headed across the hall in her flannel duck bottoms.

Are you sure, Lord? she prayed, her hand poised to knock.

Yes, child.

Her hand landed on the door as she prayed he wouldn't answer.

The door swung open, and before Reef could utter a word or she lost her nerve, she blurted out, "Can I come in?"

"Of course." He stepped inside, allowing her passage, and flipped the lights on.

She balled her hands into fists inside her sweatshirt sleeves—the fleece lining nubby from being so well worn.

He gestured for her to sit as he slipped on a shirt, and she sank onto the love seat in front of the fire.

He sat down beside her, angled to face her so their knees touched.

"While I was in vet school, Tracey was my roommate and best friend."

"And William?" he asked, his voice tender—achingly so.

"William was finishing the last year of his PhD program and was a TA in the Biology department for both environmental health and advanced anatomy. Tracey and I had him for anatomy, and we were both interested in him—though we did our best to keep things civil. Fast-forward to a few months before our graduation and he chose Tracey."

"I'm sorry."

She pulled her knees to her chest. "Not as sorry as I was. I thought I'd lost the sun, as young and blinded as I was."

"So he and Tracey started dating?"

"Yeah. It was difficult, but it was what it was. I tried to be supportive." She spoke faster, needing to get to it, get past it and let the cards fall where they would with Reef—praying he'd . . . *What?* Wrap her in his strong arms? Now she was being foolish and naive all over again.

"Kir?" He jiggled her knee.

She took a deep breath, expelled it, and continued on. "A couple weeks later, Tracey had to head home for the night last minute. Something with her family. We were supposed to go to a party with William and some friends." *And Meg.* Meg was supposed to be visiting from Anchorage that weekend, but she'd called that afternoon, said something else had come up—and now Kirra knew that something was a weekend getaway with Reef.

"And you still went?"

"When M— the girl who was supposed to go to the party with me also bailed at the last minute, I called and told William I wasn't going to go."

"But . . ."

She clutched her hands around her legs. "But William showed up at my door, begging me to go, saying we needed to talk, and . . ." She looked down. "I foolishly went." It was her greatest regret.

She got to her feet, needing to move . . . to keep moving so it couldn't catch her, couldn't strangle her the way it did in her dreams. "William told me he'd made a huge mistake. He didn't love Tracey. He loved me. He said he was going to tell her as soon as she got back, and I believed him. We talked at the party over drinks, and he started to get real friendly, so I said I needed to get back to my apartment. As much as I cared about William, I wasn't going to pursue those feelings until he broke things off with Tracey."

Her stride increased, her voice pitchy to her own ears. "He acted like that was totally cool and offered to walk me home." She glanced at Reef, at his soulful eyes brimming with compassion.

"You don't have to tell me," he said at her pause.

"I know, but I need to." She'd carried it for too long.

He gave her time, not pressing, just waiting while she gathered her courage.

"We cut through the park on the way back to my apartment, and that's when he started up again."

"With the advances?"

She nodded. "Only this time, he was more forceful." She couldn't look at Reef. She was too scared. She just continued, needing to get it all out. "He forced me behind a grove of trees and ra . . . ra . . . raped me. I screamed and cried, but he had pressed some sort of rag into my mouth."

Reef was at her side, pulling her into his arms, comforting her as the tears fell.

She swiped at her tears with the back of her hand but didn't pull from Reef's embrace. This was what she'd longed for. Someone to understand. Someone to comfort her on an intimate level. *Intimate?* After William, she never thought she'd use that word again, and now with Reef . . .

Focus. Finish. Get it all out. "Afterward," she sniffed, swiping at her tears with the back of her hand, "I was a basket case—I could hardly stand—but he acted like everything was normal. As if it'd been consensual. He even tried to kiss me good-night at the door."

Reef cupped her face in his hand, his finger grazing her skin. "Did you report him?"

Tears rolled off her cheeks, cascading to her sweatshirt. "It was the middle of the night. Tracey was gone until morning, and I was *terrified*. I locked my door and showered his stench off of me. I hid under my covers, praying for Tracey to come back. I figured she could take me to the campus police in the morning and toss William to the curb."

His jaw slackened, his heart breaking in his eyes. "She didn't believe you."

Kirra shook her head, her tears salty as they tumbled past her lips.

"William was waiting for her outside our apartment when she came back the next morning. He told her I threw myself at him at the party, that we'd both drank a lot and he'd made a stupid mistake."

Reef's brows arched. "He confessed?"

"No. He said letting me seduce him was a stupid mistake."

"He told Tracey *you* tried to seduce *him*?"

"When I tried to tell her the truth, she called me a liar and a lot worse. I couldn't believe it. I was blindsided. She was my best friend. If she didn't believe me . . ." She rubbed her arms.

"Who would?" he said, finishing her thought.

"Right."

He caressed her cheek with the pad of his thumb. "So you never went to the police?"

She looked down, the pain stabbing deeper still. "I went home."

"Surely your parents believed you and encouraged you to go to the police."

She stepped from his hold and nausea swirled inside. "My mom couldn't handle it. She listened and then asked if I wanted a slice of cake."

"What?"

She shrugged. "That's Mom's way of dealing with ugly stuff in life."

"Eating cake?"

"Ignoring it."

"And your dad?"

"He said it sounded complicated. I'd gone to the party with William. We'd been drinking . . . If I made a fuss about it, reputations could be ruined. So I needed to be really clear on what happened before I ruined reputations."

"Meaning William's?" Reef asked in outrage.

"Actually, I think he meant mine, or at least I hope that's what he meant."

"But still . . ."

"He was worried if I took it to court, I wouldn't win. People saw us drinking and being friendly at the party; they saw us leaving together being pretty chummy . . . I knew it didn't look good."

"So what? That's not what matters. *You* matter."

"My dad said I'd have tarnished my reputation and maybe gained nothing from it."

"Oh, Kirra. I'm so sorry." A mix of indignation and heartache welled in his expression.

"Uncle Frank, on the other hand, offered to kill William."

"And Meg?"

She offered a sad smile. "She felt horrible about it all because she was supposed to be with me that weekend and she'd bailed last minute."

"If she'd been with you . . ."

"I would never have been alone with William."

He paled. "Wait a minute . . . earlier you referenced the weekend Meg and I were in B.C. as *that* weekend." He swallowed, pain etched across his face. "That wasn't the weekend William . . . ?"

She nodded.

"Oh, honey. I'm so sorry."

"You couldn't have known." Nor could Meg, but that didn't ease the abandonment she felt at learning Meg was the one who'd initiated the getaway.

14

ON THE ROAD TO SEWARD, ALASKA
MARCH 13, 5:11 A.M.

Kirra felt acutely self-conscious on the ride to Seward. She'd shared the truth of her past with Reef. And amazingly, he'd responded with more kindness, support, and compassion than her own family, expressing anguish at learning he'd been in B.C. with Meg while she'd been raped.

She shifted, studying him, the bright moonlight shining in the driver's side window. He was breathtakingly handsome, but there was so much more there.

She shifted, staring out the window at towering spruce trees standing like shadowed sentinels along the roadside. She knew it was a fool's dream, but with all of her heart she hoped they'd find Meg in Seward and all of this would be some weird mix-up. But mix-ups didn't involve being chased by men with guns. Meg and, most likely, she and Reef were in grave danger, and they only had four more days before Frank should reach Nome and time would be up.

Reef glanced over at her with a soft smile. "You doing okay?"

"Yeah. Just antsy to get there."

"Me too." He looked back at the road and then glanced back at her. "I wanted to thank you. . . ."

Her forehead pinched. "Thank me? For what?"

"For confiding in me. I'm honored." He reached over and clasped her hand. "You're very brave."

"Me? Brave?" She laughed.

"You are."

"Yeah, right. That's why I was too much of a coward to confront William." His name burned acid in her throat. "Too much of a coward to press charges against him."

"You survived what he did to you. Something as traumatizing as rape could have destroyed you, but you didn't allow it to."

"Why do you say that?" In some ways that horrid event still dictated her life.

"Because look at you. You're a successful vet. You run an amazing shelter. You are active in your church. You live your life."

Guardedly.

He frowned. "You don't agree, do you?"

She shrugged, not sure she was up to delving so deeply into the issue. The fact that she'd shared what happened with Reef still surprised her, but she was glad she had. She felt closer to him, more revealed. And somehow, for some reason, the burden felt easier, lighter to bear. Some of the darkness had eased.

"I think you're a remarkable woman."

Reef McKenna believed *she* was remarkable?

They pulled into Seward a little past noon. Despite the snow and ice, commercial fishermen were out fishing Chinook salmon, while a couple dozen protestors waved signs rebuking the commercial fishing industry and its devastating effects on animal life in the area. The protestors strode in a well-defined circle around the parking lot at the edge of the pier—forcing anyone coming or going from the docks to pass through them.

According to the ROW members they had talked with in the student union, the group's trip, while officially spearheaded by ROW, had been sanctioned by the university at Professor Baxter's request—even though it pulled students away from classes for an extended period of time. It seemed Professor Baxter had a significant amount of sway on campus—probably why William had buddied up to the man. He liked to be on the good side of those in power.

Kirra stepped from the car, her heart in her throat, praying they'd find some answers. She scanned the crowd, still hoping she'd see Meg waving one of the homemade signs, but her gut knew better.

They approached the mob and snagged the first person they reached—a young man dressed in a skater hat, sleek-fitting winter coat, and skinny jeans.

"Hey, man." Reef lifted his chin in greeting. "We're looking for Sam."

"And you are . . . ?" He kept walking, and they moved to keep pace with him.

The wind blowing off the bay brought a blistering chill, stinging Kirra's cheeks and causing her eyes to water. She tightened her scarf, yanking the burgundy cashmere material higher up on her neck, the soft fabric caressing the edge of her jaw much as Reef's fingers had tenderly grazed her skin last night.

"We're friends of Meg Weber's," Reef said.

"Sam's over there." He gestured to a well-built man. Easily six foot and muscular, but not in a gawky way. His dark wavy hair ruffled in the wind, his cheeks tinged rose from the salty ocean air.

"Thanks," Reef said.

"Yup."

They let the young man pass by and then weaved their way through the swirling crowd, cutting across the snow-covered gravel lot.

"Sam?" Kirra asked when they reached the man. He leaned against the *Seward Marina* sign, one boot braced against the pylon beneath, a clipboard in his hand.

He looked up, his irritated expression quickly softening into a smile. "Yes?"

"Hi. I'm Kirra Jacobs." She extended a gloved hand and he shook it. "I believe my cousin Meg Weber is a friend of yours."

His jaw tightened. "Was."

"I'm sorry?"

"She *was* a friend of mine . . . right up until she took off in the middle of the night."

"What?"

He set the clipboard aside. "She acted so gung-ho about the cause, all raring to go for the rally, and our first night here, she just up and disappears. Nearly set the whole rally back, because she had the petition with all the signatures we'd collected. Luckily"—he tapped the clipboard—"Belinda was able to find it among Meg's stuff."

"Meg's stuff? She left her stuff behind?"

"Yeah, and if she thinks one of us is going to tote her junk back, she's got another thing coming."

Kirra swallowed and glanced back at Reef.

He rested a reassuring hand on her shoulder.

"Next time you talk to her, tell her she's not welcome at ROW anymore."

"That's the problem."

"What is?"

"We can't *find* her."

His eyes narrowed. "Didn't she head back to campus?"

"Afraid not."

"You sure?"

"We just came from there. No one's seen her."

He exhaled. "Who knows where she and Rain decided to frolic off to. I knew something wasn't right about the guy, but Meg . . . She just ran after him like a lovesick puppy." Jealousy saturated his words.

"So you're saying Meg left with Rain?"

He grabbed his clipboard, tightening his grip, the attached pages flipping up with the wind. "They were both out in the front room of the bunkhouse talking when I went to bed. Next morning there was no sign of them."

"Was there any sign of a struggle?" Reef asked.

"Struggle?" Sam pinched the bridge of his nose. "Why would there be a sign of a struggle?"

Kirra looked at Reef. How much should she say? Sam and—she gazed around at the rally team—the rest of these people were the last to see Meg before she disappeared. They needed whatever lead they could provide.

Reef nodded, silently supporting whatever approach she decided to take.

"We're afraid Meg's been abducted."

"Abducted?" He laughed. "You can't be serious."

Kirra's shoulders stiffened. "I'm afraid we are."

Sam's smile faded, and his gaze darted around the crowd before settling back on them. "Why on earth would you think something like that?" His voice was low, his fingers clamped tight on his clipboard.

Sam was edgy, shifting his weight from one leg to another and back again. Did he know something about Rain? She needed to press harder. "Let's just say we know."

His eyes narrowed. "You aren't trying to imply that Rain had anything to do with her supposed disappearance, are you?"

"You said yourself you last saw them together and assumed they took off together."

"Took off *together*, yes. Rain abducting her is a different matter entirely."

"But he was the last person seen with her."

"That doesn't prove he abducted her."

"It doesn't prove he didn't."

Sam shook his head. "This is absurd."

Kirra clenched her hands. If they were going to get anything useful out of Sam, they were going to have to be upfront. "Some men held my uncle, Meg's dad, at gunpoint and showed him a video of Meg being held hostage. They told him if he didn't do what they wanted, they'd kill her."

"Seriously?"

Kirra nodded.

"It's the truth," Reef said when Sam looked to him.

"What'd they want your uncle to do?"

"We don't know. Frank wouldn't say."

Sam cocked his head. "Are you two cops or something?"

"No."

"If Meg's actually been kidnapped, why aren't the cops here?"

"Because the men responsible said no cops."

"So you two just took it on yourselves to find her?"

"Yes. Now, can you help us?"

"I'll try, but I don't know what I can tell you."

"Tell me what you know about Rain."

He shrugged. "Not much."

"Anything is more than we know," Kirra said, fighting the desperation clawing at her, whispering this would be another dead end.

Sam raked a hand through his wavy brown hair. "I can't believe this. I just assumed she and Rain had jetted together."

Kirra supposed the possibility still existed. Meg could have been taken after they left the rally, but why would she have left the rally with Rain in the first place? Where were they headed? Had she gone with him willingly and then the situation changed? Or had he abducted her outright? Either way, Rain was the key. She could feel it. "What can you tell us about him?"

"What do you want to know?"

"Let's start with the basics. Is Rain his real name?"

"That's what he goes by."

A woman about Meg's age joined them, her gaze shifting from Sam to Kirra, and back again. "Everything okay?"

"Belinda, this is Meg's cousin Kirra," Sam said, making the introductions.

"Hi."

"And, this is my friend Reef." Who would have thought she and Reef McKenna would ever become friends? And one she trusted so dearly.

146

Belinda smiled, but it was tight. "You two here to join the rally?"

"No." Sam swiped his face. "If you can believe it, they think Meg's been kidnapped."

Belinda laughed. "What?"

"Seriously," Sam said, his countenance far less jovial than when they'd arrived.

Snowflakes flitted in the sky, clinging to Belinda's long auburn hair. "How is that possible?"

Kirra studied the woman. "When was the last time you saw her?"

"The night we arrived."

"Did you see her leave with anybody?"

"No, but last I saw she was talking with Rain." She looked at Sam, clearly looking for a reaction, but he gave none.

"What can you tell us about Rain?"

Belinda slid her gloved hands into her red pea coat pockets. "I don't know. He kind of kept to himself."

"Except with Meg, it sounds like."

She shrugged. "The two seemed to hit it off."

Heated voices coming from the parking lot drew Sam's attention. "Sorry. If you'll excuse me a moment."

Belinda waited until he was gone and then looked at Kirra with a smile. "Rain had this mysterious air, an energy a lot of the girls found attractive."

"Including you?"

"Me?" She laughed. "No. He's not my type." Her gaze momentarily slipped to Sam, but she quickly shifted it back to them.

"Were you surprised to learn Meg and Rain were gone?"

"No. I figured something grabbed Rain's attention

elsewhere. He had this habit of just disappearing and then reappearing."

"Where did he go when he disappeared?"

"No idea."

"How often did he do that?"

"I don't know. I didn't exactly keep tabs on the guy."

"So it wasn't surprising for him to just take off before the rally started?"

"I didn't think much of it."

"And Meg?"

"Figured she went along for the ride."

"Ride where?"

"No clue. But they were both that sort." She rocked back on her boot heels with a smug smile. "Unreliable."

Kirra ignored the insult to her cousin—couldn't really argue against it. "Any chance Rain took Meg against her will?"

Belinda's brown eyes widened, her thin brows arching. "You think Rain *abducted* her?"

"We don't know, but it seems he was the last person to be seen with Meg before she disappeared."

"Man." Belinda shook her head. "Never would have called him that."

"How come?"

"I don't know. Just didn't seem the type."

Neither had William. It was what made men like him so *very* dangerous.

"What about the name?"

"What about it?"

"Do you think Rain is his real name?"

"Nah."

She said it so confidently it piqued Kirra's attention. "Why not?"

"Because we went clubbing once in a while, and I caught a glimpse of his ID one time."

Thank you, Jesus.

Now they were getting somewhere. "And?"

"His first name started with a *J*." Belinda's nose crinkled. "Jacob. No . . . Joseph." She smiled. "Yeah, pretty sure it was Joseph."

Not exactly the definitive clue Kirra had been hoping for, but it was something, she supposed. "Any idea on his last name?"

"Nah. Sorry."

Kirra glanced at the crowd. "Anyone else here who might know?"

"You can ask around, but I doubt you'll learn much."

"Because Rain was uber private?"

Belinda nodded. "Yep."

Kirra and Reef spent the next several frustrating hours interviewing the entire ROW group and, sadly, came away with very little. Meg's belongings had been left—which certainly pointed to foul play—but there was nothing among her things to point to her attacker. Was Rain her abductor? Or had he been kidnapped too? Little was known about the man other than that he'd started showing up at ROW meetings several months back. No one had classes with him, but a number of the protestors had seen him on campus pretty regularly, at least over the last semester. He was tall, of sturdy build, had golden-streaked brown hair that fringed his shoulders—as one girl put it—in Brad Pitt, *World War Z* style. Beyond that no one seemed to know anything about the mysterious man—not his age, not if he was actually a student, where he lived—nothing beyond the tiny pieces they'd been able to gather. All they had was a description and possible first name.

Meg and Rain had ridden from campus with Sam, which left them sans vehicle, so Kirra and Reef were betting a third party had to be involved, or Rain had stashed a vehicle ahead of time.

One person in Meg's assigned bunkhouse said she heard a scuffling noise the night Meg disappeared, but the gal had just assumed Meg and Rain were fooling around.

Another guy in the adjacent bunkhouse thought he'd heard a vehicle pull away a little after midnight but hadn't paid it much attention.

It definitely wasn't the concrete information Kirra had been praying for, but she supposed it was a start.

Midafternoon, Reef drove away from the noise of the parking lot, but only so far as the end of the marina driveway before pulling to the shoulder. It was time to try and reach Jake again, hoping he could direct their next steps.

After the third ring, Jake answered. "Reef?"

"Yeah. I'm here." Reception was sketchy—the phone crackling—but at least he'd gotten through. "What happened?"

"Storm blew in. Lost reception. Where are you two at?"

"Seward."

"Learn anything?"

Reef relayed what they'd discovered—what little there was.

"At least you got a decent description of Joseph aka Rain?"

"Yeah."

"There's a police station in Seward that has a great sketch

artist. Landon's worked with him on a number of cases. Grab the protestor who gave you the best description and take him or her into the station. It shouldn't take long, but it could provide us with a vital lead—Rain's identity."

"Okay. Will do."

"I'll have Landon call the station to let them know you're coming, and have them scan and then e-mail the sketch to Landon and me. We can run it through our databases and hopefully get a match. After that I need you guys to head for Kodiak."

"Kodiak? Why Kodiak?"

"Is Kirra right there?"

"Yeah . . ."

"Go ahead and put me on speakerphone. She's going to want to hear this."

Reef did so with apprehension.

"All set?" Jake asked.

"Yep," Kirra said, kicking her boots up on the dash. "We're both here."

"I'm putting our end on speakerphone too," he said.

"How ya hanging in there?" Darcy asked on the other end.

Kirra smiled at Reef. "Doing okay. Reef's been a great help."

He was so thankful he could be there for her, that he could be of support. It felt good being needed, and even better being there for someone else. If only he hadn't gone with Meg to British Columbia that weekend, she could have been there for Kirra. There were so many decisions he regretted— they'd swallow him whole if it wasn't for God's grace and renewal.

"So what's this about Kodiak?" she asked.

"How much do you know about your uncle Frank's past? Back when he was a teenager and young adult?" Jake asked.

Kirra shifted, not liking where Jake's questioning seemed to be headed. "Not much." Hers was a quiet, private family. It was how her dad liked to keep things. She knew her dad went straight into the military after high school and Frank went to college, and the two hadn't been close since. She'd always chalked it up to their vastly different personalities. But no definitive reason had been given, and she knew better than to ask.

"You mentioned Frank had changed his name because he was adopted," Darcy chimed in.

"Yeah," she said slowly.

"Well, I think there might be more behind the name change than that."

"Why?"

"I did some digging and it turns out Frank had a pretty bad run-in with the law when he was eighteen."

"Frank?" She laughed. "You're kidding me."

"Afraid not," Darcy said. "He was arrested for a breaking and entering back in Kodiak."

Kirra sat upright, pulling her legs down and planting her boots firmly on the floorboard—she needed the feel of some-thing stable beneath her. "There's got to be some mistake."

"I've tripled-checked. Frank and two other men broke into a home and robbed it. Unfortunately things went very bad."

Kirra's stomach dropped. "What do you mean *very bad*?" Wasn't a breaking and entering bad enough?

"The details are sketchy, which is why we need you to go to Kodiak and do some research, but it looks like Frank got in with two guys—both in their midtwenties at the time, both with previous records. They broke into the home of a man named Phillip Webster. The owner returned home before they'd cleared out. Shots were fired and one of the burglars—Tommy Madero—was killed. Apparently they caught the ringleader, Henry Watts, quickly—as he and Madero had been busted together before—but Frank wasn't on their radar."

"Did Watts turn Frank in?"

"Apparently not. It took the police nearly a week to discover Frank was the third burglar and nearly another week to bring him into custody."

"I can't believe this." She'd thought she'd known Frank so well, but she'd thought the same about William and Tracey. When it came to people's character, she seemed doomed to blindness. Anxiety nipped at her, threatening to take over. "What does any of this have to do with Meg?"

"I don't know that it does—except Henry Watts just got released from prison last month."

"Last month? Why did he serve so long?" Clearly Frank hadn't. Had her uncle served any time in prison? The thought seemed so incongruent with the man she thought she knew.

"It was Watts's third violation in less than a year. And it was determined he injured the homeowner in the shootout and killed Madero."

"Madero was shot by Watts?" Reef's confusion echoed her own.

"He claimed it was during the chaos of the shootout, but Frank had a different story," Darcy said. "He believed it was intentional."

Jake picked up the telling. "Because of Frank's cooperation, and since he had no previous record—along with the fact he'd just turned eighteen—the judge was lenient and only gave him eighteen months for breaking and entering. Near as I can tell he changed his name when he got out, moved to Anchorage, enrolled in college, and cleaned up his act."

Kirra's mind raced through the possible scenarios, still trying to grasp what she was being told.

"Why would Watts kill his own man?"

"I don't know. The entire thing has a weird feel to it. Another house in the neighborhood was hit that same night. The alarm was triggered, but the owner claims nothing was stolen."

"Okay. So maybe the alarm scared them off before they could steal anything."

"I doubt it."

"Why?"

"Because they seemed to know what they were doing. They shut down a similar alarm at the next residence."

"Okay, so maybe they decided there was nothing worth stealing."

"That's just it. The man who insisted nothing was stolen was reputed to own a significant number of valuable antiques."

"Reputed to?"

"I found an article by a Simon Baker, a reporter with the *Kodiak Eagle*. According to the article, the other homeowner, a Mr. Bartholomew, was renowned in town for collecting the uncollectable."

"Meaning?"

"Meaning illegally obtained artifacts and antiques."

"Which would make him none too eager to report such an item stolen."

"Exactly."

"Then why hit another house if they got something of such worth?"

"Who knows? Like I said, it has a weird feel to it."

"And you're sure Frank was involved?"

"According to his conviction, yes."

"And you think this Henry Watts could have taken Meg? But why? Because Frank got away without serving much time?"

"Perhaps."

"What are you thinking, Jake?"

"I don't know. I'm not sure where this will lead, but as long as you don't have any strong leads in your search for Meg, you may as well head to Kodiak and see what you can find out about the robbery. Landon's calling the local police and giving you an intro, so they'll be expecting you."

"Looks like we're going to Kodiak after we visit the Seward police station," Reef said, and Kirra nodded, still trying to wrap her head around all they had learned.

"And now that the storm's past, Kayden and I are flying back to Anchorage to talk with the head of NorthStar Oil."

"Why fly to see him? Why not just question him over the phone?" Reef asked.

"Because he won't return our calls," Kayden said.

"Besides, *in person* is always better. You can't read expressions over the phone," Jake said.

"Gage and I will stay with the race," Darcy said. "We'll keep an eye and ear out for sightings of Frank."

"And Darcy will keep working her research magic," Gage said.

"Jake, won't people be curious about you two leaving?" Kirra asked. "First Reef and me, and now you two. What if those men are still watching? What if they figure it out and punish Meg?"

"Don't worry. We've got a cover story in place. We're flying two dropped dogs back to Anchorage."

15

Reef held the door of the Seward police station open as Kirra and then Belinda entered the one-story brick building.

"Kirra." An officer approached with a smile that made Reef uneasy—there was a familiarity there, and definite interest hovering in the man's brown eyes.

"Hey, Kevin. Good to see you." She gave him a hug, and the hairs on the nape of Reef's neck stood at jealous attention as she introduced them.

"So what brings you to my neck of the woods, Kirra?"

She pointed back at Belinda, who was sipping a soda and twirling her auburn hair. "We need to see your sketch artist."

"Oh, right. Grainger called and said he was sending somebody in. Didn't realize it was going to be you."

"Well, here I am."

"And my day just got a whole lot better." He smiled.

And Reef's just got a whole lot worse. He paced the Seward police station while Belinda described Rain aka Joseph to the sketch artist.

Kirra stood and paced in stride with him. "I know you're anxious to keep moving forward, but identifying Rain could be the first concrete piece of evidence we have."

Reef raked a hand through his hair. Getting back to their investigation wasn't the only reason he wanted to get moving. Officer Charming hadn't taken his eyes off Kirra since she'd walked through the station door. "So how do you know Officer Hoffman?"

"Kevin? Oh, we've worked a couple of SAR cases together."

"So you've worked with Seward SAR too?" Was that a regular thing? Was she in Kevin's company a lot? And *why* was he getting so jealous?

"Occasionally we team up to help each other out. I did some training here when they expanded their canine unit. Helped transition Kevin into the leader position."

"That's cool. So you work with him a lot?"

"Not anymore. . . ." She eyed him curiously. "Why the interest?"

He shrugged. "Just curious."

"Aren't you always?" She smiled.

He smiled back. "Can't argue there."

"So that would make me . . . ?"

Of course she'd make him say it. "I suppose that would make you . . . right."

Her smile widened, a playful glint dancing in her eyes. "Just as I always am."

He laughed. "Now there's the bossy Kirra I know and love."

Her brows arched. "*Love?*"

He tried to act cool, gave a casual shrug of his shoulder,

158

praying the heat flooding up his neck didn't show. "You . . . um . . . know what I mean."

"Right. It's just a casual saying. Nothing intended. I get it." She slipped her side braid behind her shoulder.

He glanced at Officer Hoffman and back to the woman who'd stolen his heart. Perhaps it was time he told her. "Actually, I . . ."

She stepped closer, her floral scent intoxicating.

What was that? Jasmine? Whatever it was, she smelled incredible.

"Yes?" she asked.

His eyes locked on hers. "I—"

"We're done here," the sketch artist said, walking smack into the middle of their moment—awkward on Reef's part as it may have been.

"Great." He shoved his hands into his pockets as Belinda strode to their side.

She slipped her purse strap over her arm. "Ready to take me back?"

"I can take her," Officer Hoffman offered. How long had he been standing behind them? How much of their conversation had he overheard?

"Are you sure?" Kirra asked. "I mean it'd get us on the way to Kodiak faster, which would be great, but I don't want to put you out."

Put him out. Reef couldn't wait to be alone with Kirra again—to have her all to himself, even if it was just while working a case.

"Anything for you," Hoffman said. "Besides, I've got to patrol the protest every few hours." He glanced at his watch. "The later-running fishermen will be returning with their day's haul soon, and that's when tensions rise. Best to have a police presence there, just to remind everyone to remain cordial."

"Wonderful." Kirra rocked back on her heels. "Thanks."

Hoffman slipped his hat on. "No problem." He leaned in and pressed a kiss to her cheek. "As always, wonderful to see you."

"You too. Take care."

The officer turned to Belinda. "Ma'am."

She smiled, taking his arm as he proffered it in gentlemanly fashion.

She glanced back over her shoulder. "Good luck."

"Thanks," Reef said, stepping to Kirra's side. He ached to wrap his arm around her slender waist, but he didn't have the right—their relationship wasn't there yet. Actually it was probably just wishful thinking on his part that they had any *relationship* at all. When Meg and Frank were safe, and this case over, he feared they'd go back to being nothing more than casual acquaintances.

He studied the gentle slope of her neck as she slipped her burgundy scarf on.

Man, he prayed he was wrong.

So they'd brought the police into it.

Anger seethed, burning through his chest, coiling his muscles as an officer helped Belinda into a patrol car. How much had the stupid broad told them?

He gripped the steering wheel, hot air blowing from the rental car's vents across his clenched fingers. He'd find out *precisely* what she told them, but that would have to wait.

Readjusting his rearview mirror, he spotted Reef and Kirra exiting the station. They were the ones who'd perpetrated all of this—questioning Belinda, pulling the cops in, interfering with their plans.

He reversed, pulling out of the precinct lot behind their rental car. They were going to pay, and the beauty of it was he simply had to sit back and watch.

Reef pulled onto the main road, thankful they were finally making progress. With any luck, they'd make it to Anchorage by nightfall. He hoped Rain's sketch would trigger a hit. They'd scanned it and then sent it on to both Jake and Landon, praying that before he and Kirra reached Kodiak they'd find a full identification—though that was being extremely optimistic.

They needed something. Meg's disappearance was wearing on Kirra, the fear for her uncle and cousin evident in her deep blue eyes, and he hated seeing the toll it all was taking. Not to mention what horror Meg may be going through. If only he could will things to go faster, figure out what was going on, know where to look, where to dig . . .

Please, Father, I need your help. I need your guidance and direction. Please let me be of help to Kirra and her family. Direct us to Meg, and bring this nightmare to an end.

He reached over and clasped Kirra's delicate hand, half expecting her to pull away, but she didn't. Instead a soft smile graced her pink lips.

Reef shifted his full focus to the road ahead, or at least tried to.

The pavement was crusted with a thick layer of ice, making

the passage back to Anchorage difficult. On such short notice, it was tough finding a flight out of Seward to Kodiak, so the two-and-a-half-hour drive to Anchorage and quick half-hour flight on to Kodiak was the fastest route there. But focus was vital. The Seward Highway was known not only for its beauty—saltwater bays, frigid blue glaciers, and alpine valleys—but also for its knife-edge ridges and rock-fall potential making it one of the deadliest highways in Alaska, or as some considered it, the most dangerous stretch of road in the U.S.

Neither he nor Kirra had much to say, so he focused on his driving, and they passed easily through the quiet town of Moose Pass and wound along the narrowing mountain walls of Canyon Creek, the seasonal steel-blue waters frozen solid.

"So . . . you were saying . . . ?" Kirra prompted. Her heart had been racing with anticipation ever since their interrupted conversation in the Seward police station. Had Reef been about to say he felt more for her than simple friendship? The sheer delight that spread through her at the tantalizing prospect hadn't stopped dancing a jig through her limbs. It was all she could do to sit still. He *needed* to finish that sentence and fast.

"Saying what, exactly?" he asked, looking rather nervous.

It was adorable. She'd never seen Reef McKenna nervous, and the thought it could be because of her felt amazing. But maybe she was getting her hopes up for nothing. Maybe she needed to settle down. But she couldn't help herself. She hadn't felt like this since . . .

She swallowed hard.

Reef arched a brow. "What's wrong?"

"Nothing." She shook off the fear, or at least tried to. What William had done to her had controlled her life long enough. It was time she took it back.

Reef's gaze fixed on her momentarily, then back on the steeply inclining road. "So . . ." He cleared his throat. "About our earlier conversation . . ."

"Yes?"

The soothing evergreen scent of his aftershave filled the compact car—reminding her of home, where her shelter and practice was surrounded by pines. "I feel like we've gotten to know each other much better, and . . ."

She found herself leaning in to him. "And?"

"And I hope when all of this is past us, and your cousin and uncle are safe, that our spending time together like this isn't over."

"Really?" She tried to maintain her excitement.

"Yes." He looked down at his right hand covering hers, caressing her skin between his thumb and forefinger. "I'd like to start seeing you as more than a friend."

Disappointment weighed heavy on her heart. So he didn't already view her that way?

"Because the truth is," he continued, "I already do."

Joy bubbled up, fizzing through her. "You do?"

He nodded, his gaze dropping to her lips, and then quickly back to the road.

"That's good," she said, summoning all the braveness she could muster, ignoring the fear pricking at her—because she could feel in her gut this was right. She'd prayed for the right man to come into her life, and God had brought Reef—crazy as it was.

"It's good?" His smile widened.

163

"Yes." She exhaled her fear. "Because I do too."

"Really?" he asked as they began the thousand-foot decline through Turnagain Arm. "No interest in anyone else?"

She shook her head. "Only you."

He smiled, but something stole it away. Was that panic?

"What's wrong?"

He clamped the wheel tight, struggling against it as the car banked hard right, straight for the side of Placer River Bridge.

"Reef?" she screeched, bracing her hands on the dash.

"I can't control the steer—"

Impact with the guardrail cut off his words, the hood of the car jutting over the edge of the bridge and tipping downward. "Hold on," he yelled as they plunged into the frigid Alaskan water.

Please don't let this be it, Lord. Not when he'd just found Kirra, when he'd just gotten his life on the right track. Discovered what mattered.

Despite the swell of panic flooding him, he trusted the Lord. If it was his time to go, then he willingly went. It was amazing how far the Lord had brought him over the past year—to a place of deep security in and dependence on his Savior.

The rapids were bone chilling, but he was confident he could last the few minutes it would take to reach shore. Growing up swimming in Alaskan waters had accustomed him to the cold.

Darkness smothered the light. Water swirled feverishly around them, marring his vision.

The open window allowed the water to pulse in at an unrelenting pace, but it maintained a route of escape against its forceful pressure. Kicking the window out with both feet, he reached for Kirra, her hair a tangled, floating mess about her face. Her arms floated above her head—leaving his gut in his throat. She was unconscious.

Wrapping an arm around her chest beneath her arms, he swam, pulling her through the open window, kicking hard against the force of the water rushing in. Finally free of the vehicle, he furiously swam for and broke the surface.

The frigid air burned his lungs more than holding his breath had. He coughed, water gurgling up his throat.

"Kirra," he choked out, swiping her hair from her face.

Her eyes were open wide, but she wasn't breathing. Spotting the riverbank twenty yards to his right, he swam.

Reaching shore, he carried Kirra up, laying her flat on the rocky surface. "Come on, honey."

Someone hollered that help was on its way. He glanced up, a figure on the bridge catching his eye. A man, his shoulders taut, his stance hard. Was it the man who was chasing them?

Turning back to Kirra, he bent, listening for breath. *None.*

He tilted her head back. "Don't die on me, Kirra." Clearing her airway, he began CPR, his lips pressing against her cold ones. "Come on."

It took several seconds, which seemed an eternity, but finally she coughed, curling toward her side, expelling murky water onto the gray rocky shore.

Thank you, Jesus.

He scooped her in his arms, cradling her against his chest. A man slid down the steep bank to their side, his boots kicking up snow and sleet in his wake. It wasn't the same man he'd seen on the bridge.

Reef glanced back in that direction, but that man was gone.

16

Red lights swirled in disorienting patterns as Kirra sat in the ambulance with Reef, thick green blankets brought by the EMTs draped over her, their scratchiness incongruent with their sickeningly sweet floral fabric softener scent.

Reef's arm was draped across her shoulders—shoulders hunched and trembling.

She was tired of being cold. Tired of being chased. Tired of being threatened.

Father, let this end.

Not yet, my child.

Why not?

It isn't time.

She fought the urge to nuzzle into Reef's chest and allow the tears buried deep inside to finally spring forth. After what had just occurred, any onlookers would attribute her reaction to the near drowning. But she couldn't let go. Not yet.

Why wasn't she ready to fully release all the pent-up sorrow and pain? Because she feared if she fully acknowledged what she'd been holding inside for so long, it would overwhelm her, flood her, and she'd break. She wasn't strong enough.

She was getting by, but healing took work, courage, strength she didn't have.

Reef rubbed her arm. "You doing okay?"

She nodded. Despite the pain, despite the shame, she always managed to keep her chin up. Maybe she had a little bit of her grandma Alice's hutzpah, as her aunt Sarah always called grandmother's special strength and vivacity. Even in her death Alice had gone with style—the only person in the hospital to wear a purple silk robe over the required gown, and a rhinestone flower pin in her thinning hair. She'd held her own right until the end, when she'd whispered, "Off to the next adventure" with her last breath.

Kirra gazed around at the ambulance lights bouncing like red fireflies off the icy road's surface. She supposed this— terrifying as it might be—was a kind of adventure. It was definitely a journey, and she was paired with the least-expected yet truly perfect companion. She couldn't have asked God for a better one.

Kevin Hoffman hurried around the end of the steadily growing vehicle line and climbed into the ambulance. "Kirra, I came as soon as I heard."

"That's sweet, but I'm fine. Really."

He squatted beside her, concern fast on his face. "What happened?"

"The steering went out," Reef explained.

Kevin's brows arched. "Malfunction?"

Reef looked down at Kirra, confirmation in his eyes. They were both thinking the same thing. Might as well say it.

"I . . ." She looked at Reef. "We think it was the man who's been following us."

"Following you?" Kevin said, confusion and alarm filling

his voice. "You never said anything about someone following you."

"We weren't sure . . ."

"Until now," Reef added. "I saw him standing on the bridge when we came out of the water."

"You saw him?" Kirra asked, turning to look up at him. "But we don't know what he looks like. Are you sure?"

Reef nodded. "When I saw him, how he was looking at us—angry and stiff—I just knew."

"But you've seen him before?" Kevin asked.

"We didn't see his face, but he tried to gun us down back at the race."

Kevin's mouth gaped. "Gun you down? Kirra, why didn't you tell me?"

"It didn't seem pertinent."

"Not pertinent? Someone tried to kill you and is following you. How could that not be pertinent?"

"I'm sorry, Kevin. I was just focused on finding Meg." She had to.

"We didn't know for certain he was still after us," Reef said.

Kevin swallowed and stood. "I see. Well, I'll need you two to come back into the station and file a report."

"There's no time for that," Kirra said, anxiety gripping her. "We need to get to Kodiak. We've already lost too much time."

Kevin looked to their car being towed out of the river. "Doesn't look like you'll be going anywhere anytime soon."

"Our next lead is in Kodiak. That's where we need to be."

"I understand," Kevin said, "but you need to file a report. I promise I will expedite the process."

Urgency flared in her throat. "But we're running out of time." Didn't he understand that?

"Kevin's right," Reef said. "We need to file a report and update Jake about what's going on. Besides, we need a new rental car. Don't worry—we'll be back on the road in no time."

"Actually," Kevin said, "I can do better than that."

Kirra reclined in her seat on the small floatplane, thankful Kevin had called in a favor. Russell Grant was taking them in his plane, directly to Kodiak.

Kevin had held true to his word—getting their report down quickly, connecting with Jake and Landon to help run a co-ordinated operation, and providing her and Reef with dry clothes as well as much-needed cell phones. Within a couple hours, they were on their way.

She shifted, pulling the wool sweater sleeves over her hands.

"You still cold?" Reef covered her with a fleece blanket—soft and blue. She nodded, doubting she'd ever feel warm. The chill of the water still clung to her bones.

He cupped her face in the palm of his hand, his skin warm, his touch commanding yet tender. "I'm sorry you're having to go through this."

She leaned into his touch. "I'm just glad you're with me."

"Me too." He caressed her cheek, his fingers brushing her skin in a featherlight motion.

His gaze dropped to her mouth and then quickly back to her eyes.

A soft, anticipatory smile tugged at her lips.

He leaned in, bringing his mouth to hers. His lips were soft, tentative.

She swayed into him, and he deepened the kiss, sending warmth rushing through her body.

Reef took her hand in his as they walked through the small metal-frame building serving as Kodiak's terminal, and his touch felt divine. She'd kissed Reef McKenna—twice now—and her heart hadn't stopped fluttering. The emotions coursing through her brought with them an exhilaration she couldn't quite describe, but she supposed the word *giddy* came closest.

She was giddy over kissing Reef McKenna. In high school she'd occasionally allowed herself to daydream about what it would be like, dreamed about him grabbing her, pressing her up against the lockers, and kissing her passionately, but this was so much better. This kiss wasn't a random act of passion; this kiss had been saturated with meaning and promise.

Unfortunately the purpose of their visit hit her anew as Kodiak's bracing sea wind lashed her cheeks upon exiting the building.

She and Reef weren't on a date. They weren't in Kodiak on some romantic daytrip. They were here to track down the past of an uncle she'd thought she'd known. An uncle she'd depended on. An uncle who wasn't what he'd seemed.

She clasped Reef's hand tighter and prayed God would supply them both with the strength needed to face whatever lay before them. Because she certainly didn't have it in herself.

17

The following morning, Reef held the door to the Kodiak police station open for Kirra. After arriving in Kodiak, they'd picked up a new rental car, checked into a hotel, and had a good night's sleep, which Kirra had desperately needed—her body nearing the point of exhaustion. Her spirit, unfortunately, wasn't close behind.

She couldn't help but continue looking over her shoulder, wondering when the man on the snowmobile, the man on the bridge, was going to surface next. The tension gripping her heart as if in a vise said it wouldn't be long. But she needed to stop expending effort on the *what ifs*. She needed to focus on what was right in front of her—and that was their next lead.

The Kodiak police station—a charcoal-colored two-story building with orange metal piping forming a canopy leading to the entrance, and orange outlining the rectangular windows running nearly the length of it—exuded a modern vibe.

Landon had suggested they speak with Officer Carson Rydell.

It took a few minutes, but they finally located the man at the last desk in the precinct office—tucked in the corner and piled high with files.

"Detective Rydell?" Kirra asked.

The man, who appeared to be about her father's age, gave a sideways glance—his eyebrows matching his salt-and-pepper hair. He was lean and fit. He clearly worked out, though his attire dated him somewhat. He wore loose-fitting Dockers, a light blue dress shirt tucked into a belted waist-band—up at his actual waist—and a navy tie with sailing boats on it.

"Hi, I'm Kirra Jacobs, and—"

"And?" he asked before she could introduce Reef, his attention fixed on the computer screen in front of him, his weathered hands typing away. Between the tie and the hands, she was betting sailing was a favorite hobby.

"I need to speak with you about a B and E involving Frank Weber."

"Frank Weber." He frowned. "Can't say the name's familiar." He continued typing.

"Oh, right." She kept forgetting. "Sorry. I meant Frank Jacobs." A man she never knew.

"Frank Jacobs?" he said in a raspy voice as he ceased typing. "Now that's a name from the past." He swiveled to face her, his gaze scanning her up and down. "What'd you say your name is?"

"Kirra." She extended a hand. "Kirra Jacobs."

He stood and shook it, his gray brows arching. "You Frank's girl?"

"No. His niece."

"So that would make you Bart's kid."

"Yeah. You know my dad?" Probably from Frank's arrest, she imagined.

"Your old man and I played some ball back in the day."

"You're kidding." Her nose crinkled. "My dad played a *sport*? Was it football?" The last few days had been full of surprises. Most of them were very bad, but at least one of them—she looked at Reef—was very good.

"Baseball," Rydell said.

"Really?" Just as surprising. Her dad had never been much into sports while she was growing up. He'd always seemed too straitlaced for them.

"Yeah. We even went to state our junior year."

"You're kidding," she murmured again. She just couldn't picture her dad running bases, sweating, or worse yet, getting dirty. He'd always had a fit when she accidentally got anything on his clothes or tracked dirt into the house as a kid.

"Yes, indeed," Rydell said, pulling over a chair for her and instructing Reef to grab a second one from the empty desk catty-corner to them. "So, what's with the interest in Frank's former ways?" His smile faded. "Don't tell me he's in trouble again after all these years?"

"No. Not in that way." At least the thought had never crossed her mind that something Frank did could have brought on her cousin's kidnapping.

"What way *is* he in trouble?" Rydell linked his arms over his chest, reclining back in his chair.

"It's kind of hard to explain."

"Why don't one of you give it a shot." He lifted his chin at Reef. "You the boyfriend?"

Kirra looked at Reef and smiled, intervening before he attempted to fumble out an answer. Not that it wouldn't be entertaining, but it was best they stick to the point. "This is Reef McKenna. He's helping me."

"McKenna?" The man paused. "As in the Yancey McKennas?"

"Guilty."

Rydell nodded. "So what's your interest in all this?"

"Kirra just learned about her uncle's past, and she was curious about what happened. Landon suggested we talk with you."

"Landon Grainger? That's right," Rydell snapped. "Nadine said he left a message saying he was sending some folks by, but she didn't give me a name. Guess that'd be you."

"Yep."

"Well, why didn't you say so?" He stood. "Hold tight. It may take me a bit to track down Frank's info. Grab a soda and make yourselves comfortable."

Kirra shifted on the metal folding chair, terrified of what she might learn about an uncle she thought she'd known so well. *Comfortable* was the last thing she could be.

18

NorthStar Oil Headquarters
Anchorage, Alaska
March 14, 9:20 a.m.

Jake followed Kayden into NorthStar Oil headquarters in Anchorage, the engagement ring still burning a hole in his faded jeans pocket. When he'd hoped for a memorable proposal, it being amidst a hostage situation wasn't exactly what he had in mind.

A woman in her thirties stood guard behind the receptionist's station—her blond hair twisted up into some kind of bun-type arrangement. Her cold green eyes fixed on them. "May I be of service?" Her words said one thing, her rigid demeanor another.

"I'm sure you can." He flashed his badge. "We need to speak with Mr. Potler."

"I'm afraid Mr. Potler only sees people by appointment." She tapped on the keyboard with her perfectly polished fingernails. "Looks like I can squeeze you in for a quick chat the end of next week, if it's truly urgent."

"It's urgent, but next week is unacceptable." Jake leaned forward—resting his arms on the granite counter. "We need to see Mr. Potler now."

She arched a frighteningly narrow brow, plucked pencil thin. The look was drastic, but perhaps that's what she was going for. "That's not possible."

"Let me put it in a way you'll understand. Either he sees us now or we camp out here in your lovely lobby with a gaggle of policemen for the day. Trust me—I think you'd rather have us gone in fifteen minutes than drawing all your high-profile clients' attention for who knows how long."

Her jaw twitched. "Just a moment." Turning her back to them, she lifted the receiver and spoke low into it. After a moment she turned back around, her ivory cheeks flushed crimson. "Mr. Potler will see you now."

Jake smiled. "I thought he might."

"You took way too much pleasure in that," Kayden whispered with a smile.

He couldn't stand uppity people who treated others as their inferiors. He'd grown up around too many people like that in high-society Boston. He no longer had a tolerance for it.

The woman led the way down the long black hall, her four-inch heels clicking along the white ceramic tiles. She paused before the double black wooden doors at the end, lacing her red manicured fingers around the ornate silver knob. She turned and pushed in. She led them through a seating area, straight to a second set of doors that opened automatically.

A man—tall, early fifties, impeccably dressed—stood to greet them. "What's this all about, Officer?"

"Detective," Jake said.

"Detective." The man's tone echoed his disinterested stature.

"Detective Cavanaugh," Jake said. "And this is Miss Mc-Kenna." Though not for long if he had any say about it. Kayden Cavanaugh had a much better ring. "We're here to speak with you about Frank Weber."

"Who?" The man returned to sit behind his mahogany desk, not bothering to offer them a seat. Jake took one anyway, and so did Kayden. Potler had brushed them off long enough. They weren't leaving without answers.

"Frank Weber." Jake handed him the picture they'd printed out from Frank's Iditarod entry. "He's an employee of yours."

Potler barely glanced at it before tossing it aside. "And . . . ?"

"And we need to know what he does for you."

"Fine." Potler steepled his fingers—his Yale graduation ring prominently displayed on his right ring finger. "I can direct you to Personnel."

"We don't have time to jump through hoops." Which was exactly what would happen if they were passed off to Personnel. "We simply need to know what Mr. Weber does for you."

Potler leaned forward with an irritated sigh and pressed the intercom button. "Audrey. Shoot me what you have on a Frank Weber."

"Right away, Mr. Potler."

"So . . ." Potler tapped his steepled fingers. "What is your interest in this man you claim is my employee, Detective Cavanaugh?"

"He's being forced to do a job and we're trying to determine what that particular job may be."

"Why not just ask him?"

"We can't locate him. He's off grid at the Iditarod, and we have great concern for the safety of his daughter."

"His daughter? I thought you said this was about Mr. Weber?"

"It's about them both."

At his computer's *ding*, he turned his attention to it. "Well, let's see. Ah, yes. Mr. Weber has been a freelance contractor with us off and on for the past"—his eyes skimmed the screen—"four years."

"Contracted to do what, exactly?" Jake asked.

"He designed the schematics for several of our off-shore oil rigs along Alaska's coast, and most recently . . . he's done the same for our interior pipeline." Mr. Potler smiled for the first time since they'd entered his office. "It's a very exciting project that will bring energy and power to the sparse interior of this beautiful state."

"Anyone not happy about the project?" Kayden asked.

"All great projects are going to have detractors."

"And the pipeline is no exception?"

He exhaled. "I'm afraid not. Whenever an oil company starts a project, we attract the environmental groups."

"Any groups in particular drawn to this project?"

"I couldn't tell you one from the other, but ask Audrey on your way out. Someone manages a file of every complaint we get. I'm sure she can steer you in the right direction. Now, if you'll excuse me, I have a teleconference in five minutes."

They waited while Audrey printed them out a list of over a hundred groups that had protested the laying of the interior Alaskan pipeline—from huge environmental watchdogs down to small campus groups.

Jake tapped one of the sheets. "What was the name of the environmental group Meg's associated with?"

"Reef said it was an acronym. Something like ROW or SEW."

He scanned the sheet. "ROW—Rescue Our World?"

"Sounds like it."

"And they're based on the University of Alaska, Fairbanks campus."

"Is there a contact person listed with the complaint?"

"Yes. Samuel Matthews. And, according to this, they did more than just complain."

"Oh?"

"ROW staged an on-site protest when the first of the pump stations went in at Anchorage. Later that night, some valuable equipment was vandalized."

"And the police think ROW was responsible?"

"Samuel Matthews was one of the prime suspects."

"You'd better call Kirra. See if she can get back in touch with Sam Matthews. He may be the key to all this."

"What we've got is a breaking and entering that went bad," Rydell said, returning nearly an hour later with a manila file folder in hand. He set it open on his desk and pushed it with his finger toward Reef and Kirra.

He went on to relay the basics of what they'd already learned—Frank had been part of a three-man team consisting of him, Henry Watts, and Tommy Madero. The men had broken into Phillip Webster's home, and a shootout had followed, resulting in the death of Tommy Madero and the injury of Webster and Watts.

"What more can you tell us about Henry Watts and Tommy Madero?" Kirra asked.

"Henry Watts had a lengthy rap sheet by the time Tommy Madero hooked up with him. Everything from possession of a narcotic to assault and battery. Real angry sort, with a dangerous chip on his shoulder. The kind that always think they're owed something."

"And my uncle? How on earth did he get involved with a man like Henry Watts, and why?" Her grandparents had been fairly well off—it couldn't have been about the money.

"At the time of Frank's arrest, I asked him the same question, knowing the family and all."

She inched forward in her chair. "And what'd he say?" She couldn't imagine anything that would make any sense out of all she was learning, but she prayed Frank had said something that would somehow bring the pieces together, and that her image of her uncle wasn't a complete lie.

"Frank was in love with a gal who was in deep to Watts."

"For what?"

"She owed him some serious money for drugs. Watts had gotten her hooked, and supposedly she'd managed to get clean before she met Frank, but not before racking up a bill with Watts she couldn't pay."

"So . . . what? If Frank worked a robbery with them, he'd wipe the debt clean?" Reef asked.

Rydell tapped his nose.

"But why *Frank*?" Kirra asked, feeling like a three-year-old repeating *Why?* over and over, but she wanted—no, she *needed*—answers. What skills did her uncle possess that made him so valuable? Or did Watts just need another warm body?

"Because Frank had a knack with mechanics even then. He could open just about any lock and disable just about any alarm."

"How? Why?" With each answer, more questions came.

"Frank said at first it was just a game. He'd gotten locked out of their house a few times and finally figured out a way in. Then he started doing it at friends' houses, just to show off."

"Watts heard about Frank's talent and snagged him into the job," Reef said.

"Afraid so." Rydell nodded.

"Was the girl a plant on Watts's part to rope Frank in?" Reef asked.

"What?" Kirra's mind raced through the scenario, wondering how Reef's mind had gone to it so quickly.

"I don't know if it started out that way, but I do know how it ended."

"How's that?"

"He married her."

"What?" Kirra was thankful for the chair beneath her. "Aunt Sarah?"

Rydell nodded with a nostalgic smile.

Reef scooted his chair next to Kirra's, the metal legs squeaking across the linoleum tile. He wrapped his arm around her shoulder, and she felt anchored for the first time in days.

She leaned into his hold.

"What can you tell us about that night? About the break-in?" Reef asked.

"I remember the call. It was my first case as a homicide detective. Tommy was close in age to me—only a few years younger. We'd attended the same grade school growing up. You know how it is growing up in a small community— everyone knows everyone."

She'd "known" Reef practically her whole life, but she felt as if she was only now truly getting to know him—the true him. And just as he'd said to her on the plane, she loved what she saw.

"Why did Watts kill his own man?" Darcy's research hadn't revealed that.

"He claimed it was an accident. That the homeowner returned unexpectedly, shots were fired, and in the confusion, Madero was killed."

"But I'm guessing by your tone that's not what you believe happened?" Reef said.

"Not according to Phillip Webster—the homeowner—or your uncle Frank. Both testified against Watts. Once we finally caught up with Frank, that is." He chuckled.

Kirra's eyes narrowed. "Our research indicated it took a while to connect him to the B and E and then bring him in. What took so long?"

"Why didn't Watts give him up?" Reef asked.

It didn't make any sense, though Kirra was hardly an expert on criminals.

"He probably feared Frank would plead out and testify against him on Madero's murder."

"Which he did."

"Yeah. But it wasn't all wrapped up in a neat package. Once we figured out Frank was our third guy, we still had to track him down."

Kirra's eyes widened. "Did he flee?" Her uncle really wasn't the man she'd thought she'd known so well.

"In a manner of speaking." Rydell gave a curious smile. "He went ahead with his Iditarod race."

"Seriously?" Reef choked out.

"A week had passed, and we still weren't on to him, so he figured why not? Probably thought some time away from

Kodiak wouldn't hurt, and he was already registered and set to go."

"So you chased him during the race?" Kirra sat back. That had to be crazy.

"No. We were waiting at the finish line."

The timing of the Iditarod being involved in both cases—following the breaking and entering, and now with Henry Watts being released from prison and Frank's daughter being held for ransom—couldn't all be a coincidence, could it? But what could Watts want from Frank? What job could he want him to do? It wasn't like there were a lot of high-end homes to steal from along the race trail—though that possibility existed. They'd have to start compiling a list of possible targets.

"We heard that Watts was recently released from prison," Reef said.

"That's right." Rydell nodded.

"Do you think he'd try and go after Frank after all these years? For testifying against him?"

"Couldn't say." Rydell sighed. "Prison either makes the need for revenge fester or it provides the distance to let it go. Weirdest thing. But you'd have to talk to Watts to see which way he went."

"We plan to."

"Be careful. I don't know what Watts is like now, but back in the day he was plain nasty."

Great. Another nasty man to deal with. As if the man chasing after them and William Daniels weren't enough.

"Thanks for the heads up," Reef said. "We were told there was something about a reporter who'd done a piece on the breaking and entering, that he claimed there was a second break-in that night, but the men were never charged for it."

"Let me guess. The reporter was Simon Baker?"

"Yeah. How'd you know?"

Rydell shook his head with an exasperated smile. "When it comes to conspiracy theories, Simon Baker's always involved. Twenty years later, nothing's changed."

"He's still reporting?"

"Yep. Actually, he runs the *Kodiak Eagle* now. Office is over on Main Street."

"Thanks," Kirra said, standing. Simon Baker had just bumped to the top of their interview list.

"What conspiracy theory?" Reef asked as Rydell shook his hand.

Rydell smiled. "I'm going to let Simon answer that one. It's his theory. Well, his and Karen Madero's."

The *Kodiak Eagle* offices were housed in a two-story converted home along Main Street. A handful of desks occupied the busy space—phones ringing, people hollering to each other across workstations, as a series of news station broadcasts were displayed on the flat screen TVs mounted on the far wall.

A man stood in front of them, his back to Reef and Kirra. Based on his gray receding hairline, she was betting the gentleman was older. His tan Dockers were rumpled, and his striped long-sleeved shirt rolled up above his elbows.

Kirra approached him, following a hunch. "Mr. Baker?" she asked.

He turned, half glancing at Kirra and half still watching the newscast vying for his attention. "Yeah? What do you want?"

He looked to be in his sixties. Tall, not exactly lean, but well built. "To speak with you about an article you wrote."

"Yeah?" He shrugged, determination fixed hard in his eyes. "Get in line." He gestured to a row of people waiting behind a half wall, most fuming. He called over his shoulder at them. "Haven't you people ever heard of freedom of speech?" He looked back at Kirra. "You don't have to like what I say, but that doesn't make it illegal to say it."

"I think there's been some confusion."

He popped the top of his soda. "That's one way to approach it."

"Approach what?"

"Whatever's got your knickers in a bunch."

"My knickers aren't in . . ." She took a deep breath and exhaled. "Look. We're just here to get your help on the Webster break-in—from twenty years ago."

The man's brows furrowed. "What about it?" He took a swig of soda.

"You wrote an article about the second break-in. Well, I suppose it was actually the first break-in, but you get my point. . . ."

He eyed them skeptically. "And?"

"And we're trying to learn all we can about the initial break-in."

"You mean you believe it happened?"

"That's what your article says, isn't it?"

He gazed around and then wrapped his arm around Kirra's shoulder, steering her to the open office in the rear. "Let's talk in my office."

They followed him in and waited while he closed the door. "Take a seat." He gestured to the two brown metal folding chairs placed on either side of a brown card table. He pulled his swivel chair over from his desk. "That break-in was years ago. Why the sudden interest?" He stiffened. "Watts didn't send you, did he? I heard he was out, but I—"

"We're not here on behalf of Watts," she assured him.

"Then why are you here?"

"Because of my uncle, Frank Web—" She caught herself. "Frank Jacobs."

"Frank's niece, huh?"

"Yes. I—"

"I get it. You're after the egg."

Kirra glanced at Reef, confused, and then back to Simon Baker. "Egg? What egg?" What did any of this have to do with an egg of all things?

"Look, kitten, that innocent look may work with the young fellows like this guy." He jabbed his thumb in Reef's direction. "But I've seen it all. If you're just in it for the treasure, I'm not interested." He pushed back from the table.

"Wait. Please. My cousin Meg, Frank's daughter, is in serious trouble, and we think it may be related to that night."

He arched a brow. "Because Watts is out of jail?"

"Yes."

"How did you know Watts is out of jail?" Reef asked.

"Because when a murderer is released back into our small community, we at the *Eagle* keep our citizens informed." He cleared his throat. "That and Karen called all freaked out, frantic he may come after her."

"Karen Madero?" Kirra asked.

"That's right."

Reef stretched his legs out, crossing one booted foot over the other. "Why was she worried Watts would come after her?"

"Because he might be under the assumption that she knows where Frank hid it."

"*It* being some egg?" Kirra asked.

Baker gave a curt nod, igniting her curiosity even more. "What can you tell us about this egg?"

"Other than the fact it's a priceless Russian Imperial Fabergé egg, nothing." He stiffened. "You want more, you'll need to talk to Karen."

She tried to move past that, to focus on what they could get out of him. "What can you tell us about that night? The police don't believe there was another break-in, or at least not one where anything was stolen. Why do you believe differently?"

"Because the security alarm was triggered at the Bartholomew residence eight minutes before the Webster break-in that night."

"That didn't give them much time at the Bartholomew residence. What do the police say about the triggered alarm?"

"They said that malfunctions happen, and even if Watts and his crew were responsible for triggering the Bartholomew residence's alarm, they didn't steal anything."

"Because . . . ?" Why trigger an alarm and not bother taking anything?

"Police say either they broke into the wrong house, realized it, and moved on . . ."

Kirra leaned forward, resting her elbows on her knees. "Or?"

"Or the alarm spooked them and they moved on."

"Not far," Reef said. "Not if it only took them eight minutes between break-ins."

"The Bartholomew residence and the Websters' are only separated by two streets."

187

"That's really risky. Two break-ins so close together."

"Risky. Stupid." He shrugged. "Take your pick."

"But you're sure an egg was taken from the Bartholomew residence?"

He nodded. "Yes."

"We were told the homeowner claimed otherwise."

"Yes, but he had his reasons."

"And what reasons might those be?"

A young man approached the office door. "Simon, it's the call you've been waiting for." He tapped the doorframe. "Line one."

Simon stood and stepped to his desk. "Sorry, folks. I've got to take this."

"But we've still got questions for you."

"Talk to Karen Madero. She'll be able to answer your questions better than I can."

"Why's that?"

"Because she was there that night."

No wonder Karen Madero was worried. If Watts had killed her husband and apparently tried to kill Frank, what said Watts wouldn't try to kill off the final witness?

19

Karen Madero lived at the water's edge in a small cabin sided with wood shingles, which Kirra guessed had once been dark and earthy in color but now closely resembled parched driftwood.

Reef held out his hand at the base of the steps. "After you."

"Thanks." She allowed her fingers to brush his, allowed her mind to drift to the moment he'd said he was falling for her, recalled the soft feel of his lips against hers—the first time in the cave, startled and hesitant, the second on the plane, confident and passionate. She wondered what the next time would be like and how long she'd have to wait.

"Kirra, the door?" Reef gestured with a tilt of his head and a soft smile curling on his lips.

How long had she just been standing in front of it? Embarrassment heated her cheeks as her gloved hand knocked on the plexiglass storm door.

The interior door opened, and an attractive woman in her early-to-mid forties stared out at them, lingering fear edging her beautiful brown eyes.

"Mrs. Madero?"

She clasped her cardigan closed, her fingers tight on the heather-gray material. "Yes?"

"Simon Baker sent us over." It seemed the less intimidating and still truthful lead-in.

"Oh?" She still hadn't opened the storm door, and as the frigid March wind blew off the bay, Kirra really wished the woman would.

"We were hoping you might be able to help us."

Her eyes fluttered. A nervous habit, perhaps? "With what?"

"The Bartholomew and Webster break-ins."

"I'm afraid that's ancient history." She moved to close the door.

"Wait. Please! My cousin's life may hang in the balance."

The woman paused, eyeing Kirra curiously. "Who's your cousin?"

"Frank Jacobs' daughter, Meg."

Karen swallowed and then opened the storm door. She looked around before shutting it behind them.

Karen Madero's home could best be summed up as quaint. A cozy front room greeted them, a navy couch and matching recliner taking up the bulk of the space, a basketful of yarn sitting next to a dark wooden rocker in front of a stone fireplace.

Kirra studied the woman's stylish wool cardigan more closely and decided by some of the intricate detailing and matching spool of wool in the basket that she'd most likely knit it herself.

"You knit?" She pointed to the basket overflowing with muted grays and bright hues of pink and purple.

Karen nodded, her arms wrapped tightly about her torso. "Can I get either of you a drink? Hot chocolate, coffee, tea?"

"I'd love a hot chocolate," Kirra said.

"That'd be great." Reef took a seat beside her on the couch as Karen headed for the kitchen.

Reef shouldered against her, threading his fingers through hers. "How you holding up?"

"Okay." It wasn't easy learning your favorite uncle had a sordid past, and she felt as if everything was going in slow motion. "I'm getting anxious. Meg's still out there, and I have no idea if we're any closer to finding her." Not to mention the man following them. Had he known they were headed for Kodiak? If not, how long would it take him to figure it out? He was never far behind, and she wanted to know how he kept managing to do that. Who was feeding him information on their whereabouts?

Karen Madero returned with two mugs in hand, passing one to Kirra and the other to Reef.

Kirra smiled. "Thank you."

"Yes, thank you," Reef said before taking a sip. The hot chocolate was rich and thick and nearly rivaled his sister Piper's—nearly, but not quite.

Karen settled uneasily in her chair, clearly bracing for the questions to come.

Kirra began. "What can you tell us about that night?"

Karen cleared her throat, staring past them both. "It was twenty years ago, but I still remember it like it was yesterday. Still see it in my nightmares."

Kirra set her mug on the coaster. "Simon Baker said there were two break-ins that night?"

Karen nodded.

"The police believe there was only one, or at least only one where they actually entered," Reef said, cupping his mug, letting the warmth ease the chill in his hands.

Karen looked straight at him. "They're wrong."

"How can you be certain?"

"Because I was there."

Just as Simon Baker had said. "You were part of the robbery?" Reef wasn't seeing it. She hardly looked the criminal sort.

"No." Karen looked down at her hands clasped tight in her lap. "I was watching."

"Watching?" Kirra asked, before taking another sip of her hot chocolate.

Reef clutched Kirra's hand as she conversed with Karen Madero. After all she'd been through, Kirra deserved to be protected.

Inhaling, anger flared inside. If he'd known when they'd been in that parking lot what William Daniels had done . . .

Exhaling slowly, Reef forced his racing heart to calm.

Kirra wasn't alone in this, not anymore. He was at her side, and that's where he'd stay.

"I knew Henry Watts was serious trouble," Karen said, reining in Reef's attention. "I begged Tommy not to get involved with him, but he didn't listen. That night, I had a horrible feeling in the pit of my stomach. I just knew something bad was going to happen, so I followed Tommy to the Bartholomew house. I saw them go inside, heard the alarm go off, and a few minutes later, they rushed out."

"Did you see them carrying anything?" he asked.

Karen shook her head. "It was dark, and they moved straight for the car, but they seemed excited—not frustrated—and it wouldn't be hard to conceal what I believe they took."

"And what's that?" They knew what Simon claimed, but he wanted to hear it from her.

"A Russian Imperial Fabergé egg."

"Why do you believe they took that?"

"Because Watts and Tommy had both heard rumors about Bartholomew."

"What rumors would those be?" Reef asked, knowing all about rumors and false assumptions, but perhaps in this case the rumors were true.

"That Bartholomew was a collector of black-market antiquities, and that he'd recently acquired a rare Fabergé egg. I heard Watts and Tommy talking about it before they left that night, and I am certain it is the reason they broke into the Bartholomew house."

"Okay, so why the second break-in?" Reef asked. "Why weren't they satisfied with the egg?" It had to be worth a fortune. His sister-in-law, Bailey, would know for sure. She continued to run her late aunt's Russian Alaskan Trading Company, and she specialized in antiques from the Imperial period.

"Watts got greedy. Before they got in the car, I heard him tell Tommy and Frank they had one more job. They argued about it as they got in, but Watts, as always, won out. I think Watts planned to make it look like Tommy and Frank shot each other at the second break-in, and then he'd just slip away with the egg. An egg that would never be reported stolen."

"But the homeowner returned," Reef said.

"Exactly. Phillip Webster returned armed and shot at and injured Watts before he could kill Frank. Watts returned fire and Frank fled during the shootout. Tommy died, Watts got arrested, and Phillip Webster spent a night in the hospital."

"So what happened to the egg?"

"Frank got away with it when he fled."

"My uncle took it?"

"It's the only thing that makes sense. After the police arrived at the Webster home, they didn't find anything on Tommy or Watts, or in the car."

"But maybe it wasn't even taken in the first place. You never saw the egg. No one admits to taking it, and even the homeowner insists nothing was stolen."

"I'm telling you, they came out of the Bartholomew house with something, and I am sure it was the egg. Besides . . . there was the rumor."

"What rumor?"

"That Frank took the egg and hid it."

"Hid it?" Kirra frowned.

"To keep the cops off his trail. To make sure no one could tie him to the break-in."

"And where, supposedly, did he hide it?"

"Along the Iditarod trail."

Kirra looked at Reef, a thousand thoughts racing across her face, and through his mind.

With obvious frustration, Karen continued, "When they arrested him at the end of the race, he insisted they didn't take anything from the Bartholomew house—but I know better. They searched his house and everywhere else they could think of. . . . Where else could it be?"

"Okay . . ." Kirra looked at Reef and then back to Karen. "So you think Watts believes my uncle hid the Fabergé egg and is holding my cousin hostage until he retrieves the egg and brings it to him?"

"Yes."

"Okay. Let's say the egg *was* stolen and Frank *did* hide it along the Iditarod trail. Once he got out of prison, why wouldn't he have retrieved it for himself?" Kirra asked.

"The egg would be too hot to sell anywhere except on the black market, which would bring Bartholomew back into it. I believe Frank just left it out there to rid himself of it and start a fresh life."

"So you believe that a Fabergé egg has been hidden somewhere along the Iditarod trail this entire time?" Reef asked, the notion highly intriguing. To think something so valuable could be out there somewhere was crazy.

"Yes," Karen said with absolute certainty to her tone.

Kirra's mind was swirling as they said good-bye to Karen Madero and headed down the front porch steps. The temperature had dropped, the sky gray and thick.

She looked up at Reef. "What do you think?"

"It's an interesting theory, but I don't know if it's more than that."

"If it is, if Karen's theory is true, then how on earth can we help Frank? Only he knows where the Fabergé egg is hidden, so only he can retrieve it. And why would others be in danger?"

"I don't know." He squeezed her shoulder. "I believe we can best help by finding Meg. By focusing on *her* trail."

"So we head back to Seward, where she was last seen, or back to the race?"

"Let's call Jake and get his input, and we should call Bailey about the egg."

"Great idea. With her expertise in Russian artifacts, she might be able to offer some helpful insight."

"Before we leave Kodiak, though, there are three more people we need to speak with."

"Henry Watts?" She wasn't looking forward to coming face-to-face with the man who could be responsible for her cousin's kidnapping. Was it his man who had been following them or the ex-con himself?

"Yes," Reef said, taking her hand in his as they made the short walk back to their rental car. "Along with Phillip Webster and David Bartholomew. Maybe after all this time and under the circumstances, Bartholomew will admit if the egg was actually stolen."

She exhaled. "We can pray." She'd been doing a lot of that lately, and it felt good.

"Excellent plan," Reef said, helping her into the car.

"Wait. What plan?"

He moved around to his side and climbed in. He started the engine, then reached over for her gloved hands.

She eyed him expectantly.

"You said we should pray."

She smiled. "Yes. I did."

"Would you like to, or shall I?" he asked.

"You go ahead." She was curious to hear what was heaviest on his heart.

He clasped her hands, dipped his head slightly, and closed his eyes. She did the same.

"Father, we come to you in need of direction. We don't know which path to follow or even if we're on the right one. Please guide us. You know who has Meg and why they have her. Don't let us waste time chasing the wrong direction; don't let us miss something we need to learn. We ask your guidance—and protection from the man chasing us. Thank you for keeping us safe, and thank you for Kirra and the amazing woman she is. We pray you'll be with Frank and Meg as they face fear we can't imagine. In Jesus' name, Amen."

Kirra kept her hold on his hands tight. "Thank you."

"My pleasure. I hope it's the beginning of a wonderful relationship between us and the Lord."

She swallowed. *Relationship?* With him and between them and the Lord? One didn't get much more serious than that.

20

KALTAG, ALASKA
MARCH 14, 2:30 P.M.

Jake entered the Kaltag checkpoint, Kayden following close behind. The warmth of the cabin compared to the frigid temps outside felt wonderful. It was good to be back with the race, good to now be what he prayed was nearer to Frank and the men who had taken his daughter than when they'd left.

Kaltag was a town of roughly two hundred, with three stores and a community hall that served as the checkpoint hangout.

"What'd you learn?" Gage asked as Darcy hurried to his side.

The front room of the community hall was empty, and Jake was thankful for it. They had a lot to catch up on. "Where is everyone?"

"Eating lunch." Darcy nodded toward the kitchen, a good ways down the hall.

They'd have some privacy, at least for the moment. Best to get to it. Jake relayed what he and Kayden had learned—that

198

Frank's latest job had been on the pipeline, and that Meg's environmental group, ROW, had staged a huge protest and possibly vandalized the first pump station.

"So it sounds like we need to have Kirra and Reef revisit Seward," Darcy said. "Find out what the students say when they call them on the pump station protest and ask about the vandalism."

"I agree." Jake dropped his duffel on the floor and placed Kayden's gently beside it.

"Any luck on the police sketch of Rain that Kirra and Reef had sent over?" Gage asked, moving to stand guard at the hall door.

Jake nodded. "Landon ran it. It matches the description of a Joseph Keller. Wanted for vandalism and trespassing."

Darcy smiled broadly. "Kirra said that they believed Rain's first name was Joseph."

"Yes." Jake nodded. "So he may very well be our guy."

Gage positioned himself sideways in the doorframe so he could see them and still keep an eye on the hall leading from the kitchen. "What do we know about him?"

Jake took a seat on the couch, pulling Kayden down playfully beside him. It probably wasn't the time for playfulness, but he needed to feel her beside him. Needed her close. Waiting for the right opportunity to propose was killing him. But the timing had to be right. She deserved *spectacular*. She molded against his side, eliciting smiles from Gage and Darcy and filling him with joy and contentment. This was where he belonged—right beside her—wherever that may be.

"Jake?" Gage prompted with a smirk.

Jake cleared his throat and tried to focus, finding it nearly impossible with Kayden so close—her lilac scent entrancing, her long, flowing hair soft against his cheek. *Get it together, man.* "Joseph Keller is twenty-six, older than the typical college student. So I called the Office of the Registrar, and there is no Joseph Keller or Rain anyone registered at University of Alaska, Fairbanks."

Gage lifted his chin. "So what's he doing hanging around campus?"

"Probably trying to get close to Meg," Kayden offered.

"You think they found out what her dad did for a living and targeted her?" Darcy asked, settling in the chair next to the sofa.

Kayden sighed. "I have a feeling . . ."

"So . . ." Darcy's brow furrowed—as it did whenever she was thinking hard. "Rain works to get close to Meg, to get her interested and involved in the cause. They win her trust and then snatch her, holding her hostage until her dad performs whatever job they've asked him to."

"Or"—Jake rubbed his chin—"she went willingly for the cause. But Kirra's convinced she wouldn't do that to her family, to her father. Wouldn't worry him like that."

Kayden tilted her head to look up at him, her brown eyes mesmerizing. "What do you think?"

"I've never met Meg, so I can't really make an informed call. I think for her safety, though, we need to assume she's being held against her will."

"I pray for Kirra and Frank's sake that's true," Darcy said.

Gage's brows shot up.

Color flushed Darcy's cheeks. "That came out wrong. I don't want her to be held hostage, but the thought of her being a part of this, of making her family think she's in danger when she's not . . . that would be awful too."

"I agree," Jake said.

"So let's focus on Frank for a minute," Gage said, shifting to face them better.

"What job could they want Frank to perform?"

"Devon Potler at NorthStar Oil said Frank worked on the pipeline. Maybe Joseph aka Rain and whomever he's working with want Frank to damage the pumps so they won't work."

"But he said others could be hurt."

"Maybe they want the pumps rigged to blow, and people could be injured in the explosion."

"Maybe, but would an environmental group really rig oil pumps to blow?" Gage asked. "Wouldn't that endanger all the animals they are so gung ho about protecting, not to mention the environment surrounding the pumps and water systems flowing through the area?"

"Are the pumps operational? Is oil already flowing?" Darcy asked.

"Potler said yes, as of last week."

"If they are extreme ecoterrorists, they want to make a statement," Darcy said. "And they might have decided the best way to show the damage a pipeline can do is to make what they believe will eventually happen, happen now. Maybe they are targeting the pump in Nome so that the damage will be somewhat contained, and at the same time—with all the reporters waiting at the finish line—will gain the most exposure."

She shook her head and continued, "It's like that guy Chaim Nissim, who fired five rockets at the nuclear power station in France—Superphénix. It was still under construction, and the rockets didn't reach the core, but under different circumstances . . . who knows the damage that could have been caused."

"The Nome station is possible, but they could be targeting any of them. We need to have the pumps checked," Jake said. "I'll call Potler's office and try to convince him of the potential risk. A NorthStar engineer should be able to detect any damage to a station, or if an explosive device has been planted. Where's the closest pump?"

Darcy pulled out her laptop and after a minute said, "The pipeline doesn't fully follow the Iditarod trail, but many of the stations are relatively close. The closest station to us is about a dozen miles east of the Old Woman cabin."

So about halfway between Kaltag and Unalakleet. At the pace Frank had been going, it was likely he'd passed by there already. "Okay. Frank couldn't have reached Nome yet, so there's no sense looking there. For now let's focus on the stations Frank could have tampered with—starting with the one near Old Woman."

Kayden sighed.

Jake rubbed her arm. "You okay?"

"Yeah. Just praying we're wrong about this. I hate to imagine the devastation that could result from one or more of those pump stations being compromised."

KODIAK, ALASKA
MARCH 14, 4:00 P.M.

David Bartholomew's home was a massive wood-framed house with a large portico under which they pulled up to the front door. Large two-story windows filled the home's front

to the right side of the door, with smaller windows on both
levels on the left. A circular room jutted out over the west
side, facing the water, windows caterpillaring the entire room

Kirra looked back at Reef. "Nice place."

He slipped his hands in his pockets. "Sure is."

They'd driven by Phillip Webster's home and learned he
no longer lived there, no longer lived anywhere. He'd passed
away five years ago from heart disease, and the house had
passed through two owners before the most recent family
took up residence. As Simon Baker had said, the old Webster
residence and the Bartholomews' were only two streets apart,
easily drivable in a minute or two.

They rang the doorbell—a deep gonging tone that signaled
their arrival. A second ring and the door opened. A man in
his upper sixties answered. He was short and stout, closer
in height to Kirra than Reef. He reminded Kirra of Mickey
Rooney, but she wasn't sure if it was his actual features or simply the hard-nosed expression on his pinched face. "Yeah?"

"Mr. Bartholomew?" Reef asked.

"Yeah."

"Hi. Reef McKenna." He reached out his hand. "This is
Kirra Jacobs." He gestured with his head. "May we speak
with you a minute?"

His gaze fixed back on Reef. "What's this about?"

"A break-in that occurred here twenty years ago."

Bartholomew laughed. "You're a little late, aren't you?"

Reef rubbed the back of his neck. "We just need to know
what happened that night."

"Why?"

"Because Henry Watts was just released from prison last
month, and Frank Jacobs' daughter has been kidnapped."

"Jacobs." He stared at Kirra, looking her up and down. "Are you related?"

"Yes." She stuffed her hands in her pea coat pockets as snowflakes fluttered around them. "Frank Jacobs is my uncle. My cousin Meg has been kidnapped."

"I'm sorry to hear that, but what would make you think her abduction has anything to do with a twenty-year-old robbery?"

"That's where you come in."

He arched a brow.

"We were told that a Fabergé egg was taken from your house that night."

"You've been listening to rumors. As I told the police that night, and everyone else since then, nothing was stolen from my house."

Rather than calling the man a liar outright, Kirra decided to take a more subtle approach. "Don't you find it odd that three men break into your home but take nothing?"

"Not really. I think they got spooked. They clearly hadn't anticipated the alarm or simply couldn't reset it in time, so they fled for an easier hit."

Kirra tried a different tack. "We're not police officers—we're here for my cousin. She's my only concern. I understand why you might not want to confide in the police, but—"

"Let me stop you right there, Miss Jacobs. I'm very sorry for the situation with your cousin, but it has nothing to do with me or that night twenty years ago."

"But Henry Watts just got out of jail, and suddenly Meg's abducted? That can't be a coincidence."

"Perhaps Henry Watts has other reasons for taking your cousin."

"Such as?"

"I can hardly surmise, but it doesn't involve my egg. Now if you'll excuse me . . ." He shut the door,

"My egg?" Kirra said with a smile. "He said *my* egg. He pretty much admitted he at least owned the egg."

"But he maintains nothing was stolen that night. Maybe he owns the egg in question but it was never stolen. Maybe it really is just a rumor. One that a distraught Karen Madero started the night her husband was murdered."

"Why? Why make up the rumor?"

"Maybe she believed it to be true. She said they discussed taking the egg. Maybe they went there with that intention but decided it was too hot of an item to fence. Maybe they simply moved on to the Webster house."

"We need to find Watts. See what story he tells."

21

"Are you sure we're at the right place?" Kirra asked, taking in the abandoned-looking trailer at the far end of the park.

Reef double-checked the address the parole officer had provided. "This is it."

Kirra lifted her hand to knock. "Here goes nothing." She rapped on the door, the thin metal creaking on its lopsided frame.

Reef scoped out the dingy windows after receiving no response.

A dog barked in the distance—high-pitched and incessant.

Kirra knocked again, a little harder. *Come on, Henry.* With her increased pressure, the door pushed open. She glanced at Reef, the question in her eyes, and he nodded.

She tipped the door open an inch and peered inside the dark trailer. "Mr. Watts?"

She looked back at Reef and shook her head.

"Looks like he's not here."

She took in the trailer's stale air. "Doesn't look like he's been here in a long while. *Great . . .*" She exhaled in frustration. They'd already checked his supposed place of employment, but nobody had seen him in several weeks. According to one of the mechanics, who seemed none too thrilled at their presence, he worked on a "consulting" basis.

Reef shrugged. "Door's open. We may as well check things out."

She smiled. "I was thinking the same thing." Perhaps inside they'd find some indication of when he'd last been there or where he'd headed.

She stepped through the rickety doorframe, Reef on her heels. Her right ankle caught on something, nearly splaying her forward.

Reef's strong arm wrapped around her waist, yanking her back out of the trailer as an explosion rent the air. Smoke and debris flew as she slammed into the ground—Reef landing on top of her with a *thud*.

The air expelled from her lungs, none reentering, her face flush with the ground, dirt clogging her nostrils.

Reef rolled off her, flipping her over. His lips were moving, but she heard nothing over a shrieking ring. She blinked, moving her jaw, trying to get her ears to pop. Reef helped her to her feet, cupping her face.

"Kirra"—his voice finally broke through the vibration churning in her ears—"are you okay?"

She nodded, unsure if she really was. What had just happened? "Was that . . . ?"

"A trip wire. Guess Watts *really* didn't want any visitors."

A smile curled on her lips.

He arched a brow. "Are you smiling?"

She nodded.

"Why?"

"Because it means we're on the right track."

"How do you figure that?"

"Watts clearly doesn't want to be found, which means . . ."

"He's hiding something," Reef finished for her.

Reef and Kirra waited at what was left of the trailer until the local authorities arrived and took their statements.

"Where now?" she asked once they were finished.

Officer Bohart, a friend of Landon's, handed her a slip of paper with an address scrawled across it.

She looked up at him.

"Watts's ex." Bohart shrugged. "It's been a couple decades since he went in the slammer and she divorced him, so who knows if she'll have any clue of his whereabouts, but she might have an idea."

Kirra smiled, clutching the paper. "It's worth a shot." Anything was at this point. Desperation was setting in, and Kirra hated the well-known feeling.

Camille Watts lived in a two-story-bungalow-style home in the downtown section of Kodiak, one street over from Main Street. Similar-looking houses now remodeled into businesses surrounded the home. Apparently she'd been unwilling to sell when the neighborhood turned commercial.

According to Officer Bohart, the two had divorced a year into Watts's sentence and there was nothing on the surface to indicate they'd had any contact since—no recorded visits to the prison or mail between the two. The only thing that connected them still was their now twenty-three-year-old daughter, Mallory. And that gave Reef hope that maybe Camille had some idea of where Watts was residing. If not, perhaps Mallory had a clue.

Reef let Kirra take the lead and stood back as Camille opened the front door. She looked them both up and down. "Yes?"

"Mrs. Watts?"

"Ms.," she said, her jaw tightening.

"I'm Kirra Jacobs, and this is—"

"What are you two selling?"

"We're not selling anything. We're here about your ex-husband."

"*Ex* as in he don't live here anymore."

"I understand, but perhaps—"

Her eyes narrowed. "Did you say Jacobs?"

"Yes, ma'am. My uncle is Frank Jacobs."

She shook her head. "Two decades and Henry's still trying to drag me down. What'd he do now?"

"We think he may be responsible for my cousin's kidnapping."

"Kidnapping?" She shook her head. "That don't sound like Henry."

Kirra explained the situation as Camille ushered them inside and settled them in at her kitchen table—round, with an orange-and-lime-print plastic cloth covering it. "And you really think Henry's involved in a kidnapping?"

"The timing would suggest so."

"Not to mention our close call at his trailer," Reef added.

Camille plopped two glasses on the table and reached for a pitcher of tea. "I wouldn't put it past Henry to hold a grudge, but . . ."

"But?" Reef nudged.

"Kidnapping a girl seems a bit extreme, even for him."

And murder didn't? The man had killed his own partner.

"Do you have any idea where we might find him?" Kirra asked, the hope in her voice nearly bringing Reef to his knees. If only he could fix this for her.

Camille sighed. "I don't know if my telling you is the right thing. Not for Henry's sake, mind you, but for yours. You have no idea the kind of man you're dealing with. When he feels cornered . . . it ain't good."

22

Kirra waited in the rental car while Reef entered the Roadside Bar. Camille had told them she'd heard Henry had been frequenting their old haunt. Kodiak being a small community was working to their advantage, though Kirra couldn't help but wonder if it might work to their disadvantage too. Watts had to know they were coming. Had the trip wire been intended for them?

She shifted restlessly, not thrilled with the idea of sitting this one out, but from the look of the clientele she'd seen come and go since their arrival ten minutes ago, it had probably been the wise call. Though she doubted Reef looking like a model out of a Hollister catalog would blend in well with the roughneck crowd.

Ten minutes later, she started tapping a crescendo on the plastic dash, needing to get out the antsy energy coursing through her. What was taking him so long?

Another ten minutes and she got out of the car, striding to the front door. She pushed through to find near darkness, despite it being the middle of the day.

Cigarette smoke infused the air, AC/DC blared over the

speakers, and every man in the joint turned to give her a once-over. When her eyes fully adjusted, she searched frantically over the L-shaped interior. No Reef.

A chill tingled down her spine. *Where is he?*

The only other female in the place was the bartender—slender with short brown hair. "Let me guess," she said, her eyes on Kirra as she set a beer in front of the man at the end of the bar. "You want the good-looking one that was in here?"

Was? "Yeah."

"He's out back." She gestured to the rear door.

"Thanks." Her heart pounding in her throat, Kirra strode for the back door, a hundred different scenarios racing through her mind, none of them good.

She burst through the exit door, the sun glinting bright in her eyes. She lifted her hand to shield them. "Reef?"

"Over here, Kirra."

She followed the sound of his voice to find him sitting on the open bed of a truck with a large man.

Reef stood and walked toward her.

She looked past him at the man, who smiled back at her. "Everything okay?" she whispered as Reef reached her side.

"Yeah. Sorry. Emmett and I got talking."

"Emmett?"

The tall man stood and strode toward them. He extended a thick hand. "How ya doing?" He was nearing six-five, easily two hundred and eighty pounds, broad shoulders, bulging biceps.

She shook his hand, his grasp sturdy, though she could tell he was trying to be gentle.

"Emmett used to help my dad with fishing excursions way back when."

"Yeah." Emmett raked a hand through his tangled dirty-blond hair. "Last time I saw Reef he was about yay high." His large hand hovered near his thick waist.

Kirra smiled, her heart finally settling. "Is that right?"

"Emmett was telling me he saw Henry Watts in here last week."

She tried to contain her excitement. "Oh?"

Emmett folded his massive arms across his burly chest. "Yeah. No idea where he's holed up at, but like I told Reef, I'd be careful. Prison did nothing to settle Henry down."

Kirra waited until she and Reef were pulling out of the parking lot before getting directly to the point. "So we keep an eye on this place hoping Henry shows up?"

"Emmett had a better idea."

"Oh?"

"Suggested we talk to Watts's girlfriend."

She hiked her brows.

Reef smiled. "Emmett works as a short-order cook over at O'Dell's Diner. He said one of the waitresses has been spending a lot of time with Watts lately."

"Great. Let's go."

"She's off today, but Emmett said she will be in for the breakfast crowd first thing tomorrow."

She hated to wait another second. "Any chance he knows where she lives?"

Reef shook his head. "Nope. Said Charity likes to keep to herself."

"So our chances of getting anything out of her . . . ?"

"Are probably not great, but you never know. We can pray, when you explain about Meg, that her conscience will kick in."

Kirra looked back at the bar as it faded in the distance. "So what's the story with Emmett?"

"He had it rough growing up. My dad took him under his wing, but after Dad passed, Emmett stopped coming around."

"That's too bad."

"Yeah. Selfish as it may have been, I was too preoccupied with my own pain to think of anyone else, but Cole tried to keep him on as we transitioned Dad's fishing business into Last Frontier Adventures."

"But Emmett wasn't interested?"

"I don't know. He was comfortable with my dad, but I got the feeling he wasn't around us kids . . . Maybe felt like he didn't belong."

"That's a shame."

"Yeah. It is. I told him next time he's visiting Yancey he needs to stop by for dinner."

"I hope he does."

Reef tapped the wheel as he pulled back onto the main road. "Me too."

Reef saw Kirra settled before returning to his room, uneasiness tugging at his gut. He was right next door, but it didn't feel close enough, not when they were being hunted.

He gazed out the window, checking the nearly empty parking lot. There'd been no sign of the man chasing them since their near drowning, but he doubted the man had given up. Question was—had they finally eluded him or was he simply biding his time before closing in? Reef shut the curtain, moved to the bed, and dropped to his knees.

I'm out of my league, Father. I'm not a cop like Jake or Landon. I just want to protect Kirra, to help her find Meg, to keep Frank and her safe. Please guide us. You know the men responsible. You see through all of this. Please lead us in the right direction and wrap your arms of protection around us. In Jesus' name. Amen.

Turning out the light, he crawled into bed, stretching his arms behind his head. He'd be surprised if he slept at all.

Kirra opened her eyes, the space around her disorienting. Everything within her screamed something was wrong. Her gaze fixed on an object poised about a foot over her head.

"Hello, darling."

She blinked. The voice was rough, foreign.

She scrambled back, her head bumping hard against the thick wooden headboard, the room dark except for the flash-light glaring in her eyes, illuminating the silver-toned bat.

"Easy there." He held the bat steady—now inches from her face, black lettering imprinted along its sleek metal surface. "See this?"

She nodded.

"Stop looking for Henry Watts, or next time I come swing-ing."

Reef's feet hit the floor before his brain processed what he was hearing.

He yanked the door open, and Kirra rushed into his arms.

Not that he was complaining, but . . . "What happened?"

His blood boiled as she relayed the terrifying event.

A quick call had the local police on site within seven minutes, but there was little to report. Kirra hadn't gotten a good look at the man—he'd been shrouded in shadows, the bat he held the only thing she could describe with any certainty.

"You heard his voice," Reef said.

"Yeah." She nodded.

"Did it sound like the guy on the snowmobile?"

Officer Bohart frowned. "What guy on a snowmobile?"

Reef explained—what was pertinent at least.

Kirra cut in. "This guy's voice was different. Distinct."

"Distinct how?" Reef asked.

"Gravelly. The other guy's was simply deep, and his inflections were different."

"Great." Reef sighed. "Now we have two guys threatening us."

"I spoke with Officer Bohart," Jake said over the phone as Reef paced the hotel room after explaining all that had happened since they'd talked that afternoon.

"Yeah, I told him it would be a good idea if he touched base with you. Anything on your end?"

"Well, we found something new about Rain—or should I say, Joseph Keller. He's got a long rap sheet, including being a principal suspect in a vandalism case involving NorthStar Oil and their newly laid interior pipeline."

"Is that right?"

"Police didn't have enough evidence to make it stick, but they are convinced it was the work of Joseph and his *accomplice*."

"Who . . . I have a feeling you're going to say we know."

"You got it—Samuel Matthews."

"Are you kidding me? Sam acted like he barely knew Rain, let alone partnered in vandalism with him. He made it seem as if Rain was just some guy who showed up when he wanted and no one except the girls really liked."

"And that makes Sam a prime suspect in my mind. When Kayden and I got back to Kaltag, we discussed the pipeline angle with Gage and Darcy. We're concerned Frank is being pressured by ecoterrorists to sabotage one or more pump stations. I've arranged to meet a NorthStar maintenance engineer at one of the stations, but if nothing comes of your search for Henry Watts, we think you should head back to Seward to question the students—especially Sam Matthews— about ROW's involvement in any vandalism."

"We can do that. But Kirra can't see her uncle sabotaging a pump station, Jake."

"A desperate man will do a lot to save someone he loves."

"I guess." Reef would do nearly anything to protect his family, but endangering others . . . ? It wasn't right. They needed to find Meg before it came to that. Before whatever job Frank was supposed to do was complete. "You know what I'm thinking . . ."

"What?"

"I'm starting to think we are off track with this whole Henry Watts chase. Frank said other people might get hurt. How does retrieving a Fabergé egg endanger others?"

"I don't know, but as long as you are this close, let's keep at it. Maybe it is somehow connected with the ecoterrorist angle."

"How?"

"I don't know. Maybe Henry assessed his options. Maybe he found another plan already in action and offered his services to the environmentalists."

"Meaning?"

"I'm just spit-balling here, but maybe Watts promised to give Joseph Keller or Sam Matthews or the *cause* a percentage of his proceeds from the Fabergé egg once he fenced it in exchange for something he needs from them."

"I suppose it's possible."

"At this point I'm not discounting anything."

"Well, I should probably get some shut-eye. Any sign of Frank?"

"Grabbed more of his dogs' and his food rations sometime during the night. Must be hitching his team and tracking in by foot, because no one saw him come or go. One of the checkpoint volunteers just noticed his ration bags missing after her break."

"So he's keeping up with the race front runners for the most part, just off course."

"So it would seem."

"Which leaves us little time."

"You need to find Henry Watts ASAP."

23

KODIAK, ALASKA
MARCH 15, 9:30 A.M.

Reef held the door for Kirra as she entered O'Dell's Diner, where Emmett and, more importantly, Henry Watts's girlfriend, Charity Driver, worked. Kirra hoped her personality held true to her name. They could use all the charity they could get.

Reef had tried to convince her to stay at the hotel or police station while he continued to track Watts's whereabouts, but that wasn't happening. She was the one Henry's man had threatened, it was her uncle being used as a puppet in some criminal's scheme, and her cousin was being held hostage. She was not sitting this one out.

"Table for two?" the hostess asked.

"Actually—" Kirra began, only to be cut off by Reef's affirmative, "Yes, and could we sit in Charity's section?"

"Whatever floats your boat." The hostess removed two laminated menus from the bin fixed to the hostess station and shuffled Reef and Kirra through the maze of tables to a booth by the front window.

"Thanks," Kirra said as the hostess handed her the sticky menu smelling of grape jam and syrup.

"Your server will be right out."

Kirra looked at Reef. "Smart. Getting us seated in her section."

He smiled. "Harder to avoid us if she has to wait on us."

Charity took her sweet time before approaching with two glasses of ice water—though Kirra doubted the two misshapen chips of ice bobbing in the lukewarm water classified it as *iced*.

"What can I get you folks?"

Reef started the conversation, charming as always. "Actually . . . we're trying to get in touch with an old friend and heard you were the lady to talk to."

She smacked her chewing gum, the sugary scent of grape infusing the air. "Is that right?"

"Henry Watts," Kirra said, trying to keep her voice even.

"'Fraid I can't help you. Henry and I are no longer an item."

Kirra tried to smother her joy. That little fact greatly lessened the likelihood of Charity's desire to protect the man. "That's too bad. Know where we can find him?"

Charity stopped tapping the order pad with her pencil and eyed them skeptically. "Whatdya want with Henry?"

"Just to talk," Kirra said. "We think he may be able to help me find my cousin."

Charity chuckled. "Henry ain't much of a talker."

"Please," Kirra said. "My cousin's in serious danger."

Charity glanced around the diner, and after a moment's hesitation she leaned in. "Okay, but you didn't hear this from me. Henry's right-hand man, Curly, makes a daily drop-off at the post office right about this time. If you hurry, you may be able to catch him."

"What does he look like?" So they knew they had the right guy.

"You can't miss him. Six-two, with a mop of curly brown hair."

"Great. Thanks." Kirra stood and moved to slide past her.

She tugged hold of Kirra's arm, her skin dry, cracked. "A word of advice?"

"Of course."

"Curly ain't no peach, but he's nothing compared to Henry. Watch your step."

"Thanks, Charity."

Reef and Kirra rushed out of the diner to their car, driving the short distance to the post office. Better to be sheltered by the car than sitting ducks in the open. Plus they'd have transportation to follow the man, praying he led them to Henry.

Reef held Kirra's hand as they pulled to a slow stop five hundred feet away from the old garage Curly had parked in front of. They'd stayed far enough back to avoid detection, or at least Kirra prayed so.

They waited in their rental car until he entered through the front glass door covered with thick paper that had once been black but was now a faded shade of grayish blue.

Approaching the building quickly, they pressed against the stucco side.

"What do you think? Should we call Officer Bohart?" Kirra asked, unsure of the best way to proceed.

"Let's confirm Watts is here first," Reef said, signaling for her to move around the building with him.

All the windows were covered with the same fading and curling black paper, leaving small slits at the windows' corners for peering in. The first two revealed nothing but an empty storage room. It wasn't until the window by the back entrance that they spotted two men—neither of them Curly. The fact that the only picture they'd seen of Watts was his booking photo twenty years ago—combined with the dimness of the room—made it impossible to tell if one of the men was Watts.

"What are they doing?" she whispered.

The two men were bent over a workstation—one appeared to be studying something beneath a large lit magnifying glass.

Reef pointed to a long brown string running between two metal shelving units. "Looks like passports hanging on the line."

"Document fraud," Kirra whispered as they turned from the window.

"Call Officer Bohart," Reef said.

She dialed, heard the operator answer, and then froze as Curly appeared around the edge of the building with a gun in hand.

"Put down the phone, darling."

The gravelly voice of her night visitor with the bat.

"Kodiak police station. Hello?" the operator said again.

Kirra did the best she could to stall. "Look, we don't want any trouble."

"I said, drop the phone!"

She put the phone in her pocket, careful not to turn it off.

222

"I don't think so." Curly shook his head. "Put the phone on the ground."

She moved slowly, trying to give the police enough time to find their location.

"Now!" Curly roared.

She reluctantly did as instructed.

Curly took a few long strides over and crushed her phone with the heel of his boot. "Both of you inside." He waved the gun toward the rear door, which opened for them, a grizzled man waiting on the other side.

"So you're the two that have been looking for me."

"Henry Watts," Kirra said, trying to keep her gaze on the man and not on all the document-fraud equipment and evidence surrounding them.

The man held out his hands at his side. "Live and in the flesh, which is more than I can say for you two in a bit."

"What have you done with my cousin?"

"Your cousin?" He looked genuinely confused. "I don't know nothing about some cousin."

"Not *some* cousin. Frank Jacobs' daughter."

He looked up for a moment and then grinned broadly. "Now there's a name from the past. What's ol' Frank up to these days? I heard he went all straitlaced."

"Don't play dumb with me. You kidnapped Meg and are holding her hostage so Frank will retrieve the Bartholomew Fabergé egg for you."

"What?"

"You're forcing him to do '*the job*.'"

"Look, lady, I don't know who's got Frank's girl or what *job* they want him to do, but it's got nothing to do with me or that egg."

"And we're just supposed to believe you?"

"I don't care what you believe, but Frank can tell you I got nothing to do with any of that."

"How's that?"

"Because the stupid guy returned the egg to Bartholomew the same night we stole it."

"What?"

"Said he didn't want a man like Bartholomew after him. He never cared about the haul in the first place. He was just there for Sarah."

"And he just told you this?"

"Yeah. At the trial. Knew otherwise I'd come back for it. Said I could check out his story myself if I didn't believe him."

"And did you?"

"Yeah. I wasn't just taking his word. I sent a friend into Bartholomew's place. He confirmed the egg had been returned. Stupid Frank—that thing was worth millions."

Kirra tried to grasp what that information meant to them. "So . . . if you aren't after the egg, what are you after?"

"Nothing, when it comes to Frank."

"Then why the elaborate measures to keep us off your trail?" Reef asked as he glared at Curly.

He gestured around them.

"Document fraud?"

He tilted his head. "I get caught, I go back to the pen, and that ain't happening. I already lost twenty years of my life in that place."

"We don't want any trouble. We're only trying to find Meg. This has nothing to do with us," Reef said.

He was trying to get them out of a tight spot, but Watts's

glare told Kirra he knew full well the minute they walked out of there, they'd contact the police.

"I'm afraid it's too late for that. Curly, tie them up in the next room while I decide how to take care of them."

Kirra swallowed. *Take care of us?*

Reef pulled against his bonds, the frayed rope tight and biting into his now raw wrists. He had to figure out a way to free them.

"I can't believe we've been chasing down the wrong trail this whole time," Kirra said. "I kept believing we were getting closer to finding Meg, and we were only getting further away."

"That's not completely true. Jake is following a hunch on the pump stations."

"I was so sure Watts was playing a role."

"Me too, but how could we have known your uncle returned the egg?"

"It explains why Bartholomew just let the situation go."

"And Watts wasn't stupid enough to steal the same piece twice, even if he hadn't been in jail."

"But he's stupid enough to start a document-fraud business."

"No wonder he didn't like us poking around."

"Without us in the picture, his secret stays safe."

"But Officer Bohart knows we were searching for Watts, and the police operator surely heard Curly threatening us. Our disappearance will only bring the heat on him."

"He's not just going to let us go. I saw it in his eyes." The malice.

"Which is why we need to get ourselves out of here."

"How?"

"I'm working on it." Reef surveyed the room for anything that might be of help. The man who tied his restraints knew how to tie a secure knot. He wondered if Curly had done as thorough a job on Kirra's bonds. "I've got an idea."

"What?"

"Hop your chair over to mine as quietly as you can."

The men were still arguing in the next room, which he hoped would cover any noise she might make.

"Okay." She did as he asked, moving more silently than he'd expected. *Impressive.* The woman seriously just rolled with the punches.

"Now, I'm going to shift my chair around so we're back to back." He did, scooting backward until his hands reached the knot binding Kirra's delicate hands. He set to work and, after what seemed an eternity of painstaking tugging and finagling, finally managed to loosen the knot enough for her to slip one hand free.

She turned, undoing the other, and then set to work unknotting his. He'd just started loosening the knots binding his ankles to the chair when the door opened and Curly entered with a gun.

"Down," Reef hollered, swaying his chair back, knocking Kirra to the ground.

"What do you think you're doing?" Curly slipped his gun in his belt and moved for Reef.

Reef twisted sideways, grabbing at the ropes on his feet. He'd managed to get one free and kicked out as Curly bent to right him. His boot collided with Curly's jaw, knocking the lumbrous man off balance.

He quickly untied his remaining binding and moved for Kirra, who'd already freed herself. He helped her to her feet and pushed her into a run for the nearest window, chair in hand.

"Enough!" Curly roared, swiping blood from his mouth, his shoulders hunched as he lurched for them, gun poised to shoot.

Commotion sounded in the next room, and as Curly's gaze shifted, Reef flung the chair. It knocked him in the chest, and he staggered back. Reef rushed him as his gun went off, tackling him to the ground, the bullet lodging in the ceiling.

Officer Bohart rushed in with support covering his back.

Kirra exhaled, tears beading in her gorgeous eyes. "You got our location."

Officer Bohart smiled.

Kirra sat in the Kodiak police station clutching a Styrofoam cup of tea. Henry Watts and his men were being booked for documentation fraud, assault, and attempted murder. Watts was headed back where he belonged, but she was no closer to finding Meg, and the despair biting at her was nearly overwhelming. Where did they go from here?

24

OUTSIDE OF UNALAKLEET, ALASKA
MARCH 15, 3:30 P.M.

Jake approached the Kaltag pump station after a fifty-five-mile trek on the snowmobile. Kayden had offered to fly him in, but it was tough terrain for landing a plane close to the station, and after a little discussion they all decided a snowmobile would not be as high profile—in case they were still being watched.

He'd stopped at Old Woman cabin, hoping to find Frank or some sign of him. It was clear musher teams had passed, and at least one had bunked out in the cabin, and another off in the woods behind the cabin. If Frank had stopped at that site, Jake bet he had camped up in the woods, out of sight.

There was also a set of snowmobile tracks, fresher than those of the sleds. It appeared Frank was still being followed.

Frank had picked up more of his dogs' rations from Kaltag sometime during the night, but again, no one had seen him. Jake had tracked the boot prints back to where he'd left his team harnessed and waiting.

He moved on to the pump station, which appeared quiet. A wire fence enclosed the one-story concrete building, two large circular containment tanks, and what Jake assumed was a smaller cylinder-shaped overflow tank. He approached the gate and pulled his snowmobile to a stop beside another one. So the engineer from NorthStar had already arrived—at least he hoped that's who had ridden in on the other snowmobile.

He climbed off and looked around. A crisp wind blew in from the east, snow preparing to fall again. A large animal— he was betting caribou—was lumbering in the woods just to his north. He turned back to the pump station. Someone was approaching the gate from the inside.

A man in navy coveralls and a bright-orange down jacket lifted his goatee-covered chin in Jake's direction. "You Detective Cavanaugh?"

"Yep."

"You got some ID? Boss is all squirrely now that there's the possibility of equipment tampering."

"Sure." He pulled out his badge, thankful he'd brought it with him. It was habit. Badge and gun at all times. "You got ID?" he asked in return.

The man pulled his ID badge off his pocket clip and handed it to Jake through the gate slot.

Jake scanned the info—Andrew Ross, maintenance engineer. It appeared legit and matched the name and position NorthStar had provided of the man he'd be meeting. Jake handed it back. "Thanks for coming all the way out here."

Andrew opened the gate. "I do whatever they tell me, as long as I'm getting paid." He shut the gate behind them.

"You typically work on this pump?" Jake asked.

"Nah. I helped Frank install them, but this is his responsibility. He's the designing engineer, and until the entire pipeline is running smoothly for the agreed-to amount of time, these are his babies."

"Have there been any problems with any of the pumps?"

"Not that I'm aware of, but I haven't been out here since we installed it."

"Were you at the Anchorage pump during the protests?"

Andrew unlocked the building door. "Unfortunately."

"That's got to be frustrating," Jake said, trying to build a rapport with the man.

"Annoying is more like it. But it's the vandalism that gets under my skin. You want to protest, make your voice heard, fine. I don't think it ever results in any change, but it's not my breath wasted. But destroying property—that's crossing a line."

Jake agreed. He had no problem with people voicing their concerns—he shared some of them. He loved his adopted state and wanted to see the wilderness and the creatures residing in it protected.

People had every right to voice their opinion, and he had seen great change come from it over the years, regardless of what Andrew said, but he *did* agree that breaking the law was not to be condoned, no matter the cause.

Andrew led him down a flight of concrete steps, the metal railing cold beneath Jake's hand.

"Pumps are over here." Andrew directed, handing Jake a flashlight. "What are we looking for exactly?"

"Any kind of tampering, or an incendiary device."

"Great." He shook his head with an exasperated and slightly nervous sigh.

They spent the two hours searching every inch of the pump

and machines surrounding it, and found nothing. Jake wished he felt relief, but all he felt was a sense they were missing something.

His sat phone rang. *Reef*. He looked to Andrew. "I need a minute."

"Take your time." Andrew took a seat on a thick metal tube and pulled out his phone. "Angry Birds." He smiled. "Darn kids got me hooked."

Jake lifted his phone to his ear. "Hello?"

"Jake, it's Reef. We're finished here."

"And?"

"Watts isn't involved." Reef went on to explain all that had happened and everything they'd learned—including the dead end they'd hit.

"Looks like it has nothing to do with Frank's past and everything to do with Meg's present."

"Such as?" Reef seemed tired and frustrated. But Jake knew he was game for the next step.

"Her connection to ROW, and whatever they are involved in. You and Kirra need to pay Sam Matthews a visit—find out what he has to say about his role in the pipeline vandalism. I can have Landon call Officer Hoffman and have him accompany you, if you think it might make Sam more cooperative."

"No. I think it would have the opposite effect."

"Okay. Let me know if you change your mind."

"Will do. How's it going on your end?"

"Not seeing any tampering or incendiary devices at this station."

"You sound disappointed."

"Not disappointed. Concerned we're missing something."

"Think outside the box. Sometimes it helps."

Jake rubbed the back of his neck. Reef was right. He was looking at this straight on. Maybe it was time to flip things sideways.

"Andrew."

The man half glanced up from his phone, his fingers still gliding over the screen.

"How else could the pumps be compromised?"

He shrugged. "Internally, I suppose."

"Meaning sabotaged from the inside?"

Andrew slipped his phone back in his pocket and stood. "I suppose."

"How would that work? For instance, if you wanted to sabotage a pump, what would you do?"

"I don't know . . . I guess I'd misadjust the settings."

"How?"

"The pumps run according to the settings we enter into the controls via the computer. Those settings are programmed to vary on a daily, even hourly basis, depending on expected conditions."

"Can you pull up the settings that are in place, not just for today but for the next week? See if anything is set to change."

Twenty-five minutes later, Andrew looked up at Jake, his face ashen.

"I'm guessing you found something?"

He nodded. "Looks like new flow rates have been entered and are set to be remotely triggered."

"What do you mean *remotely triggered*?"

"I mean Frank recoded the system, and it looks like its being controlled remotely."

"How do you know it's Frank?"

"Because he's the only one with the access necessary to make a change like that."

"Okay, so what happens when the new flow rates are triggered?"

"The pump will overheat rapidly."

"Meaning?"

"It will explode."

"Can't you just reset the codes, the flow rates?"

Andrew swiped his perspiring brow. "I tried, but I'm blocked out."

"Isn't there an override function?"

"One only Frank now has access to."

"What about securing the power?"

"That was my first thought too, but Frank's way ahead of us. He rigged it to blow if we attempt to cut power."

Jake swallowed. "How many pump stations are there between Anchorage and Nome?"

"Ten."

"Get on the phone. Call out whomever you need to. Each and every pump station needs to be checked ASAP. We need to know what level of disaster we're facing."

25

Reef held Kirra's hand as they crossed the tarmac to board their puddle-jumper flight from Kodiak back to Seward. Fortunately they'd been able to arrange a flight out within an hour of Jake's call.

He took the first of the metal steps up to the plane as his phone rang. Kirra glanced back.

"Jake," he said to Kirra. "Hope he hasn't changed his mind about us going to Seward." They'd pulled a lot of strings and called in a lot of McKenna-family favors to arrange this last-minute flight. "Yeah, Jake?" he said. "We're about to board our flight. What's going on?"

"It's not good, Reef. At least this pump station is set to blow."

His heart sank. "Are you sure?"

"Positive. And we don't know how widespread the problem is. The oil company's calling people in, but it's going to take time to get enough qualified people out to cover each of the stations. Andrew, the engineer with me, is estimating at least a day just to get them to all the stations. Frank has set up a remote trigger that only he has control of. If we can't find him, the company's engineers need to figure out a way to rewrite or override the codes Frank's changed."

"We've only got two days before Frank reaches Nome."

"I know. That's why it's critical you get whatever information you can out of Sam."

"Do you think he's part of Meg's kidnapping? It is quite a jump from vandalism to kidnapping."

"Even if he's not playing a direct role, he knows more than he's letting on. We need to know where they might be holding Meg and who else is involved. Joseph Keller can't be pulling this off on his own—you saw at least one other guy with him, and somebody appears to be herding Frank. But I have a feeling they're just players and someone else is calling the shots. We need to find out who."

"Why? I mean, why do you think someone else is calling the shots?"

"I'll explain later. Andrew needs me, and you have a flight to catch."

Reef nodded and pressed the disconnect button as Jake's line dropped. He glanced across the tarmac at a man standing by the metal terminal building.

He squinted.

It was *him*. The man who'd nearly drowned Kirra. The man who had been following them since the beginning of this nightmare was back on their trail. The hairs on the nape of Reef's neck bristled. He stepped for the tarmac, rage bubbling inside. He was going to end this *now*.

"Reef," Kirra hollered above the *whoosh* of the propeller.

He turned. She was standing in the open doorway, her blond hair whipping about her face. "The pilot says we need to go."

"I'll be right there." He looked back at the man—at least at the spot where the man had been standing—but he was gone.

"Reef, come on," Kirra called.

He scanned the tarmac, frantically searching the surrounding area, but there was no sign of the man. With a nervous twinge in his gut, he turned and boarded the plane to Seward.

"They're headed back to Seward."

"Why?" His cousin's voice cut deep with displeasure.

"I'm guessing Sam."

"Is he still there?"

"As far as I know. I tried reaching him, but he doesn't have his cell on him. I told him how stupid that was." He watched as Reef and Kirra's plane flew over his rental car and flicked his cigarette in the snow.

"Get on a plane and make sure Sam keeps his mouth shut."

Yay. Another flight. Why was he the one flying everywhere? "I'm on it."

"You'd better be, or this entire plan could come tumbling down."

"You mean *cause*." It was starting to irritate him. He preferred to view their plan as a cause—though the true intent differed greatly from what the others believed.

"What?"

"You keep saying *plan*, but this is so much bigger than a plan. It's a chance to right a great wrong."

"Why are you wasting time preaching to the choir? Now get on that plane before I'm forced to."

Maybe it was time *he* got on a plane instead of playing babysitter to Meg. "How's the girl?"

"Surviving. For now."

"What's wrong?" Kirra asked as Reef shifted restlessly in the seat beside her.

"I saw him."

"Who?"

"The man who's been following us since the race."

Anger raked through her. "Where was he?"

"By the hangar, but he was gone in the blink of an eye."

"So he knows we're headed back to Seward."

"Yes." Reef nodded on a sigh. "Which means we need to get to Sam before he does." He stood and moved the few feet to the cockpit.

"What are you doing?"

"Getting a call patched through to Jake."

"Why?"

"I'm going to tell him to have Officer Hoffman pick up Matthews and hold him until we get there."

"But if they're watching and see us bring the police in, they said they'd kill Meg."

"I don't think we have a choice anymore. If whoever is in charge of all this reaches Sam Matthews before us, it could cost us our only chance at finding Meg. I'll make sure Hoffman pulls him in on suspected vandalism or something unrelated to Meg's kidnapping. Something that won't tip off whoever might be watching that we are, in fact, working with the police."

Kirra closed her eyes in prayer, needing to release the fear crushing her heart.

Please protect Meg, Father. Only you know where she is and what she's going through. Only you can keep her safe. Please don't let them hurt her. Please lead us to her. I hate feeling so afraid. I've felt this way for far too long.

Then she heard it, as if whispered in her ear—*It's time to let Me carry you past your fears.*

Reef sat back down beside her and she opened her eyes. Could she trust those words? He reached for her hand, his fingers caressing her skin. "It's going to be all right."

"How can you sound so certain?"

"Because I trust God's Word that says He is at work in all things for those of us who are in Christ Jesus."

She'd heard that before. But if God was at work in even the darkest parts of a Christian's life . . . what did that mean for the pain she'd experienced? Had God been with her during her rape? Had He allowed it? Would He ever bring the healing she so desperately desired? What about Meg? What if her abductors killed her? She wasn't a Christian. What then? The truth of it pierced a deep, stabbing pain in her soul.

Please, Father, don't let her die.

Why hadn't she shared Christ with Meg every chance she'd had? She squeezed her eyes shut. The slightest thought of her cousin spending eternity in hell was beyond horrific.

"Kirra, what are you thinking?"

"That just because He's at work doesn't guarantee a happy ending, at least not in this life." And that terrified her. In this life parents got Alzheimer's, children died, couples divorced—a multitude of horrid things happened.

"No, and that's a part I still grapple with, but God is with us through it all. He tells us we're going to have trouble because this world isn't paradise—because of our sin, we live in a fallen world."

She knew that. "But how does that help with the loss and the pain?"

He looked at her, the subtle shift in his heartfelt expression saying he understood what she was really asking—he was speaking to the anguish she'd carried since William raped her.

She'd been trying to heal herself for so long. Trying to find wholeness in being a good vet, in taking care of her dogs, in volunteering. Trying to keep busy so the fear wouldn't sink in.

She was determined to be in control. To not let what William did control her.

Her frustration flared.

But that was exactly the problem. She was trying to control what she couldn't because she wasn't the one in control. God was. Maybe it was time she handed her hurts and fears fully over to Him.

Reef exhaled, his voice soft as he responded to her question after a moment of thought. "This life is the blink of an eye compared with the eternity we will spend with our loved ones—with all believers. I take hope and comfort in that—and in the knowledge that God is at work even in the painful things of life—and Christ himself can empathize with our hurt. Think of the pain, betrayal, loneliness, and sorrow He endured. He understands, Kirra."

"I know you're right." She did. "I know that God's Word tells us, but I still . . ."

"Hurt?" he asked, his voice choked.

She nodded, finally releasing the fear that had dwelt inside for so very long. Tears burned her eyes, streamed down her face, bouncing off their joined hands.

"Come here." He didn't give her a chance to move, just engulfed her in his sturdy embrace, as she now realized Christ had done so many times throughout her sorrow. "I don't have a perfect answer, honey. I wish I did. But I do know that God's love is everlasting, and I truly believe He wept the day William raped you. He loves you, Kirra, and one day William will answer for what he's done."

She breathed in his evergreen scent, taking comfort in the coziness of his plaid flannel shirt brushing her cheek, absorbing her tears.

He caressed her back. "For what it's worth. I love you too."

She sniffed and pulled back in shock. "You . . . *love* me?"

He smiled that smile that had first garnered her attention all those years ago—the quintessential lopsided Reef McKenna grin that did funny things to her insides.

He brushed the hair matting to her tear-stained face behind her ear and dipped his head to look her straight in the eye—a deep and abiding love shining back at her. "Quite desperately, I'm afraid." His smile widened, but there was nervousness there. Was Reef McKenna actually nervous? Over *her*?

"I . . ."

"You don't have to say anything. I didn't mean to just spring that on you, but I wanted you to know."

"But how? When?"

"I think it started that day last summer when Rori got hurt because I'd let her off the leash while we were hiking."

"But I totally laid into you that day."

"I know." His smile twitched. "But I deserved it."

She smirked. "So . . . you're a glutton for punishment?"

He lifted her hand joined with his and pressed it to his

chest, reining her focus fully in. The gorgeous, intelligent, inspiring man sitting right beside her was *in love* with her.

"That day I saw your passion and love for animals, for your job and shelter, for my family. I saw your skill as a vet—which was quite impressive—and most importantly, you weren't afraid to put me in my place." He smiled. "Not that you ever have been shy about putting me in my place. The point is, I saw what a strong, smart, vibrant, and passionate woman you are. Every moment with you since then has only confirmed what I felt first stirring then. I love you, Kirra Jacobs."

She bit her bottom lip, terrified to take that plunge. A plethora of *what if*s danced through her mind, the fears singing loudly in an attempt to drown out her elation.

"I love you too," she blurted out, breaking past her fears. She loved him. She'd loved him on some level since kindergarten, but it had deepened since that first kiss in the cave—her heart knowing way before her head. But wasn't that always the way?

Before she could voice, let alone fully articulate, her feelings, his warm, soft lips were pressed to hers. His kiss was slow, tender, and oh, so full of promise.

26

Jake returned to the Kaltag checkpoint, his heart heavy. He only had bad news to share. Kayden spotted him first as he stepped through the door, the warmth of the building a welcome and stark contrast to the frigid temperatures outside. A handful of mushers were propped against the walls asleep—several sacked out across the kitchen floor beyond the tables—their dogs bedded down on hay piles outside.

He wiped the matted snow and ice from his boots and pulled off his hat, clutching it in his hands.

Kayden approached him, her voice low when she spoke. "I know that look, and it isn't good."

"Gather everyone up." He glanced around, looking for the most secluded spot. "Probably best we talk outside."

Within minutes he, Kayden, Gage, and Darcy were congregated out by the snowmobiles in the barn-turned-garage.

"I'm afraid to ask," Darcy said, huddling closer to Gage—her five-foot-two frame next to Gage's six-foot-three always made Jake chuckle, but this wasn't the time for laughter. "We have a serious and, I believe, imminent threat." He went on to explain what he and Andrew had discovered at the Kaltag pump station and that they feared Frank had done the same at the earlier stations along the Iditarod route.

Kayden, always the pragmatic one, asked, "How quickly can the other stations be checked?"

"Andrew's heading back to the pump station outside of Iditarod now. If it's also been tampered with, then I think it's safe to assume that each one Frank's passed since the restart has been as well."

Gage rubbed Darcy's arm. "How many pumps are we talking?"

"Ten total spread out from Anchorage to Nome, which"— Jake swallowed—"unfortunately means it's going to take some time for the oil company to check them all out."

"Time we don't have," Darcy said.

Jake nodded, clasping Kayden's hand. Every living thing throughout the interior of Alaska would suffer from the resulting tainting of the water supply and ecosystem—an ecosystem many inhabitants along the interior and out west on toward Nome relied on for subsistence living.

Gage cleared his throat. "What do we do? How can we help?"

"The only thing we can do with the pump stations at this point is help prepare for the worst and pray NorthStar Oil's mechanics figure out a solution in time. But we can continue our search for Frank and Meg."

"We need help," Gage growled.

Darcy leaned into him. "But the kidnappers are still watching us. If we call backup in, we're sure to draw their attention to the fact that we've figured out their plans."

"Which," Jake said, sighing, "is why I'm praying Reef and

Kirra are able to get some useful information out of Sam Matthews."

Gage cocked his head. "Sam Matthews?"

"The ROW leader?" Darcy asked, confusion dotting her brow.

"Yeah. He—" Jake stopped midsentence at a crunching noise toward the rear of the barn. Had someone been eavesdropping? Was there a plant among the volunteers, as they had feared? He indicated for everyone to be quiet as he crept to the open doorframe and sprang through it.

Xander jumped, dropping the pile of snow goggles he'd been holding. "Jake! Man, you sure know how to sneak up on a guy."

Jake stiffened, surveying the area. "I could say the same about you."

"Me?" Xander bent, retrieving the goggles, shaking the snow off as he scooped them back up in his arms. "I just de-iced these bad boys." He stood. "Was bringing them back out." He stepped in the barn and glanced around. "What are you all doing out here?"

"Just making sure the snowmobiles are gassed and ready to go," Gage said, holding a red gas can.

Darcy was busy checking the snowmobiles' instruments, while Kayden appeared to be inspecting the windshields for any damage.

"Oh?" Xander's face scrunched. "I thought it was my turn on snowmobile maintenance."

"I just got back from a sweep and figured I might as well take care of my ride." Jake stood beside the machine he'd recently driven.

"A sweep, huh?"

"Yeah."

Xander dropped the goggles back into the tub. "If you say so."

"What's that supposed to mean?" Jake asked, concerned at Xander's sudden level of interest.

"I just heard one of the mushers say earlier in the day he saw you head south past Old Woman cabin."

"Is that right?"

"Yeah. And it's strange, because the trail heads north. So what were you doing heading south?"

"We still have a missing musher who hasn't been spotted on the trail for days, so I widened my sweep radius." Xander worked communications not SAR. What concern was it of his?

"Ah. Any luck?"

"Unfortunately, no."

"That's too bad. But it looks like we've got another missing musher, so you won't be expending all your effort on locating Frank Weber."

"A second musher?" Gage set the gas can down.

"Yeah, just came in over the radio. Brad Abbott missed the Eagle Island checkpoint."

"Maybe he's just running behind."

"Doesn't look that way. He left Grayling checkpoint yesterday a little after three a.m. Even barring a rough ride, he should have reached Eagle Island by this morning. We're twelve hours on."

"Any sightings?" Kayden asked.

"Afraid not."

"I'll check with the air force. See how they are dividing up the search grids and sweeps."

Xander linked his arms across his chest. "Probably good if you start giving all the mushers the same attention you've been giving Frank Weber."

Jake's jaw tightened. What was his problem?

After Xander finally left, Darcy asked, "Is it just me, or was that totally awkward?"

"Yeah, but my concern is another missing musher." Jake shook his head. It happened, but something about the timing felt too coincidental. Were the men behind Meg's kidnapping trying to distract them from Frank's trail and their interest in the pump stations? And what was up with Xander's attitude? "We need to find Brad Abbott as soon as possible, not just for his safety and that of his team, but so we can get back on task."

"You don't think they . . . ?" Gage said.

Jake sighed, knowing exactly where Gage was going. "That's my concern, and if it's true, I fear what may have happened to Brad Abbott."

27

Kirra followed Reef down the metal stairs from the plane to find a police cruiser waiting for them on the dark tarmac.

A deputy stepped from the car and waved. "Kevin said you two could use a ride."

"Thanks. That will help a lot."

The drive to the station was short—under fifteen minutes—but it felt long and slow. Perhaps because the weariness was creeping into Kirra's heart and mind. Weariness over Meg, over the news about the pipeline Jake had shared with them.

How could her uncle have rigged the pumps to overheat, knowing that would cause them to blow? She understood his desperation to save Meg—it clawed at her too—but threatening the lives of innocent people, as well as vast wildlife, was too much.

All of it was too much—facing Tracey, seeing William, learning it had been Meg's idea to take off with Reef for British Columbia, leaving her in the lurch the weekend William raped her . . . And discovering her uncle's shady past—even if he'd done it for Aunt Sarah—made everything worse. Wrong was still wrong. Didn't he see that?

Reef clasped her hand. "You doing okay?"

"I don't know." It was the most honest answer she could give.

When they pulled up to the station, Reef hopped out, moving around to get her door.

"Thanks." Who would have thought God would have sent Reef to help anchor her, but he'd been steadfastly at her side since the whole mess started, and she knew in her heart he was a gift from God, and that he wasn't going anywhere.

She knew the same was true of God, but why did she struggle to accept that fully? To know it not just in her head but in her heart?

Maybe it was because so many people she'd trusted and depended on had let her down, shattered her heart. But she had to let that harsh reality go, because God *was* different. He would never let her down. The truth of that washed over her like a cool downpour on a hot summer day, bathing her afresh in the beauty of God's nature and promises. He was always with her.

"I have loved you with an everlasting love."

Reef cleared his throat. "Kirra?"

She looked up to find Kevin Hoffman standing in front of them.

"Sorry." She swiped off her hat and smoothed her hair. "I was . . . distracted."

"No problem," Kevin said. "You've got a lot on your mind."

If he only knew.

"I've got Matthews in Interrogation." He ushered them into a room. On the other side of the two-way glass, Matthews paced a tiny room, agitation spewing from his frantic hand motions.

"Has he said anything yet?" Reef asked.

"Other than to himself?" Kevin rested his arm against the glass as Matthews continued pacing. "I brought him in under the guise of questioning him about an act of vandalism we had out at the docks a few months ago."

"Any chance he actually was involved?"

"It's possible, which is why I didn't hesitate to bring him in when you asked, but he claims he was nowhere near Seward at the time. I also questioned him about his involvement in the pump station vandalism up in Anchorage."

"And?"

"Claims he was only a peaceful protestor."

"Does he realize he can walk anytime?" Kirra asked, knowing they didn't actually have enough to keep holding him.

"Hasn't figured that out yet, but he did know about his right to a phone call." Kevin smoothed a hand over his head with a sigh. "I could only stall him so long."

Kirra swallowed the lump forming in her throat. "He made a call out?"

"Afraid so. Said he hadn't brought his cell phone to Seward, so he asked to use ours."

"Any idea who he called?" Reef asked.

"We traced it. Went to a burner cell, which I imagine by now has been discarded."

Great. She was putting money on his call going to Joseph Keller. Which meant they'd been tipped off that they were closing in, and that the police had been brought in.

Fear seized her chest. What if they harmed Meg because of their actions?

"I hovered when he made his call," Kevin said.

"Did you overhear anything useful?"

Kevin smiled. "He kept most of the conversation fairly

quiet, but at one point he seemed to freak out over something the other person said—asked what he should say if he's questioned about the stations."

"Station*s*? Plural?" Reef said.

Kevin nodded.

"He must have been tipped off by the person he talked to," Kirra said. "It's the only way he could know Jake found out about the rigged pump station. Someone inside the race had to tell him."

"So they *do* have a man on the inside." Reef reached for his phone. "I better let Jake know for certain."

"You may want to wait until after you talk to Sam," Kevin said, gesturing with his chin.

Sam's pacing speed had increased dramatically.

"I worry he may figure out he can just walk out of here any minute."

Reef slipped the phone back in his pocket. "You're right. And I'm sure, or at least hope, we'll have more to tell Jake after we talk with Sam."

"One more thing," Kevin said as Kirra's hand rested on the doorknob.

"Yeah?" She paused.

"He's pretty upset about another missing ROW member."

"Someone else has gone missing?"

"I'm afraid so. Belinda Morrison."

Kirra swallowed, looking back at Reef. "Belinda? What if our talking to her caused . . ."

He cut her off gently. "We could play the *what if* game all day, but it won't help anybody." He stooped, his big blue eyes full of love and support. "Let's do what we *can*. Let's talk with Matthews."

Reef was right. Taking a steadying breath, she entered the interrogation room, utterly grateful Kevin was allowing them to question Matthews.

Sam halted, his gaze jumping from Reef to Kirra and back again. "What are you doing here?"

"Why don't you take a seat," Reef suggested, pulling one out for Kirra and then one for himself.

"If it means I can get out of here faster . . ." Sam slid into the chair opposite them.

Reef swung his chair around and straddled it, resting his arms across the back. "What can you tell us about Joseph Keller?"

Sam swiped his nose. "Who?"

So that's how he was going to play it. Kirra leaned forward, planting her palms on the table. "Rain."

"Like I said"—he reclined—"not much."

His nonchalant, arrogant attitude rubbed her wrong. It took great restraint for her to remain calm and collected, at least in appearance. If this man knew anything about her cousin and was taking it so lightly . . . "That's funny, because we learned you two were part of the NorthStar protest back in Anchorage."

"So?"

"So it appears you two took things further than just protesting."

"Says who?"

"Anchorage police."

"They're wrong."

"That's not how we heard it. We heard you and *Rain*"— she added extra emphasis to the alias—"were arrested for vandalizing NorthStar equipment later that night."

He straightened. "We were brought in for questioning, not arrested."

"Still proves you lied to us."

"How do you figure that?"

"You said you didn't know Rain's real name, didn't know him at all until he recently showed up on campus. But the two of you protested together months ago, and if you two were brought in for questioning together, surely you would have learned his real name at the time of interrogation, if you didn't know it before."

"So what if I did?"

"So that's just the tip of the iceberg, isn't it?" She shifted in her chair. "What happened to Belinda?"

Pain flashed across Sam's face. "I don't know. She just disappeared."

"After talking with us."

He pinned an angry gaze on them. "Yeah."

Kirra's stomach flipped. So Belinda's disappearance *was* a result of her talking to them. Had she been silenced? "What did you do to her?"

"Me?" Color raced up his neck. "I'd never hurt Belinda."

"So who did?"

Sam looked away. "I don't know."

Kevin stepped into the room, clearly deciding this was the time to apply some pressure. "If anything happens to Meg or Belinda while you keep your mouth shut, you'll be charged as an accessory."

Sam's face paled. "I want a lawyer."

"Fine," Kevin said, linking his arms across his chest. "But the accessory charges, along with obstruction of justice, will still hold if anything happens to them in the meantime."

Sam swallowed, the defined Adam's apple in his narrow neck bobbing.

"On the other hand," Kevin continued, "if you help us out, we'll pass that info along to the DA, and in exchange for what you know, you might just get off—or at least get a reduced sentence. Not to mention the satisfaction of saving two ladies' lives." Kevin placed his palms on the table in front of the young man and leaned forward. "So what's it going to be, Mr. Matthews?"

He sat in yet another rental car across the darkened street from the Seward police station, rage seething inside. If Sam gave him up . . .

His fingers tightened around the steering wheel.

"Yeah?" his cousin answered on the other end.

"They've got Sam," he gritted out, irritation burning his veins. All because of a stupid girl.

"What?" The timbre of his cousin's voice vibrated.

"He called. They're questioning him."

"About?"

"Word from the race is they are checking out the pump stations."

"Are you kidding me?"

He adjusted his side mirror, watching an attractive woman cross the recently snowplowed street. "Don't worry. Frank knows what to do and what's at stake. Even if they figure it out, they won't have time to do anything about it."

"And Meg? How much does Sam know about her?"

He swallowed, preparing for a rant. "Enough."

"Then you better find out how much he tells them and if he's really loyal to us."

"He's loyal to the cause."

"Cut the *cause* junk. You and I know why we're really doing this. You can call it a *plan* or a *cause* or whatever you choose, but you know the truth."

"But Sam doesn't, and that's how it has to stay if we want to maintain his loyalty, especially after taking Belinda out."

"I told you not to involve anyone else."

"We needed to know what she told Reef and Kirra, and she could have identified me. I had no choice."

"Well, you ticked off Sam, and now we might have a loose cannon on our hands. It's essential you find out what he told them."

"I will, and don't worry about their interest in the pump stations—we've thrown in a nice diversion."

"At least you did something right." The line went dead.

He chucked his new burner cell onto the empty seat beside him, the old one tossed as soon as Sam's call came in. If their plans fell apart all because of a nosy cousin and her boyfriend . . .

His grip tightened on the wheel.

Well, then more than one pretty cousin was going to have to die.

"So, what's it going to be, Sam?" Kirra asked, struggling to keep the desperation from her voice.

"I want it in writing—I'm cleared of charges in exchange for what I tell you."

Hoffman chuckled. "Let's see if what you got is worth anything first."

"Fine." Sam leaned forward. "I know who took Meg Weber, and I'm pretty positive Belinda too."

An unsettling mix of fear and hope coursed through Kirra. She looked back at Kevin, praying he knew how valuable that information was and how time was of the essence.

28

After a grueling two-hour wait, the regional assistant DA had the papers drawn up and faxed over.

With only a modicum of hesitation, Sam signed and Kirra pounced.

"Where's my cousin? Where's Belinda?"

He slid the papers to Hoffman with his index finger. "I don't know."

Panic shot through Kirra. "But you said . . . ?"

"That I knew who took her . . . *them*." He swallowed. He clearly cared about Belinda.

Reef rested a hand on Kirra's shoulder, steadying her. "And . . . ?"

"Joe took Meg our first night in Seward. I imagine he took Belinda after she went to the police station with you. I'm sure Joe was watching."

"Belinda?" she asked.

He shook his head. "No. You two."

Kirra swallowed the fear that invoked.

"Joe, as in . . . ?" Hoffman asked.

They needed him to be precise.

"Joseph Keller. I told him I didn't think we needed to snatch the stupid girl for our cause to be effective, but he was persuasive and insistent. I ain't going down for his choice, though, especially not after Belinda."

Irritation flared in Kirra that Sam apparently attributed worth to Belinda's life but seemed to attribute none to her cousin's. Besides, they already knew Keller was involved, or at least suspected as much. What if they'd made a horrible mistake by making a deal with Matthews? What if he was of no actual help and they'd just let him off the hook for his role? Nausea waffled through her stomach.

"You mentioned that he and Meg had ridden up to the protest with you," Reef said, keeping them on track.

"That's right."

"So what car did he move Meg in? Is someone else involved?"

"There are lots of us involved at varying levels, but that night it was just me and Joe. He had a car stashed up there ahead of time."

"We're going to need a make and model on that vehicle," Hoffman said.

"It was an old beater. Something Joe paid cash for."

Hoffman frowned. "I'm afraid you're going to have to do better than that."

Sam sighed. "It was a red Fiat."

"So what happened?" She was desperately trying to envision how that night had played out, praying some detail—any detail—would lead them to Meg.

"Joe slipped something in Meg's drink. Once she was out, I helped him carry her to the car."

"And then you started the rumor the two of them had just taken off together during the night?"

"Yeah." Was that a hint of a smirk on his lips? Did he not grasp the seriousness of this? Or did he actually not care when it came to her cousin?

"Where'd he take her?" Reef asked, his tone deepening in intensity.

"Like I said . . ." Sam shrugged. "I don't know." He rocked back in the chair, the front two legs lifting off the floor.

Hoffman stalked around behind him and shoved the chair down. "Not good enough!"

"I can't tell you what I don't know."

"You know more than you're saying."

"No I don't. All Joe said was they were taking her someplace safe."

"They?" Reef prodded.

"I assume Joe's cousin. He's the one running things."

"Let me guess," Hoffman said, his jaw tight. "You never got a name?"

"Actually, I did."

Kirra straightened. *Finally.*

"Jay."

"*J* as in the letter?"

"I always assumed *Jay* as in *J-A-Y*. But either way it was short for something."

Maybe Jacob or Jason.

"Same last name?" *Keller.*

"I assume so."

"How'd you meet Joe?"

"He approached me on campus in Anchorage."

"Anchorage? You're at Fairbanks," Kirra said. That's where they'd found him or at least heard of him from the ROW students there.

"I am now. Joe approached me on campus last fall and said he and his cousin have been fighting environmental injustice for years and they had something monumental planned. Something they hoped I'd be a part of. They were familiar with my vigor for the cause and wanted me to join them."

"So you just hopped on the bandwagon. No questions asked?"

"I asked."

"And?"

"They were sick of the oil companies like NorthStar taking over native and private land, destroying the environment so big corporations could get richer. They wanted to teach them a lesson."

"And kidnapping my cousin was the way to do it?"

"Like I said, that wasn't my idea, but Joe and his cousin were convinced we needed somebody on the inside to rig the pump stations to overheat."

"So it would look like a company malfunction rather than an act of ecoterrorism?" Reef said.

"We're *not* terrorists. We're just fighting back for those who have no voice."

"What about all the people that will get hurt when those stations overheat and blow?"

He shrugged. "Cost of the cause."

"And how did Meg get pulled into all this?"

"They learned your uncle Frank was the one they needed to rig the pumps. He designed them and laid all the grid work, not to mention he maintains them. He even had a background in B and E. You couldn't get much more perfect than that."

"How'd you know he had . . . ?" She shook her head. "Never mind." That wasn't important. If anything, it'd been a total diversion. Meg wasn't being held as ransom for a Fa-bergé egg. She was being held so Frank would rig the pumps to overheat and blow.

"But you needed leverage," Reef said.

Sam smiled. "Exactly. They found out that Frank's daughter was a junior at Fairbanks, and that the campus had a particularly strong environmental group, so I transferred from Anchorage to Fairbanks over winter break."

"And sought Meg out?"

"Yes. She already had an interest in the cause from a class she'd taken the previous semester and had focused all her energy on learning as much about environmental rights as she could, so that was helpful."

"But you took it a step further and made sure she got interested in you as well," Kirra said.

"Yeah. At least until Joe started hanging around campus."

There was a sore spot to nudge. "And Meg fell for him?"

Sam swiped his nose. "No biggie. Turned out he was the one she needed to be attached to anyway."

But he clearly wasn't happy about it. Maybe that's why he didn't seem particularly concerned about Meg's well-being.

"Say Frank does as they instructed and the pumps blow—what happens to Meg then?"

He looked away. "That's up to Joe's cousin."

"Why's that?"

His frame stiffened. "He's calling the shots."

Kirra stood, intercepting his line of sight, forcing him to look her in the eye. "This is Meg's life we're talking about. Are you sure you have no idea where they're holding her?"

He swiped his nose.

"You nervous?" Reef asked.

"No." Sam shoved his hands into his pockets, his right knee bouncing.

"If they kill her, you're going to have to live with the knowledge you sat back and did nothing to help."

"Fine! They took her to some family cabin near Nome, but I'm sure they've moved her by now." He frowned and stuck out his chin. "That's all I'm saying."

"And Belinda?"

Were those tears beading in his eyes? "I don't know."

29

Gage watched Xander step from the room as Darcy moved to his side with her backpack. The communications and SAR team were packing up to head for the next checkpoint located at Unalakleet—the lead mushers having pulled out about four hours ago, the slowest ones not to arrive for another eighteen hours. They'd hang back for a little while and then move on with the rest of the crew.

Unalakleet marked the first checkpoint on the coast of the Bering Sea, and the weather and terrain shifted dramatically. Brutal storms could suddenly hit off the sea without warning, the soft, drifting snow reaching rooftops. Many mushers would make the change to lightweight racing sleds there—preparing to face the windblown landscape for the remainder of the race.

"Any word from Jake and Kayden?" she whispered once she was sure they were alone.

"Nothing positive," Gage said, "but the search is just getting started." Jake and Kayden, along with several other air force pilots and some snowmobilers, had left in plenty of time to arrive in the search area when dawn broke. The sun was rising behind the cloud cover, bringing filtered light onto another day of the Iditarod. Unfortunately they'd found no sign of Brad Abbott.

Darcy collected the remainder of her things into her backpack. "I know he needs to be found, and I want him to be, but so does Frank. Why has all the SAR effort shifted to Brad?"

"Because"—Gage zipped up his duffel—"Ben believes Frank scratched and didn't bother telling anyone. Scratched mushers aren't Iditarod SAR's responsibility. With another musher missing, one who's still part of the race, he gets full SAR support. Until Brad Abbott is found we don't have the go-ahead to resume searching for Frank—and we might not even get it then."

"What if we tell Ben what is really going on? Might he see the importance and change his mind?"

"No . . . Jake and I discussed that. Ben would just argue that the threat to the pipeline isn't Iditarod SAR's responsibility—and he'd be right." Gage shook his head. "NorthStar Oil isn't willing to call in the authorities yet, and even though we're pretty sure the kidnappers are well aware of our activities and that we have been in contact with the police, we can't take the chance of ticking them off by making law enforcement's involvement official." He picked up his duffel and Darcy's backpack and walked toward the door. "So for now . . . we wait."

Jake opened the throttle on the snowmobile as he entered the woods blocking any view of the ground from the Iditarod pilots searching for Brad Abbott.

Kayden had dropped him at the Grayling checkpoint, where he and two other volunteers had climbed on snowmobiles to begin an adjacent ground search for the missing musher.

The temperatures were holding at around five below, but Jake's internal fire had been set aflame. The thought of someone posing as Iditarod staff—or even worse, someone who actually *was* part of the Iditarod staff—watching them chewed him up.

He had Darcy running a background check on Xander Cook while they were searching for Abbott. Perhaps the relative newcomer had a few red flags in his background.

The thick patch of woods surrounding him provided an effective shield from the grueling winds plaguing this portion of the race route.

Animal tracks on top of sled ruts showed it had been some time since a musher had passed this way. Jake slowed to study the freshest tracks of the bunch. A bear had rumbled past within the last hour, and a trail of blood leading into the woods said he'd had a recent kill.

Something in his gut prompted him to stop. He turned off the snowmobile, climbed off, stretched, and then proceeded to follow the blood trail.

A handful of steps in, Kayden's voice broke over the radio. He moved it to his mouth. "Yeah, sweetheart?"

"Abbott's team just pulled in to the Eagle Island checkpoint."

"Oh, thank goodness." He'd started to imagine the worst.

"Jake . . . his team pulled in, but not Abbott."

Concern tracked through Jake. "What?"

"Ben just radioed. Apparently, the team was pretty shaken and tangled up, but they stuck to the course as trained."

"Anything to indicate what happened to Abbott?" Mushers sometimes fell off their sleds and weren't able to stop their teams. Perhaps that was the worst of it, but the uneasy feeling tugging at his insides said otherwise.

"No, but Ben said one of the volunteers still camping out there saw what he believes is dried blood on the sled mount."

Jake swallowed and turned his attention back to the blood trail. He exhaled. "Let me call you back."

Seward Airfield
March 16, 9:16 a.m.

"Another musher is missing?" Kirra asked as she and Reef boarded the . . . third . . . no fourth . . . ? She shook her head. She couldn't even remember how many planes they'd boarded since this nightmare had started. She and Reef were headed back to Anchorage, where Kayden would be making a dog drop after the search for the missing musher was over, and she'd fly them back to the heart of the race.

"Yeah, he called right before we left."

"Did he say who it is?"

"Brad Abbott," Reef said, settling in beside her. "You know him?"

"He's one of the new guys. Well, relatively new. I think he's run the past couple years."

"Older? Younger?"

"Forties. Teacher, I think."

"How'd he finish the past few years?"

"Couldn't tell you exactly, but nowhere near the top."

"So it's possible he's fallen behind or encountered some difficulty?"

"Sure. I suppose, why?"

"Gage seemed spooked when he called."

She shifted to face Reef better. "Spooked, how?" That wasn't a term usually associated with the go-with-the-flow Gage.

"I don't know. It's like he thought someone may be listening. He spoke in basics."

"Do you think something happened to make them even more certain they are being watched and reported on?"

"Maybe. I wonder who it is?"

She hated to imagine. Volunteering with the Iditarod for years—starting as a teen with her dad—she couldn't imagine someone working by her side could be capable of kidnapping her cousin, or working with the men who had. "You told him what we learned from Sam—about the car and the cabin?"

Reef nodded. "Of course."

"What did Jake think?"

"He wasn't there. He's already out searching for Abbott."

"And Frank?"

Reef shook his head.

So for the time being they were on their own in the search for her cousin and uncle.

"Did you ask about what was found at the other pump stations?"

"Yes. No word from Jake's contact yet."

She took a deep breath and released it, along with her anxious thoughts, finally verbalizing them. "I'm afraid we're running out of time."

"I know." He cupped her face, caressing her cheeks. "But we won't give up until we find them. I promise."

She smiled, knowing he meant it from the bottom of his heart. "I believe you." She truly did. "But what if we're too late? What if they're already . . ."

"We need to pray we make it in time."

She closed her eyes and they prayed, asking God to provide a miracle, because that seemed their only hope for a good outcome.

With trepidation, Jake continued following the blood trail. With each step, the burden on his spirit increased. Before he stepped beyond the last copse of trees obstructing his view, he knew what he would find. Finally he stopped. He squeezed his eyes shut as he stood over the mauled body of Brad Abbott.

30

They'd only had to wait three hours for Jake and Kayden to arrive. When they did, their grim expressions said they had horrible news.

Kirra rushed toward them. "What happened?"

"Let's talk on the way," Jake said.

"I'm so thankful you were able to pick us up," Kirra said. Otherwise reaching the Unalakleet checkpoint could have been tricky, especially with another storm threatening to hit—soon.

"We were already in Grayling as part of the search for Brad Abbott and after Jake's discovery . . ." Kayden swallowed.

"Discovery?" Reef asked, just as she was about to.

"Brad Abbott was mauled by a bear," Kayden said.

Kirra's chest rose with a sharp intake of breath. "How awful."

"I think he was fortunate, in a weird way . . ." Jake looked embarrassed to have said that but then continued, "Mauling would be a horrible way to die"—he settled into the copilot seat beside Kayden—"but I'm pretty sure he was dead before the bear reached him."

"Why do you say that?"

"There wasn't nearly the amount of blood I would expect if he were mauled alive."

Kirra blanched. "You don't think . . . ?" That the men responsible for kidnapping her cousin had killed Brad Abbott to create a diversion. Things were escalating, and fast.

"Yes, I do think. I think someone close to us is a plant," he said. "My bet is on Xander, but it could be anyone. I think the men responsible for your cousin's kidnapping were concerned we were getting too close to the truth, and they wanted to divert us from the trail for a while."

"Poor Brad." Her heart went out to the man and his family.

Reef clasped her hand, steadying her. "What about the other pump stations?" he asked. "Any word?"

"Yes." Jake sighed. "Andrew just called, and the pump station between Iditarod and Shageluk is also rigged to overheat and blow."

Kirra swayed into Reef as the full impact of what that meant hit her.

Reef ushered Kirra into the Unalakleet checkpoint and waited for Kayden and Jake to enter before closing the door on the howling storm behind them. They moved farther into the front room and joined Gage and Darcy as they sat in a grouping of chairs in front of the fire. Reef was thankful to be back with the race—and hopefully closer to finding Frank and Meg.

The winds had picked up to nearly forty miles per hour. It was a wonder Kayden had been able to safely land the plane. Snow had been falling since Anchorage, the deluge growing in intensity as they touched down. Well, skidded down was more like it. His sister was a gifted pilot, but he couldn't help feeling God had been watching out for them—that He had been ever since the start of the race.

Reef had felt Him spurring him on as he declared his love for Kirra, felt Him guiding them to Joseph and Jason Keller—whose name Darcy had been able to recently confirm—and he prayed He would guide them to Meg.

Kirra shivered beside him, and he put his arm around her. "Your jacket is wet. You should take it off and sit by the fire."

She moved to sit by the stone hearth. The Unalakleet checkpoint was one of the cozier along the circuit, and with the harsh and burgeoning winds outside, Reef was thankful to be in it.

Ethan stepped in the room with three mugs in hand. "Heard you were coming back." He handed the first mug to Kirra. "Thought you guys could use something hot." He handed the remaining two mugs to Reef and Kayden. "I'll go grab one for you, Jake."

Reef cupped the mug. "Wait. How'd you know we were coming in?"

"I heard Gage talking with Kayden on the radio as she was bringing you down. Quite a bit of flying, little lady."

Reef sat uneasily as Ethan exited the room, wondering just what else he may have heard. But Ethan had been part of the Iditarod for years, according to his siblings. Jake was right—if they had a spy in their midst, it was far more likely the relative newcomer Xander Cook.

Kirra leaned forward, desperation heavy on her pinched brow. "Please tell me one of you has heard from Hoffman or Landon with a solid lead on Meg's location."

"We have more information on Jason Keller," Darcy said as Gage kept his gaze fixed on the door, making sure no one was lingering in the hall.

"What can you tell us about him?" Reef asked, stretching out beside Kirra, kicking his boots off to let the fire warm his feet.

"He's an accountant, most recently living in Anchorage."

"An accountant?" Kirra frowned. "And living in Anchorage. What on earth is his tie to Nome or any of this?"

"It's definitely taking some digging," Darcy said, retrieving her laptop from her satchel. "But"—she turned on the Mac—"it looks like the Keller family is from Nome. And here's the interesting part. . . ."

Kirra leaned forward, and Reef rubbed her back, thankful to find her sweater dry and warm.

"Jason's father, Stanley Keller, died not long after North-Star purchased a huge section of the land for their pipeline project."

"Okay . . ." Reef said, his brows furrowing. "Was any of it owned by the Kellers?"

Darcy smiled. "A bunch of it."

"So do you think this is about more than the environment?" Kirra asked. "Perhaps some revenge mixed in?"

"That's what I'm thinking," Darcy said. "But I'm going to have to do a little more digging on the Keller family to be sure."

"In the meantime," Jake said, rezipping his coat and slipping his gloves back on, "I'm meeting Andrew back out at the Iditarod station. We've got to come up with a response plan in case we can't prevent Frank from remotely triggering the codes or, more than likely, handing the trigger over to Jason Keller."

"And Meg?" Kirra asked.

"We're searching for property still owned by Jason Keller," Darcy said. "So far nothing but a family home in Nome is showing up. It's in the middle of town, so it wouldn't be the cabin Sam Matthews mentioned, but Landon is contacting the local police to have it checked out."

"Have you searched under the father's name?" Reef suggested. Oftentimes titles took a while to get properly changed.

"Good idea." Darcy smiled. "Searching now . . ." Her fingers glided over the keypad. "It's going to take me a bit to comb through the records."

Kirra rubbed her arms. "Any sign of Frank?"

Reef hated the heartache he heard in her voice. If only he could fix this, somehow make everything better.

Please, Father, protect us. You are in control. I beg your mercy and protection. Don't let these men succeed.

The Lord replied silently in Reef's heart. "*Some trust in chariots and some in horses, but we trust in the name of the Lord our God.*"

Reef reaffirmed, *We are trusting in you, Lord.* He *would* carry them through.

"I'm sorry," Kayden said, moving to sit on the hearth beside Kirra. "No sign of him recently."

"Which station do you expect him to sabotage next?" Reef asked.

Jake looked at the race map, comparing it to the pump station locations they'd received from NorthStar. "I'd say this one—fifteen miles outside of Shaktoolik."

"Kayden, can you get us out there?" Kirra asked. "If we can reach it before Frank and wait inside . . . maybe we can at least catch him and update him on what's going on. And, maybe, just maybe, we can convince him to relinquish the trigger."

Jake lifted his hood. He was probably cutting it close for his meeting with Andrew, but he kept on subject. "I imagine he'll only do it if he truly believes Meg's no longer in danger. And unfortunately, until we find her, that's not the case. But we won't give up." He looked to Darcy. "Find me that cabin."

"Sam said they probably already moved her." Kirra bit her bottom lip to keep it from quivering.

Reef's heart broke. He loved her so deeply. Seeing her in pain was infinitely worse than experiencing it firsthand. If only . . .

Please, Father. Give me the strength necessary to be the man Kirra needs. I'm ready to take the plunge, to be fully dependent on you.

"Sam may have been bluffing," Jake said.

"And if he wasn't?"

"Then they would have left in a hurry, and that means they could have left a trail behind."

31

Gage tugged at Kayden's arm, the scope fixed in her hand as they crouched in the waist-deep snow, a hundred and fifty yards outside the Shaktoolik pump station. "Let me see."

"Stop being so impatient." She swatted his hand away, then cocked her head. "Do you hear that?"

"Hear what?" He stilled, listening. "Snowmobile?" He frowned. "We better go take a look."

Shockingly Kayden agreed, and without argument followed him across the frozen terrain.

Moving felt good, blood and warmth pumping through his cold legs as they neared the east side of the station, where he thought he'd heard the snowmobile stop.

Gage crouched in the bushes beside his sister, his chest tightening at the sight of the unmanned snowmobile. Whoever had arrived was most likely already inside. Was it the man who had been following Frank? Was he still on his trail? Had they missed Frank's arrival?

Kayden reached for her sat phone. "I'll call Jake."

"Good." He stood. "I'm gonna head in."

"Wait!" She tugged his arm.

"What?"

"You don't know what's going on in there. We don't want to do anything that could possibly endanger Reef and Kirra more."

"What do you suggest?"

"First, we disable the snowmobile, so even if whoever is inside makes it out, he'll have nowhere to go."

"Nice plan," a man said, right as something hard *thwack*ed into the back of Gage's head and everything went dark.

Kirra huddled next to Reef inside the concrete pump station outside of Shaktoolik, praying they'd chosen correctly. Kayden had flown them in, and if they weren't careful, the storm would quickly snow them in. Frank had better show— and soon.

Kayden and Gage were positioned outside with scope in hand, keeping an eye on the station, watching for Frank.

Darcy had remained at the checkpoint, digging through online files and trying to connect with the Records Department in Nome.

Jake was on his way to meet with Andrew Ross at the Iditarod pump station—close to a hundred and twenty-five miles away as the crow flies.

Kirra desperately prayed at least one of them would have good news, but the unsettling motion writhing in her belly suggested otherwise.

"He'll be here," Reef said, rubbing her tightly coiled neck.

She nodded, thankful for his touch and comfort. "I pray you're right." But even if her uncle showed, how would he react? Surely he had to realize the madness of rigging the stations. If they could just talk to him . . .

But what if it wasn't enough? What if he wouldn't give up the kidnappers' assignment?

She looked at Reef, wondering, if it were her being held hostage, would he do as the kidnappers demanded, or would he refuse and pray for God's intervention?

What would *she* do if she were in Frank's shoes? She'd like to think she'd do the right thing—go to the police, try and find Meg, but definitely not endanger all the lives Frank was by rigging the pumps.

The front door opened, a cold gust of wind blowing snow in above them—the flakes dropping through the metal catwalk overhead. Boots clanged along the walkway, heading for the stairs.

Kirra held her breath. *Here goes nothing.*

The man turned, moving down the steps with precision . . . dragging . . . a body . . . behind him?

Horror engulfed Kirra as she stepped from the shadows. "Uncle Frank?" *What have you done?*

The man released the body and stood there, a gun in his hand, hood hiding his face. "Afraid not, sweetheart."

Jason Keller drove the thirty miles to the ghost town of Solomon, passing the last train to nowhere with his cargo in the rear of his vehicle.

Solomon. It seemed a fitting place for Frank and his daughter to die.

His family had once thrived in this shadow of a town, had once owned the surrounding land before NorthStar scooped it up, but he'd be getting it back—at least the vital part of it. And nothing—or no one—would derail his plans again.

The man pushed his hood back, exposing his face.

"Ethan?" Kirra stumbled back into Reef's arms.

Reef stepped in front of her, shielding her with his body, his gaze fixed on Kayden's still form.

"What'd you do to her?"

"Just a little bump on the head."

"And Gage?"

"Him too, though his bump was a lot harder."

Reef looked past him.

"Don't worry, he's on ice for now, but you all need to be disposed of, eventually. You've gotten too close."

"To who?" Kirra moved around Reef.

Was she crazy? Was she *seriously* pressing an armed man?

"Jason Keller?" she said, taking another step.

Reef grabbed her arm.

"His cousin Joseph?" she yelled. "How can you be involved in this, Ethan?" She shook her head. "You've been working the Iditarod by my side for years."

"Yeah, and I've also been working to prevent companies like NorthStar from raping our land."

"Wait a minute." Her eyes narrowed. "How'd you know we were headed here?"

"Oh, come on. You really think it takes that long to make another cup of cocoa? I was listening the entire time."

"But Gage was watching the door."

"What, do you think we're amateurs or something?"

"Ah. Yeah," Reef said. This was Ethan Young, after all.

"I told you." His gun arm stiffened. "I've been at this for a while."

"Kidnapping people?" she asked.

"Fighting companies like NorthStar."

"And Meg?"

"Your cousin was just a piece of the puzzle."

"Did the Kellers recruit you?" Reef asked, curious how Ethan had gotten involved with the cousins.

"One of them."

"Which one?" Kirra asked.

"Does it really matter?"

"It does to me," Kirra said.

"Well, that's too bad. You're just going to have live . . . or I guess, in this case, *die* without knowing. Now over there." He waved his gun, backing them into a corner by the pump. He pulled out handcuffs and tossed them to Reef. "Her first, then Kayden, then you."

"I won't cuff her."

Ethan aimed the gun at Kirra. "Then I'll shoot her now."

Reef looked at her, knowing he needed to buy time. "Fine." He cuffed her to the metal pipe running into the pump as instructed and then did the same with Kayden, who was still unconscious.

Ethan tossed him a third pair of cuffs. This guy really came prepared. "Now you."

"I don't understand," Kirra said, shaking her head.

"What's to understand? You guys thought you were so smart, planning to beat Frank here. I heard everything, have been hearing everything. I've got bugs planted at all of the checkpoints. I set up the communication center, remember? Every time you thought I was listening to my iPod, I was listening to you all. Face it, you're too late."

Her face paled. "What do you mean *too late*?"

Reef's chest constricted. Was Meg already dead?

"Frank's already been here. This pump is rigged to blow. And, lucky for you, you'll all get to witness firsthand the devastation companies like NorthStar cause."

Reef struggled against the restraints, metal clanging against metal as he scanned the space for a means of escape. He had to act fast.

Ethan aimed the gun at him. "Settle down." He shifted the barrel back to Kirra. "Or I shoot your girlfriend."

Reef stilled. *Please, Lord. Help us.*

"NorthStar didn't cause this," Kirra said, rattling her cuffs. "You and your crew did."

Ethan shook his head. "Nah, we only upped the timetable. Something like this was bound to happen. It always does. Need I remind you of the Valdez oil spill?"

"But that was an accidental spill."

"Which would've eventually happened here, but maybe after three or four years of NorthStar getting rich off our land. Nah, this way is much better."

"You're mad." She jangled her cuffs, her cheeks reddening with fury. "How can you justify kidnapping an innocent woman?"

"Innocent?" Ethan laughed as he backed toward the stairs. "You forget I know Meg. Hooked up a time or two with her when she was here at the Iditarod, cheering her dad on. She's far from innocent. As for you two, if you'd just kept your noses out of our business, everything would have been fine."

"Minus numerous explosions and oil spills meant to look like a machine malfunction, right?" Reef bit out.

"You won't get away with this," Kirra yelled.

"Yes we will."

"The police know about the Kellers."

"Yeah? So too bad for them, but other than you guys, nobody knows I'm involved."

"It's only a matter of time before Sam Matthews or one of the Kellers talk."

"I'll deal with that then. But it's all a moot point anyway. We'll have already won."

He finished climbing the stairs and ducked out the door.

32

Kirra wrestled with the restraints, frustration fueling her agitated and useless attempts to break free. She wondered if her cousin was feeling anything similar, and her heart welled for Meg even more. If Ethan knew they were on to them, then surely the Kellers did too—Sam had no doubt seen to that.

What did that mean for Frank and Meg?

Had they ruined their chances of rescuing Meg and keeping Frank safe?

Tears streamed down her face.

"Breathe, honey," Reef said, handcuffed beside her. "I'll get us out of this."

She appreciated his conviction and compassion, but how on earth would they get out of *this*? They were handcuffed to an oil pump that was rigged to overheat and blow. And Ethan had gone to drag Gage in and cuff him up as well. Jake would come looking for them, eventually, but Ethan probably had a plan

281

to get rid of him too. That left Darcy. How long would it take her to figure out something was wrong and rally the troops?

Reef squirmed, pulling his legs toward his chest.

She eyed him curiously. "Should I even ask?"

He twisted to press his shin up to his cuffed hand. "I've got a knife strapped to my calf. If I can just reach it"—he maneuvered—"I can get us out of this."

Somehow he managed to finagle it out of its sheath, and set to work.

"Do I want to know how you came to possess the skill of breaking out of handcuffs?" she asked.

He smiled. "Probably not."

With a little effort, he managed to open his and then moved to work on hers.

The door creaked open overhead, and they both stilled.

"He's back," she whispered, sweat beading on her brow.

Ethan had returned and was dragging Gage behind him.

Reef lifted his index finger to his mouth. "Stay here."

"What?" Why wasn't he releasing her? And where was he going?

"Trust me." He winked as he wove between the machinery.

"And . . . the last of the bunch," Ethan said, rounding the corner with an unconscious Gage—none too carefully. He stopped short at the sight of Reef's empty handcuffs. "Where'd he—"

Ethan's cramped expression went blank, his hold on Gage slack as he fell face-first to the floor.

Reef quickly cuffed Ethan to the pipe in his place and freed Kirra and Kayden—his sister waking as he picked her handcuffs open.

She smiled drowsily. "I see that questionable talent of yours came in handy after all."

Reef smiled.

Kirra wasn't even going to ask.

"I'll alert Jake," Kayden said, rubbing her wrists, "while you tend to Gage."

Reef nodded and knelt by his brother.

"If Frank's already been through here, that only leaves two pump stations to go before Nome," Kirra said, stooping beside Reef. "We're running out of time, and they clearly know we're on to them."

He bunched his jacket up like a pillow, rested it under Gage's head, and turned to Kirra. "So what's our next move?"

"We should check in with Darcy," Gage said, jolting Reef.

"Sorry." Gage opened his eyes with a smile. "Didn't mean to startle you."

Reef shook his head. "All good. You were saying?"

"We should check in with Darcy. She was on to something when I left. Maybe she's found it." He sat up, swaying slightly.

Reef steadied him. "Easy. You took a good knock. How do you feel?"

"Seeing stars." He blinked. "But otherwise good to go."

Kayden returned from contacting Jake and insisted on performing a concussion test on Gage. Afterward, she sank back on her heels with a sigh. "You better have Doc Graham check you out when we get back to Yancey."

Gage moved to stand. "I'm fine." He wobbled but made it to his feet. "I'll go outside and put in a call to Darcy. See if she has some place for us to start looking in Nome."

"It's a good plan," Reef said. "But aren't we overlooking the obvious?" He gestured to Ethan cuffed to the pipe. "When he wakes up, he may be full of information."

Kirra smiled. "So let's help his awakening along."

A few slaps to the face that she took way too much pleasure in did the trick.

Ethan's eyes fluttered open. He took a minute to assess his situation, and then grimaced. "This doesn't change anything."

Reef rested his boot on the pipe by Ethan's head, holding a wrench in his hand. "I beg to differ."

"Do what you want with me. Keller still has your cousin," he said to Kirra. "And the pumps are still rigged to blow."

"But we know what we need to do to stop them," Kirra said.

Ethan paled. "You're bluffing."

"All we have to do is intercept Frank and make sure he doesn't press the trigger."

"You really think Frank would risk the life of his only daughter and just hand over his only leverage?"

Reef bent down, his eyes level with Ethan's. "Kayden's notified law enforcement to pick you up . . . but we're in the middle of nowhere. That's going to take some time."

Kayden picked up where he left off. "That's right. Time for you to sit and stew."

"And time," Kirra said, "for the pump beside you to blow if we don't stop the Kellers from carrying out their plan."

Ethan looked at the machine, horror crossing his face. "You wouldn't just leave me here."

"You mean . . . like you were about to leave us," Kirra said, kneeling down beside him. "It depends on how helpful you choose to be."

Okay, she was bluffing, but he didn't need to know that. "Where are they holding my cousin?"

Ethan ground his teeth.

"You can take the rap for all of this, if you like, but I'd suggest you play along," Reef said, keeping his boot a breath from Ethan's face.

"I'm not a rat like Matthews is."

So they did know Matthews had talked.

"Where *is* she?!" Kirra roared.

"I don't know. They had her at some cabin up by Nome, but by now they've moved her."

"Where?"

"I don't know."

The door swung open and Gage clomped down the steps. "Anything?"

"Nothing useful." Kirra sighed. "Please tell me you've had better luck."

"Let's talk out of earshot." He gestured to the stairs.

Kirra and Reef followed Gage back up the steps and outside while Kayden maintained a watch over Ethan.

"What'd Darcy find out?" Kirra wrapped her arms around her waist, pulling her jacket tighter against her. Man, the temperature was dropping.

"The Keller family owned land stretching from the outskirts of Nome out a hundred miles west, including Solomon."

"The ghost town?" Kirra asked.

"Yep. Apparently it belonged to their family as far back as records go. And it looks like they got quite wealthy during the mining craze and while the railroad ran through there."

"And then?"

"Not so well off, but they managed to hold on to their ancestral land until—"

"NorthStar stepped in?" Reef guessed.

"They were about to be foreclosed on and had no choice but to take NorthStar's lowball offer. Seems NorthStar does quite a bit of business with the lending bank."

"So they probably had a hand in forcing the foreclosure," Reef said.

"Or at least speeding it along."

"So this is payback?" Kirra asked.

"Darcy thinks there's more to it than that. Jason Keller's father, the head of the family, didn't just die. An article in the Nome *Gazette* suggests that selling the land broke Stanley's heart and . . ."

"He took his own life," Reef concluded.

How sad. "Let me guess," Kirra said, shifting her weight to keep warm. "Jason and Joseph weren't on board with the sale?"

Gage shook his head. "Not as far as Darcy can tell."

"So this *is* about revenge rather than the environment."

"That's what it looks like."

"So why are Ethan and Sam involved?" Reef asked. "They seem to believe this really is about saving the environment, even if it means flooding it with oil. Explain that one to me."

"No way to answer that one, but I do get the feeling they truly believe this cause, as they like to call it, is about protecting the environment. They didn't seem to know that Jason and Joseph are playing them. But . . ." Kirra smiled, glancing back at the station door. "Knowing the truth might change how Ethan feels about remaining silent."

Reef smiled. "Smart lady."

"Now." She exhaled. "We just have to convince him we're telling the truth."

33

Agitation and anxiety whirled inside Kirra. She wanted to move, to keep searching, but Kayden had explained that Jake, who had much more experience and instinct when it came to matters of law enforcement and criminal apprehension, felt it best that he meet them at the pump station—and so that's what they were doing. Three hours had passed, but Kayden assured her that Jake and Andrew would be arriving soon.

And . . . she admitted to herself, they had already decided to wait until the closest police arrived to take Ethan into custody—they couldn't risk the remote chance of him escaping and warning the Kellers—although they were only too happy to let Ethan think he would be left on his own once they finally did leave. A man who felt his life was threatened was much more likely to give up information—though he had provided nothing in the time they'd been waiting. He refused to believe what he called their heinous lies.

Just as Kirra felt she was about to blow her top, Jake and Andrew finally arrived. Jake pulled off his gloves, kissed

Kayden, and turned to the uncooperative Ethan. "Let me take a whack at him."

Kirra sat back and watched Jake interrogate the man with a finesse she'd never witnessed. He really was as good as everyone claimed. Ethan coughed up a few more details, remarks made between the Kellers, talks of regaining their rights, and their plan to punish NorthStar in the process. Unfortunately, as for where Jason Keller may have moved Meg, he was at a loss.

"Think," Jake said. "Did they ever talk about someplace they liked to go as kids, a weekend retreat, a hunting cabin?"

"No. They always talked in code, it seemed. Now I know why."

"In code. Give me an example."

"They used the words *plan, cause, rights, corporate America, home base.*"

"Home base?"

"Yeah. I assumed it meant their family cabin near Nome."

"Where they were holding Meg?"

"Yeah, as far as I knew. I mean they kept me on a need-to-know basis. I was to watch you guys, monitor the communications. . . . If anyone got near Frank, I was to call it in. If anyone started looking for Meg near Nome, I was to call it in."

"And this cabin near Nome. Have you been to it before?"

"Once. We had a meeting out there before all this began."

"Where?"

"On the southeast coast outside of Nome."

"Near the water?"

"Yeah."

"Did Jason or Joseph Keller own a boat?"

"I think so. Everyone in Nome does."

"Did Joseph ever confirm that's where they'd be holding Meg?"

"No, but it was pretty secluded, and I just assumed."

"So . . . what makes you think they moved her?"

"I told them that you were on to them and they should consider moving."

"Moving where?"

"Wherever they had as a backup place."

"So you know they had a backup?"

"Sure. I mean they never said it outright, but it's just how they worked. They covered their bases. They've been working on this for years. Ever since NorthStar broke ground in Anchorage."

"If they had a backup location, would it be near Nome?"

"I don't know. They seemed awfully familiar with the area."

"What about Solomon?"

Ethan frowned. "The ghost town?"

"Yeah."

"What about it?"

"Did they ever mention their family used to own the land?"

"No. It never came up, but . . ." He straightened.

"What?" Jake pressed.

"They had this weird saying."

"Yeah?"

"'To nowhere.'"

"'To nowhere?'"

"Yeah, it didn't make any sense. I figured it was some family inside joke. They'd just say it and smile, but now that I think about it—that's what the locals call that defunct train in Solomon."

"The last train to nowhere." Jake clapped Ethan's shoulder. "Thanks, Ethan. Let's go, guys."

"Wait!" Panic permeated his voice as they all moved toward the stairs. "Hello? Aren't you forgetting something?"

Jake paused at the base of the steps. "I don't think so." He looked at the rest of them. "Any of you?"

They all answered in the negative.

"This isn't funny." Ethan's cheeks flared red. "Seriously! Aren't you going to uncuff me?"

"Not until the police arrive," Jake said.

"Don't worry," Kirra added. "I'm sure they'll arrive before Frank reaches Nome, or at least you can hope so."

34

After leaving Ethan handcuffed at the Shaktoolik pump station, knowing the authorities were already waiting outside to take him into custody, Kayden flew them through the night to Nome, hoping to intercept Frank and locate Meg.

Everything pointed to her being in or near Nome—their best guess being Solomon. So that's where they'd spend the rest of the race—what little was left of it—searching and praying.

Reef stepped off Kayden's plane to find Cole, Piper, and Landon waiting. "What are you guys doing here?"

"We heard you and Kirra needed all the help you could get," Cole said.

Kirra's eyes welled with tears. "That's so sweet of you, but Cole, you have a three-month-old at home. I don't want to put you in any danger. If anything happened to you . . . to any of you . . ."

He smiled. "Then it'd be our time to go."

Reef was still amazed by his big brother's depth of trust and dependence on God. Cole, and all of his family, had shown him it wasn't about church attendance and checklists; it was about a personal relationship with Christ. He understood that now. Well, he understood it *better*. It was about a daily walk with Jesus. A walk he hoped to share with Kirra. Side by side. For years to come. The thought of not being with her, of not helping her through hard times like this, of not being there *for* her, choked him.

"How's she doing?" Piper nudged his shoulder as they all moved for the rental van Cole had procured.

"She's tough like Kayden, but tenderhearted like you."

"Sounds like a good mix."

A smile curled on his lips. "The perfect one."

Piper pursed hers in a ridiculous attempt to hide the gargantuan smile spreading across her face. As resident Yancey matchmaker, he knew she'd be all over his and Kirra's new relationship. But strangely enough, it didn't *seem* new.

They'd known each other for most of their lives—but their relationship had changed in what seemed like the blink of an eye . . . for the better. He loved the woman, plain and simple. Timelines didn't matter—only his love for her did.

"Looks like we've got our work cut out for us," Landon said as they all piled in the van. "The Kellers owned thousands of acres of land, so we have a lot of ground to cover."

"And they're probably very familiar with every inch of it," Cole added.

"We have a second vehicle where we're bunking," Landon said. "I suggest we split up into teams so we can scour a wider area. Local police are currently moving through town, but there's no sense starting a full-scale SAR rescue outside of the town's limits in the dark. It's too barren, the weather too brutal, and it'd be too easy to miss something.

"Come dawn we'll start by trying to intercept Frank between the last pump station outside Elim and Nome. And, of course, looking for the Kellers' backup location for holding Meg."

"How do you suggest we split up?" Reef asked.

Landon shifted in his seat to survey everyone. "Jake's the best tracker. He and Kayden should search for Frank. Piper, Cole, and I will accompany you and Kirra out to Solomon."

"You think that's where they're holding Meg?"

He nodded. "If I were a betting man."

Reef scooted closer to Kirra as they made the short drive through town to their lodgings—not that he imagined they'd get much sleep. He wrapped his arm around her shoulders. "How you holding up?"

She shook her head. "I just can't believe your family would come out here and risk so much to help me."

"That's what they do."

"That must be nice, having such a supportive family."

"It is, and now you're a part of it."

"What?" Her forehead creased.

"I love you, and I know Kayden and Piper think the world of you. Trust me, I've seen it happen with Bailey, Landon, Jake, and Darcy. You're part of our family now."

"But . . . we haven't even gone on an official date."

He grinned. "Since when is tracking down leads and being threatened by thugs not considered a date?"

She laughed for the first time in days. "Oh dear. Should I be frightened by what our futures dates might hold?"

"Frightened. Never." He grazed her chin with his finger. "Not with me at your side, and that's exactly where I plan to stay. Curious, perhaps, but definitely not frightened."

How Reef managed to lighten her mood during such a difficult time still surprised and amazed her. Who would have thought she'd have found love during hardship?

Wasn't love supposed to be about happiness and warm fuzzy feelings? At least at the start?

Instead she'd gotten straight-to-the-deepest-well-of-her-heart intensity and an inside look at the beautiful man standing strong beside her through it all. He truly was beautiful—not just his swoon-worthy physical appearance, but his hunger to know God better, to love his family deeply, and to live fully. He'd captured her heart amidst the most difficult of circumstances, and she had to admit God couldn't have planned it better.

Love in the difficult parts of life. God in them—in the sorrow and pain. He was right there, carrying her through.

She squeezed her eyes shut.

Father, I don't . . . I haven't wanted to think about where you were when I was raped, because no answer to that question is easy. I've been holding you at arm's length since that day, because I believed you turned your back on me, looked the other way when I needed you most. But your Word says you've never left my side, that nothing—not even hell itself—can separate me from your love. But what does that mean, then? That you loved me but allowed it to happen? Why? Why didn't you stop him, stop them?

The rape hadn't ended with William—she had been destroyed over and over again as family members let her down, abandoned her in her darkest hour. How did she reconcile a loving God with an act of such hatred on William's part?

On William's part.

William was the one full of hate and harm. He was the

one who'd sinned, who'd harmed her with *his* choices. She lived in a fallen world, with fallen people.

Maybe Reef was right. Maybe God *had* wept that day.

She swallowed, emotion roiling through her.

Maybe God was finally bringing the healing she so desperately needed in the worst of times, and in a way she could never have anticipated.

"I know the plans I have for you . . . plans to give you hope and a future."

Was this it? She looked over at Reef with love. Was he the hope and future God had for her?

Thank you, Father.

Deep and abiding peace, beyond description, beyond explanation, flooded her. God met her in that moment. Her Savior met her at her well, overflowing her cup with living water that quenched the deep ache inside of her, finally bringing the healing she so desperately desired.

FIFTEEN MILES OUTSIDE OF ELIM, ALASKA
MARCH 17, 8:00 A.M.

Kayden circled around in her Cessna, the weather clearing long enough for them to actually see the ground below in the early morning light. They'd decided the best way to continue searching for Frank was by air. It allowed them to cover the most ground.

While the race route took a straight western course past Koyuk, they were following the pipeline, which ran at a southwest angle to the circuit.

"I think he really cares about her," Kayden said.

Jake kept his eyes on the ground, searching for any sign of Frank. "Who cares about who?"

"Reef cares about Kirra."

"Yeah." He chuckled. "I'd say so."

"It's sweet."

He couldn't help himself. He took his eyes off the ground and looked at the woman he loved. "Did my no-nonsense girlfriend, Kayden McKenna, just use the word *sweet*?"

She stuck her tongue out at him, and he chuckled.

"Keep your eyes on the ground, mister."

"Yes, ma'am." He turned his gaze back to the vast tundra stretched out below the Cessna.

"I'm just saying all my other siblings have found their mates. It'd be nice to see Reef settle down too."

"And you? Are you ready to settle down?" He rubbed the ring still in his pocket.

She glanced over at him with a heartfelt smile. "You know I'm here to stay."

He slipped his hand in his pocket, his finger hooking the ring. "Care to make that offi—?"

"There!" Kayden hollered, pointing out her side window.

You've got to be kidding me. He leaned over her shoulder, peering down at the musher team below.

He exhaled, releasing his hold on the ring. "Set her down when you can."

"We need to get past this small inlet or we could end up landing on an ice floe." It took a few minutes of circling and searching, but she landed on a solid piece of ground about a mile ahead of the musher. Now the trick would be intercepting him.

They slipped on the cross-country skis they'd borrowed from local law enforcement and headed toward the musher.

Kayden, the more-experienced skier, quickly moved ahead. Jake prayed it was Frank, but who else could it be?

About a half mile in, Jake heard the howl of dogs. He took a moment to appraise the sparse, hilly terrain. In the distance he saw what appeared to be the pump station behind a small copse of trees. A wooden bridge spanned the narrow inlet of the Bering Sea before the landscape transitioned to full tundra on the other side—white and vast, stretching on for miles. He heard the dogs again, much closer this time. He whistled.

Kayden stopped, turning back to look at him.

"Get off the trail! He's going to cut through those trees any moment."

She looked to the copse of trees, then back at him. "What about you?"

"I'm going to make him stop." Or at least try his best.

"What? Are you crazy?"

"Trust me."

"You're lucky I do." She hurried off the path.

He planted his poles firmly in the snow at his sides, bracing for impact.

Within seconds, just as anticipated, the sled-dog team burst out of the woods and barreled straight for him.

"Anything?" Landon asked Reef over the radio.

"Not yet." He and Kirra had covered the first two search grids they'd broken the Solomon area into, and so far nothing.

Kirra wrapped her scarf tighter about her neck and face as the wind whipped across the barren plain.

The abandoned mining town rather resembled those in

New Mexico and Arizona. But there was one vast difference—Solomon was on the Bering Coast of Alaska, where temperatures could hit lows of thirty degrees below zero.

The air bit crisp through Reef's layers. If Jason Keller had Meg somewhere out here, it was somewhere without electricity. Unless a generator was being used, their only heat source would be fire—which meant smoke for them to follow. Reef scanned the area. Were they searching in the wrong spot? He heard no generator, saw no smoke.

At the next abandoned building, Reef and Kirra worked their way in through a loose board across what at one time had been a window.

The interior was cold and dim, and the frozen floor planks creaked beneath them.

Reef swung his flashlight around the empty space, moving for the stairs.

They swept the top floor and found nothing.

Kirra rubbed her arms, shifting her weight from foot to foot, her breath white in the beam of his flashlight. "Do you think they'd really be holed up out here?"

"Seems like an awfully barren place. Not a bad place to hide out, but we may be thinking about this all wrong."

"What do you mean?"

"Systematic doesn't work for me." He grinned. "I like to go by instinct. If it were me, and I was familiar with this area, I'd pick a place of high ground—a place with open sight lines and a back way out."

They walked down the rickety stairs and stepped outside, and Reef took a moment to really survey the landscape.

"Where would you pick?" she asked, standing beside him.

Reef once again scanned the area, his gaze finally settling

on the gold-dredge building—windows blacked out and boarded up.

"The dredge?"

"It's the largest building, and it has the best view."

"Minus the boarded-up windows."

"Which would prevent people from looking in."

He radioed the others and explained his idea. "We're going to check it out."

"Be careful," Landon radioed back.

He and Kirra moved across the barren plain toward the hill where the dredge building sat. As they mounted the rise, an explosion shook the ground, vibrating the earth beneath them. Reef pulled Kirra into his arms and covered her with his body as they dropped down.

Terror recoiled through him as he glanced up to find metal parts spewing through the smoke-filled air. *The train.* Keller had rigged the train that sat in the center of the ghost town to explode, knowing its placement would cause the most widespread damage.

As soon as parts stopped flying, he lifted his head and surveyed the ground below, searching through the smoke for his siblings.

His ears ringing, he released his protective hold on Kirra and helped her to her feet.

"You okay?"

She nodded. "Your family?"

"Cole?" he called, his voice hoarse, his throat burning. "Cole?" he tried over the radio.

Nothing.

Panic clawed through his chest. "Piper?"

"Down here," she hollered. "Landon's hurt."

They rushed down the hill, stumbling, climbing over scorched train parts to find Landon crumpled in a heap.

Piper rolled him over, and he coughed.

"I'm fine." He coughed some more. "Just landed awkward. But I saw them."

"Them?" Kirra asked, looking back at the dredging building.

"When the explosion went off, through the smoke, we caught a glimpse of a man yanking a woman out back behind the dredge building."

"Meg?" Kirra asked, hope infusing her words.

"I couldn't say for certain, but I think so."

"Where's Cole?"

"He went after them, over that ridge," Landon said, struggling to get to his feet. "Let's go."

"You're not going," Piper fussed. "You've got a broken arm."

"Fine, then you all go. I'm good, really."

Reef and Kirra ran back across the plain and up the hill around the back of the building. They crested the first ridge as a gunshot fired.

Reef's heart dropped. *Cole.*

"Stay back," he urged Kirra, but she didn't listen, just kept barreling on beside him.

They rounded a hill and found Cole ducking behind an old mining cart as a second shot flew overhead. Relief swarmed inside.

"Get down," Cole hollered, waving them to the ground.

He yanked Kirra down beside him, and they crawled to Cole's side.

His brother peered around the cart's edge. "Looks like he's got help."

Another bullet whizzed overhead, and Reef cradled Kirra close. "What do you mean?"

"They're climbing into a black Tahoe. I'd fire at them, but I don't want to risk hurting Meg."

Car doors slammed shut, and they looked around to see the vehicle pulling away—Meg gagged and staring out the rear window, terror rampant in her wide eyes.

They gave chase—Reef racing beside Cole and Kirra, his lungs and thighs burning.

Meg's name tore from Kirra's lips as the vehicle pulled out of sight.

There were no license plates, but at least they'd gotten a good look at the vehicle and could provide a decent description.

"We were so close," Kirra said, stooping to catch her breath.

"We'll get them. It's only a matter of time."

Reef couldn't help wondering if it would take more time than they had.

Landon and Piper crested the ridge, Landon's arm braced across his chest with Piper's scarf.

"They got away."

"How?"

"In a waiting vehicle," Cole said. "But we've got a description."

"Great. I'll alert SAR along with police in Nome and the state troopers." Landon fished his phone from his pocket awkwardly with his left hand.

Tears welled in Kirra's eyes. "We were so close."

35

"Frank, you've got to listen to us," Jake pleaded with the man, thankful he'd stopped short of running him over, which exhibited great command over his dogs.

Frank shook his head. "Not until you have Meg safe and sound."

"Reef and Kirra are closing in on her now. We know the men behind this and the area they're hiding in."

"That's all well and good, but until Meg's safe and sound, I'm doing as I'm told. You've got to understand. She's my baby girl."

"I understand," Jake said, looking at Kayden. "Believe me, I do. I've had the woman I love held hostage."

"And I bet you'd have done whatever it took to get her back."

"Yes, but think of the lives you're endangering."

"Until Meg is safe, I'm finishing the job." Frank's right leg jiggled, his gaze fastening on the path beyond.

Jake knew he had better find a way to break through, and fast. "Why Nome? What happens there?"

"I turn over the trigger so he can remotely kick in the code changes I've programmed into the pumps."

"And then?" Maybe if he said it out loud he'd realize the devastation his actions would cause.

"Then he gives me Meg in exchange."

"You really believe he'll just let you both go?"

"It's the only hope I have."

"So none of this had anything to do with the Fabergé egg," Kayden said more to herself than to him.

"The Fabergé egg?" Frank frowned. "I haven't thought about that in years. How'd you know about that? And why'd you think any of this had anything to do with that?"

"Because rumor was you hid the egg worth millions along the Iditarod trail and Henry Watts just got released from jail."

"Watts knows better."

"Meaning?"

"He knows I returned the egg to Bartholomew's place later that night. But none of that has any bearing on Meg . . . unless Henry wants revenge for my testifying against him." Panic swelled in his voice. "Is Henry connected to the men who have Meg?"

"No."

His shoulders dropped in visible relief. "That's good."

"Why?" What was so upsetting about the possibility of Henry Watts being involved?

"Because Henry Watts would kill Meg just out of spite." Frank's dogs pawed the ground—antsy like their master. "Now, if you'll excuse me, I'm due in Nome."

"If you hand over the trigger to Keller, we'll be looking at the worst chemical spill in Alaskan history," Kayden said.

"And if I don't, they'll kill my girl."

"Please," Jake pleaded. "Let's find another way."

"There is no other way. You failed to rescue Meg, and now I have no choice."

"You *always* have a choice," Kayden said.

"And I'm choosing the one that protects my girl. I already lost her mother. I can't lose her too." He gave his dogs a signal, and they took off in a flash, mushing up along the hillside past Jake.

He'd never seen anyone keep a sled upright on such a steep incline.

Frank mushed over the narrow bridge and stopped on the far side. "Sorry," he yelled, "but Meg's my choice."

Jake rushed for the bridge, Kayden following at a close clip.

"Don't come any closer," Frank screamed, his dogs howling.

Jake heeded his warning, stopping Kayden just shy of the bridge. "What did you do, Frank?"

"Made good time. Got here early and did what I had to before rigging that pump." He gestured back to the station on the other side of the trees. "Now, I won't tell you again. *Get back.*"

A snowmobile roared behind them.

Frank shook his head grimly. "He's never far behind. This was meant for him, not you. Now! Move!"

As the snowmobile burst past them, Jake grabbed Kayden's hand and yanked her away from the bridge, running as far and as fast as he could until an explosion knocked them to the ice-packed earth.

Landon's phone rang as they approached the outskirts of Nome.

Reef squeezed Kirra's hand. Maybe someone had spotted the SUV.

"What?" Landon said, his gaze shifting to Piper, then back to the road. "When? All right. Thanks for the call."

"What is it?" Kirra asked, a tremble quivering in her voice.

"A member of the Iditarod air force searching for Frank spotted an explosion out by the Elim pump station. He called it in to Iditarod SAR headquarters, and Ben forwarded it on to Nome SAR, as they're the closest responders to Elim, and my friend there in turn called me."

Reef swallowed hard.

"Elim?" Kirra said. "Isn't that where Jake and Kayden were headed?"

Reef closed his eyes as nausea rumbled through his gut.

Please, Father, let Kayden and Jake be okay. The thought of losing someone else he loved was devastating.

"I'm afraid so," Landon said, reaching for Piper's hand.

They tried reaching them via Jake's satellite phone but had no luck. They only got static.

"We need to get out there," Piper said. "Now."

Reef looked at Kirra, knowing she was torn. She wanted to help his family, but hers was still very much in danger.

"Here's what we'll do," Landon said. "We'll drop in at local SAR headquarters. Piper and I will find a pilot to take us out to Elim while you, Cole, and Kirra continue the search here."

"Are you sure?" Kirra said. She turned to Reef. "Your family is only out here because of me."

He silently prayed for wisdom, and God filled him with assurance to stick with Landon's suggestion.

"I'm positive."

Her eyes welled with gratitude. "Thank you."

Nome SAR headquarters was situated in the fire station. Once there, it didn't take long for Piper and Landon to co-ordinate a flight out. Working SAR provided the McKennas with wide-reaching contacts that came in particularly handy in these situations.

As they were getting ready to split up, Kevin Hoffman rounded the corner.

"Kevin," Kirra said, "what are you doing here?"

"After we released Sam Matthews, he caught a flight headed out here."

"Sam Matthews is in Nome?"

Hoffman nodded.

"Any idea where?"

"I asked a local cop friend, Dave Carter, to keep an eye on him. So far he's made a couple stops, including the post office and the general store."

"Any idea why those places?"

"I think he's trying to make sure no one is following him, but Dave's good. If we're lucky, we'll get a call anytime."

"We've also got everyone keeping an eye out for a black Tahoe that Keller left Solomon in—with Meg," Reef added.

"That's great," Kevin said. "You found her?"

"Yes," Kirra said wearily. "But Keller triggered an explosion and got away with Meg in the chaos."

"Don't worry. We'll find them."

She looked at Reef, clutching his hand. "I know we will."

They'd do this together. It seemed insane to be thinking so long term when, as Kirra had pointed out, they technically hadn't even been on a first date. But after what they *had* been through, had come through *together*, with the Lord's strength, they were so far beyond first dates.

The thought of not being with her for the rest of his life terrified him far more than any thought of commitment did. He prayed she felt the same. They could take things as slowly as she wanted. Just as long as they were taking the journey together—side by side.

Jake lifted his head once the explosion settled.

Tendrils of smoke rose in vapor-like streams above where the bridge had stood moments earlier—its planks now bobbing in the water, spread out across the narrow inlet. Frank and his team were nowhere to be seen.

He loosened his death grip on Kayden, brushing her hair gently back from her face and examining her for injuries. "You okay, baby?" Other than some snow matted in her hair, she looked untouched.

"I'm good." She tugged his jacket, pulling him back to her, and laid a kiss on him that had his knees wobbling, and he wasn't even standing.

She released him with a satisfied smile on her face.

"Not that I'm complaining, but what was that for?" The lady kept him spiraling, and he wouldn't have it any other way.

"Can't a girl kiss her man?" She stood and pulled her gun from her side holster. "Now, we better see what happened to our snowmobile friend."

A kiss and a gun. The woman was an intoxicating mix of feminine strength and sensual appeal—the heady kiss still rattled his bones.

He stared at Kayden—her taste still on his lips—in awe of how deeply he loved her. "Hold up." He tugged her into his arms.

She smiled. "Another kiss first?"

"Actually . . ." He pulled the velvet pouch from his pocket. "I can't wait a moment longer."

Her brows arched, her pink snow-kissed nose crinkling.

He lowered to one knee and dropped the ring from the pouch onto his flattened palm.

Her almond eyes widened. "What are you doing?"

He cleared his throat. "Asking you to do me the honor of being my wife."

Love welled in her eyes, her smile, and the surprised blush caressing her cheeks. "Now?"

"We could have died right here, just moments ago. So, yes, now. I can't wait another second to make you mine forever."

Tears, actual tears, welled in her eyes. "In that case." She dropped to the ground in front of him and looked him straight in the eyes. "Yes. Jake Westin Cavanaugh. I'd love to be your wife."

He slid the ring on her finger, kissing her with all the love in his heart.

"I love you," he whispered against her mouth.

"I love you too," she whispered back. But then she jumped up. "Now, let's go get our man."

He chuckled. "And that's exactly why I love you."

"Any word?" Kirra asked as Reef reentered the fire-station bay.

His downcast expression said it all.

"How could they just disappear? Nome's not that big."

Cole hurried in from the chief's office. "Our luck may just

have changed. The Tahoe was spotted out by an old cannery warehouse on the southwest side of town."

Jake and Kayden approached the unconscious man splayed out on the snow, his snowmobile a dozen feet away and on its side.

Jake searched him, finding a high-frequency radio. "This could come in handy." Their satellite phone had ceased working after the explosion. He slipped the radio inside his jacket pocket.

"What do we do with him?" Kayden asked.

"Let me right his snowmobile—see if it still works. If so, I'll tie him up and throw him across the front. He may have some useful information when he comes to."

Jake and Kayden righted the snowmobile and thankfully found it still in working order. They tied up the man, and Jake loaded him onto the front of the snowmobile seat, climbing on behind him but keeping careful control over the machine. Kayden slid on the rear—their skis across her lap. He hated having her teetering on the edge, but she seemed perfectly comfortable with it—which should have come as no surprise. Using the snowmobile, even if he had to take it slow, would allow them to reach her plane so much faster, and bring their new baggage along.

A mile or so into the ride, the man's radio garbled. "Bruce, we need an ETA on Frank."

Jake stopped the snowmobile and looked at Kayden. He had no idea what Bruce sounded like.

Keeping the snowmobile idling, and trying to mask his voice with added static and garble, he responded, "Soon."

"Good. We're in place at the warehouse."

"Okay."

"Come around the rear. We don't want to draw too much attention. We've already got extra baggage."

Them too? "Oh?"

"We had to detonate the train ahead of time. The girl's cousin and friends were closing in."

Jake squeezed his eyes shut. Kayden now joined in with static of her own. "And . . . ?"

"We got away but had to bring the girl along. At least this will be over soon."

Jake quickly switched frequencies and patched in to Nome's SAR headquarters, having them patch him on through to Landon.

"Grainger," Landon answered.

"It's Jake."

"Oh, thank you, God. We heard there was an explosion. Are you all right?"

"Yes. We're both fine, and we're headed into Nome."

"Okay, we'll turn around."

"Turn around? What, were you headed out here?"

"Yeah, with Piper. We got word of the explosion. So what happened?"

"Frank blew a bridge to cut off us and the man following him."

"Smart. He wanted to force anyone chasing him to have to go the long way around the inlet."

"You got it. On the plus side, we have the man who was herding Frank with us—unconscious."

"Great. We'll take care of him when you get back to Nome. Where is Frank headed now?"

"To meet up with Keller."

"At the warehouse?" Landon asked.

"Yeah. You know about the warehouse?"

"Keller's vehicle was spotted approaching the abandoned cannery out on Frasier's Pass. How'd you know about the warehouse?"

"Keller just radioed our downed man. And he gave me the scoop."

"He have any idea it was you talking?"

"No. I left the snowmobile idling and used my hand to muffle it, and Kayden added in some great static."

"Great. We'll turn around and head straight for the warehouse."

"What about Reef and Kirra? Do they know?"

"Yes. They're already on the way to the warehouse."

36

Reef held Kirra's hand as they entered the warehouse. It was large and still filled with cannery equipment—the cold temperatures the majority of the year preserving the equipment in fairly good condition.

They entered through one of the side doors, bringing them into the central section of the warehouse.

Kneeling behind a production belt, bat in hand—it was the only weapon they had handy at the fire station, besides an axe—Reef scanned the space, his eyes taking a moment to adjust to the dimness. He looked to the rafters overhead and then to the open sliding doors across the way.

Joseph Keller stood in the center of the open space with a gun to Meg's head, as a man he assumed was Jason Keller paced impatiently.

A man entered through the rear.

Jason turned. "Bruce?"

"Try Sam."

"Sam? What are you doing here?" Jason leveled his gun on him. "I ought to kill you for talking."

"I've got some questions I want answered. Starting with what happened to Belinda?"

"Seriously? You expect me to answer your trivial questions?"

"I think I deserve that much."

"Deserve?" Jason scowled. "What do you know about deserving? I oughta *give* you what you deserve."

Announced by the barking of dogs, Frank's team pulled up at the side doors. He commanded his dogs to stay as he walked inside.

"We'll continue this conversation later, Sammie boy," Jason said, turning from Sam to Frank. "Frank, glad you could join us."

Frank surveyed the surroundings, his eyes filling with tears as his gaze fastened on his daughter bound and gagged. "Hey, pumpkin. It's going to be all right."

"Well, that all depends on you," Jason said. "You have the remote trigger?"

"I do."

"Then hand it over."

"Not until you release Meg."

Jason waggled a finger. "That's not how this works."

"I want her first," Frank reiterated.

Reef looked at Kirra, fearing her uncle would get Meg killed if he pushed too hard.

"Fine," Jason said with an eerie smile. "How about this? I shoot you both and then take the trigger off your cold, dead body."

"That'd be interesting," Frank said. "Since you need a password to make the trigger work."

"What's he talking about, Jay?" Joseph asked, his gaze frantically switching between the two.

"Shut up, Joe. I'll handle this." He turned back to Frank. "What are you talking about?"

"Password's only up here." Frank tapped his head. "You release Meg or the trigger is useless."

"You're bluffing. No way you're willing to chance your daughter's life like that."

Reef slipped from Kirra's side. "Stay put," he whispered. She nodded.

"Please," Frank said, "I'm not a fool. I give you the trigger and the password and you kill us both."

"I don't capitulate to demands." Jason glanced at Joseph and then Meg. "Shoot her."

Reef crept behind boxes and crates, trying to get as close to Joseph and Meg as possible without being seen. Joseph pressed his gun against Meg's temple.

Meg whimpered, her eyes fastened on her dad, tears streaming from her panicked eyes down over the duct tape covering her mouth.

"Wait!" Frank hollered.

Joseph eased his gun back.

"Down, Meg," Reef yelled as he sprang from cover.

Shaking, Meg dropped to her knees as Joseph swung around in Reef's direction, just in time for Reef to whack him across the face with the bat.

Joseph fell backward to the ground with a thud.

Looking around, Reef saw Jason aiming his gun in Reef's direction. "You're dead."

Reef ducked as he spotted Cole approaching Jason from behind.

Jason spun around, shooting.

Cole dropped to the ground, clasping his side.

"No!"

Jason rushed past Reef, his gaze fastened on—

Reef turned to look and found Kirra kneeling at Meg's side. He'd asked her to stay put.

Jason yanked her up to her feet, gesturing for Sam to take hold of Meg. He kicked Joe's gun over to him, and Sam did as instructed. After all that, how could he obey the crazy man?

Kirra struggled as Jason dragged her back toward the wall, his gun waving across the warehouse as he tried to figure out how many people were present. "Enough. This is between me and Frank."

Frank stood paralyzed in the center of the room, his hands held up in surrender as Sam kept the gun pointed at Meg's head.

Reef moved for Kirra.

Jason tightened his hold on her. "No closer or she dies."

"Then you will never get access to the pump codes," Frank said.

"Yes, I will." He shot Frank.

Frank dropped to his knees, clutching his shoulder as Meg cried and Kirra screamed.

"Oh, quit your sobbing," Jason said, striding to stand over Frank. "I only shot him in the shoulder. I need the password, Frank." Blood oozed down Frank's arm. "Next will be your knees."

Reef scrambled to Cole's side, his gaze still fixed on Jason and Kirra.

"I'm okay," Cole whispered. "Just a flesh wound."

Reef nodded and rose to his feet, lifting his hands in the air. It was time for a diversion. "If we could all just calm down."

"Reef, no!" Kirra said.

"Calm down?" Jason roared. "That's what NorthStar told my father when he realized they'd swindled not only our land but also our mineral rights out from under us."

"Mineral rights?" Sam frowned. "So it's true. None of this was about protecting the environment?"

"Only the minerals found in it."

"And Meg?" He slackened his grip on her, lowering the gun to his side. "You said you'd let her go after Frank gave you what we needed."

"You're not part of *we*. This is between Joe, me, and North-Star. And I'll do whatever I deem necessary with the girl and her father."

Sam's jaw tightened. "Just like you did with Belinda." He lifted his hands. "I'm outta here."

"I'm afraid it's too late for that."

"What are you going to do? Shoot us all?"

While Jason was distracted with Sam, Reef moved around behind him, smiling as he caught sight of Jake and Landon weaving in through the equipment to intercept Sam and Jason.

"Yes, I'll kill you all if I must. I was going to kill Frank and place his body in a pump station before it blew, but I've learned the value of backup plans. This warehouse is also rigged to blow, if need be. The authorities will be so overwhelmed by all the pumps exploding and the oil spill, it'll take them forever to search an old, abandoned cannery."

"Too many people know you're involved—responsible," Kirra said.

"Well, aren't you just the mouthy one. Much bolder than your cousin." He chuckled. "It's no matter. I'll simply disappear and eventually purchase the mineral rights back using a shell corporation. I've set up plenty during my years as an accountant. But I'm finished with this chat—this has gone on long enough."

"I agree." Reef lifted his bat.

Jason shifted his gun, moving from Kirra to Reef but not quickly enough. The bat made contact first, knocking Jason back. The gun fired as he stumbled to the ground.

Jake moved in to cuff Jason while Landon did the same with Sam and the unconscious Joseph. What an awakening he'd have.

Once unbound, Meg raced to her father's side, dropping to her knees. Kirra joined her.

Reef assessed Frank's injuries. "We should get him to the clinic."

Frank grasped Kirra's arm. "I'm so sorry." Tears streamed down his face. "I just couldn't live without my Meggie. Please forgive me."

Reef wrapped Kirra in his arms as they stretchered Frank out with Meg at his side.

"Do you think he really would have handed over the trigger?"

"He did his best not to. Even took a bullet in the process."

"But if it had come to the password or Meg . . . ?" Was her uncle capable of something like that?

Reef pulled her against his chest. "We need to thank God that he didn't."

Epilogue

THREE WEEKS LATER

Kirra stood on what had once been the McKenna family porch but was now the home of Mr. and Mrs. Landon Grainger.

Mr. and Mrs.

She glanced down at the princess-cut diamond on her ring finger. To some, her and Reef's engagement would seem too fast, but to them, after what God had brought them through together, it only made sense. They'd known each other the majority of their lives and there had never been a commitment, other than hers to Christ, that had felt more divinely blessed.

Reef approached from the house, his agile footsteps quick across the squeaky porch boards. He wrapped his arms around her from behind, scooping her tightly to him.

"Mmm. You smell incredible."

She laughed as his breath tickled the nape of her neck.

"I never asked. What is that scent?"

"Jasmine."

"Exotic and precious, just like you."

She turned in his arms to look up at him. "So is this the kind of treatment I can always expect from my husband?"

Reef smiled. "Husband . . ." His grin was not lopsided in the least, but full and broad. "I love the sound of that."

She smiled. "Me too." Who would have ever thought a few months ago that God would have brought her to this place—a place of deeper relationship with Him, a place of inner peace despite circumstances, and a place of genuine love the way God created it to be among family.

The McKennas were a family full of love and laughter, one she could trust and depend on as she and Reef strove to love each other as the Lord loved them. People weren't perfect, she understood that, but thankfully God was. He was her source of security. He would never leave her side. He would carry her through whatever valleys may still lie ahead and would rejoice with her on the mountaintop.

"Hey, guys . . ." Gage leaned out the kitchen door. "Cole's ready."

"Be right there," Reef said.

Gage smirked and ducked back inside.

"You heard your brother," Kirra said at Reef's reluctance to let go.

"Just another minute . . ." He snuggled her closer.

Yet another blessing—being totally comfortable in a man's arms. After William she never thought she'd experience that again, but God had been at work. Not just in her, but with William.

Soon after their return from Nome, Meg had called to tell her that one of the onlookers in the parking lot the day of Tracey's vicious attack was also a victim of William's.

And discovering she wasn't the only one gave that woman the courage she needed to go to the police. William was being charged with rape, and Kirra had offered to add her testimony if it would help put him away. Justice was being served. Even if he beat the charges, Kirra was not the only voice speaking out against him—and it felt so good, like a blessing from God.

"Guys!" Gage called.

"Coming." She nudged Reef toward the door.

"Okay, but I'm not happy about it."

They entered the family room to find all the McKenna siblings and their significant others: Cole and his wife, Bailey; Piper and her husband, Landon; Gage and his soon-to-be fiancée, Darcy—Kirra wasn't supposed to know, but Reef couldn't keep his ring-shopping trip with Gage a secret—and Kayden and her fiancé, Jake.

It had been a crazy couple of years for the McKennas—both good and bad, but as she sat and took in the joy, love, and laughter filling the room, she knew good had most definitely won out. Two weddings last summer, two engagements thus far this spring with another imminent one; she wondered what else they'd do in multiples.

Unfortunately, Emmett hadn't lingered much past the meal, but they'd all been thrilled when he'd taken Reef up on his invitation to join them. Kirra suspected they'd be seeing a lot more of him now that Reef had reconnected Emmett with the McKenna family, and with Piper's hospitality in particular. Dinner had been fantastic. Hawaiian chicken, mango-coconut rice, and grilled pineapple. A Hawaiian feast in the middle of winter—clearly Piper had been in charge of the menu.

Cole stood and moved to the fireplace as Reef pulled Kirra down on the couch beside him. "So glad you lovebirds could join us." He chuckled. "Now, while Calvin is still napping . . ." He looked at their youngest sister. "Sorry, Piper. He'll wake up soon."

Almost as if his words had caused it, a soft cry spilled from the adjacent room, and Bailey rose. Cole rubbed his hands together and continued, "Bailey and I wanted to take this time to thank you all for coming to Calvin's dedication today, and for being the amazing aunts and uncles you are. I know we all wish Mom and Dad could have been here, but I know in my heart they are so proud of you all."

"*Us* all," Kayden added.

Cole smiled with a nod. "They taught us the importance of walking with the Lord, of loving your spouse as yourself, striving with dedication in everything you do, including work and service, and—most pressing on my and Bailey's hearts—teaching the next generation."

"Speaking of the next generation . . ." Bailey said, entering with Calvin, bundled in her arms, wearing a red-and-white *Divers Rule* onesie. "Look who's here."

"Ah." Piper rushed Bailey, nearly barreling her over. "Let me see my adorable nephew."

Bailey laughed and handed Calvin to an elated Piper. It was a daily routine. Piper cooing over Calvin, though Kirra could not blame her—the little dude such a gorgeous mix of his daddy's sandy blond hair and his mommy's big blue eyes. She wondered what her and Reef's children would look like.

"What?" Reef nudged at her spreading smile.

"Just thinking . . ."

He laughed. "That's dangerous."

"You have no idea."

"Bring it on." He winked. "I'm up for any adventure, as long as you're at my side."

"Remember you said that."

He pulled her into his embrace. "Wouldn't have it any other way."

"Don't worry, Bay," Landon said, standing and moving toward Piper. "One day we'll have a baby of our own, and Piper will stop stealing yours."

Piper grinned—her smile oozing with mirth. "*One day* may be sooner than you think."

Landon laughed, then slowly stilled. "What?" He studied his wife. "Are you saying? Are you . . . ?" A mixture of fear and elation spread across his flushing face.

She nodded, her eyes glistening. "Doc Graham confirmed it."

He swooped her, baby and all, up in his arms. "I can't believe it."

"I wanted to tell you when we were all together. The look on your face was priceless—how could I keep that to myself?"

"How long have you known?"

"I've suspected for a while, so I took a home pregnancy test this morning. It was positive, so I dropped by Doc Graham's before the dedication. He did the initial ultrasound."

She pulled the sonogram picture from her pocket.

Landon clutched it. "I can't believe we're having a baby."

"Babies."

Landon stilled. "What? Did you just say . . . ?"

Piper waggled two fingers.

"Twins?" Landon swallowed, staggering backward.

Piper nodded.

Kayden swooped in and lifted Calvin from Piper's arms so she could tend to her husband.

Piper waved her hand in front of Landon's blank face. "Are you in shock?"

He blinked. "Yes, but I'm thrilled." He scooped her back in his arms, the whole room erupting in laughter.

Kayden laughed. "Actually, what's shocking is that my sister actually kept a secret for a few hours."

Piper pursed her lips at Kayden. "Very funny."

"I must say," Jake said, moving to Kayden's side and handing Calvin his moose blanket—a gift from Aunt Piper, of course. "You look mighty fetching with a baby in your arms."

"Whoa there, mister. We *just* got engaged."

Jake grinned. Clearly he had a quick engagement in mind.

Reef nuzzled beside Kirra as Piper started quizzing Bailey on everything baby related.

"You know," he said, fiddling with her ring, "my mom would have loved that we ended up together."

"Really? Why's that?"

"Because whenever I'd come home from school and complain about you, my mom would always say that only someone you really love can manage to get you that fired up."

"Is that right?" She smiled.

"At age five, I thought she was crazy, of course. I mean, me, love a girl? And a bossy one at that?" He tickled her playfully.

She laughed. "Sounds like your mom was a wise woman."

He wrapped her in his arms, bringing his lips to hers and hovering momentarily, then whispered, "I couldn't agree more."

Acknowledgments

Jesus—Thank you for creating and equipping me do something I love so very much. May each word be for your glory, always.

Mike, Ty, and Kay—For all your love and support. Couldn't do this without you guys.

Dave and Karen—I can't believe we've completed our first series together. It's been a joy and honor. Here's to many more!

To the brave and fearless men, women, and sled dogs of the Iditarod. You are an amazing inspiration.

Dani Pettrey is a wife, home-schooling mom, and the acclaimed author of the ALASKAN COURAGE romantic suspense series, which includes her bestselling novels *Submerged*, *Shattered*, *Stranded*, *Silenced,* and new release, *Sabotaged*. Her books have been honored with the Daphne du Maurier award, two HOLT Medallions, two National Readers' Choice Awards, the Gail Wilson Award of Excellence, and Christian Retailing's Best Award, among others.

She feels blessed to write inspirational romantic suspense because it incorporates so many things she loves—the thrill of adventure, nail-biting suspense, the deepening of her characters' faith, and plenty of romance. She and her husband reside in Maryland, where they enjoy time with their two daughters, a son-in-law, and a super adorable grandson. You can find her online at *danipettrey.com*.

Have you read the rest of the ALASKAN COURAGE series?

To learn more about Dani and her books, visit danipettrey.com.

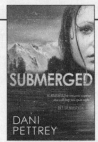

Bailey Craig has reluctantly returned to her Alaska hometown to bury a loved one. But when dark evidence emerges surrounding her aunt's death, can she and Cole McKenna overcome past hurts and catch the killer?

Submerged, ALASKAN COURAGE #1

Piper McKenna would be overjoyed at the sight of her brother Reef—if he wasn't covered in blood. She knows he's innocent. But when her closest friend, Landon Grainger, arrests Reef on charges of murder, can they discover the truth before it's too late?

Shattered, ALASKAN COURAGE #2

On the trail of a missing friend, reporter Darcy St. James is shocked to find Gage McKenna—handsome and unforgettable as ever—on board the cruise ship she's investigating. She'll have to enlist Gage's help when it becomes clear that one disappearance is just the tip of the iceberg.

Stranded, ALASKAN COURAGE #3

After Kayden McKenna discovers the body of a fellow climber, she and Jake Westin team up to investigate the death—provoking threats on her entire family.

Silenced, ALASKAN COURAGE #4

You May Also Enjoy

Researcher Gina Gray is on the verge of a breakthrough in sonar technology, but she fears that her impending discovery will only put the lives of those she loves in greater danger.

Undetected by Dee Henderson
deehenderson.com

When Sarah's sister suddenly reappears, only to disappear again—in the same manner as her parents—can Deputy Sheriff Paul Gleason help her to solve the mystery that's still haunting her?

Deadly Echoes by Nancy Mehl
FINDING SANCTUARY #2
nancymehl.com

Answering a plea for help from an old flame, Drew and his fiancé, Madeline, discover murder and more behind the scenes of a theater production of *The Mikado*.

Murder at the Mikado by Julianna Deering
A DREW FARTHERING MYSTERY
juliannadeering.com